Dear Readers,

The late great Toni Morrison mentored me early in my career. She was an editor at Random House at the time. As busy as she was, she found time to read and critique my work. Her editorial input was priceless. She advised me to write books *I'd* like to read, and to write about what I know. Well, as a former battered woman, *Bent but Not Broken* is very personal.

Unlike the long-suffering wife Naomi Purcell in this book, who remains with her brutal husband for twenty years, I ended my toxic marriage in less than a year and a half. I was still a teenager so I had plenty of time to restart my life. Like Naomi, I thought a new man would "fix" me. Unfortunately, she jumped from the frying pan into the fire and so did I. The next man after my husband was even more brutal! When I ended that relationship six months later, he became my stalker. He made death threats over the telephone and in crudely written notes he would slide under my living-room door during the night. I escaped by leaving Ohio on a Greyhound bus to California in the middle of one cold January night. It was a while before I felt comfortable enough to date again. The *first* time a new boyfriend waved a red flag in my face, I sent him on his way.

Naomi goes through hell with the two men in her life. But karma steps in and "rescues" her. A massive stroke brings her evil husband down. The ex-lover who stalks her meets a fate even worse. Despite the violence in my books, I don't have a violent bone in my body and I don't condone it. However, during my ordeals I used to wish that I could "do away" with my abusers . . .

Readers frequently ask me what it's like to be a writer. Some even suggest that it is not a "real" job, but a glorified hobby. Not only is writing a real job, it is not easy. There is a lot of hard work involved. But for me it's also fun, therapeutic, and empowering. I feel like a director because I "tell" my characters what to do. Whenever my friends hear that I am working on a new book, they gasp when I reveal the shenanigans I have in store for my characters. *Bent but Not Broken* even made me gasp when I finished reading the final draft. I hope you will enjoy it!

Very truly yours,

Mary Monroe

Bent But Not Broken

Mary Monroe

KENSINGTON PUBLISHING CORP.

kensingtonbooks.com

DAFINA BOOKS are published by

Kensington Publishing Corp.
900 Third Avenue
New York, NY 10022

Copyright © 2025 by Mary Monroe

CONTENT WARNINGS: Emotional abuse, animal cruelty, animal abuse, animal death, murder

All Kensington titles, imprints, and distributed lines are available at special quantity discounts for bulk purchases for sales promotion, premiums, fund-raising, educational, or institutional use. Special book excerpts or customized printings can also be created to fit specific needs. For details, write or phone the office of the Kensington Special Sales Manager: Attn. Special Sales Department, Kensington Publishing Corp., 900 Third Avenue, New York, NY 10022. Phone: 1-800-221-2647.

The DAFINA logo is a trademark of Kensington Publishing Corp.

Library of Congress Control Number: 2024949732

ISBN-13: 978-1-4967-4318-3
First Kensington Hardcover Edition: April 2025

ISBN-13: 978-1-4967-4320-6

10 9 8 7 6 5 4 3 2 1

Printed in the United States of America

This book is dedicated to the following queens: Maria Sanchez, Elizabeth (Liz) Tyler, Hazel Lynch, Priscilla Shipstad, Sarah Nicholson, Mona Lisa Williams, Ellen Tate, and Vella Mae Woods.

ACKNOWLEDGMENTS

I am so blessed to be a member of the Kensington family. Thanks to Leticia Gomez, Steven Zacharius, Adam Zacharius, Michelle Addo, Lauren Jernigan, Robin E. Cook, the crew in the sales department, and everyone else at Kensington. I love you all! Thanks to Lauretta Pierce for maintaining my website.

Thanks to the fabulous book clubs, bookstores, readers, and libraries for supporting me for so many years.

Andrew Stuart, you are the best literary agent in the world for me. Thank you from the bottom of my heart.

Please continue to email me at Authorauthor5409@aol.com and visit my website at www.Marymonroe.org and my Facebook page.

All the best,

Mary Monroe

CHAPTER 1

My daddy warned me on a regular basis when I was growing up that if I made bad choices, the Devil would come for me. I thought it was just old man talk, so I didn't pay him no mind. Well, I would find out he was right all along. I would make choices so bad, TWO devils came for me.

May 13, 1916

THAT SATURDAY MORNING STARTED OFF LIKE EVERY OTHER SATUR-day for me. I did a few chores and then I cooked breakfast for me and Daddy. The only thing different about this day was that I had woke up with a overwhelming sense of dread. The only other times I felt this bad was when somebody close to me had died. I couldn't figure out what was causing it or what I could do to shake it off.

At one point it was so bad, I went into my room and read my Bible. That didn't help . . .

The ominous feeling was still with me when I walked the six blocks to the market after me and Daddy finished eating breakfast. Colored folks was only allowed to shop at this place on certain days and hours. The days and hours would change at random, so we never knew if we'd be allowed to shop until we got there.

Lady luck was on my side today. When I walked into the cluttered, musty-smelling store, I went to the meat counter first. I frowned at the chicken wings with a few feathers still attached, gimpy pig tails, and discolored hot links dangling from strings tacked to the ceiling. Behind me was a barrel filled with assorted fruit. Some was bruised or had already started to rot. Gnats hovered above the barrel. Some white merchants put out expired and undesirable food products during the colored shopping hours.

The redheaded, sharp-featured old man behind the meat counter stared at me and didn't bother to ask what I wanted. The pig ears looked fresh, so I pointed to them and told him how many I wanted. I watched him real close because the last time I came to buy some liver, he had the nerve to try and sell me a piece with a big green spot on it. He tried to hide it by folding it in two. I told him to forget the liver and give me some pork chops instead.

I'd been coming to this store since I was a little girl, and it was just as scary and uncomfortable today as it had always been to me. "Add two more pig ears, sir," I requested with my heart beating fast and hard.

The man still didn't say nothing. He just rubbed his pointy nose, wrapped up my order, slapped it down on the counter, and walked off. I shook my head, grabbed my pig ears, and shuffled over to the produce section. While I was rooting through the bin that contained the yams, somebody tapped me on the shoulder. My heart started beating harder and faster because the only time I got tapped on the shoulder in a white-owned store was when they thought I was stealing. They would check my purse, socks, shoes, and pockets. The last time, this store's manager even looked in my mouth to make sure I hadn't swiped some candy and hid it inside my jaw like some of my friends did. I had never stolen nothing in my life, and I would get naked if they wanted me to so they could see I hadn't swiped a thing today.

I sucked in my breath and reminded myself that no matter what, I had to remember my place. Colored folks wasn't allowed to sass, argue with, or disrespect white folks in any way. If we did, we could end up in jail, beat to a pulp by the sheriff and his deputies, even murdered. A lot of the folks buried in the colored cemetery was there because they had riled up white folks in one way or another. Me being just a teenage girl didn't matter much. Our church choir director's thirteen-year-old daughter got beat to death in broad daylight in the middle of Main Street by a mob of white boys for snatching a white woman's purse.

I forced myself to smile before I turned around. I was surprised to see Jacob Purcell standing there with a wall-to-wall smile on his cute, coffee-colored, baby face. He looked more like sixteen than twenty-six, but his well-developed body belonged to that of a full-grown man.

I breathed a deep sigh of relief. All of a sudden, the dread I'd been feeling was gone. But I was still concerned as to why I'd had it in the first place. "You frightened the daylights out of me," I said in a stern tone. "What do you want?"

"I'm sorry if I spooked you." Jacob suddenly looked nervous. "I been trying to catch up with you for a long time." He snorted and scratched his head, which contained some of the thickest, blackest, curliest hair I ever seen on a colored man. He had on a pair of bibbed overalls and a brown plaid shirt with the sleeves rolled up.

I'd left my house at 10 A.M. and didn't think I'd run into anybody I knew that early, so I hadn't bothered to put on no makeup or none of my cute clothes. I looked like a frump in my faded gray blouse with the top button missing, and a limp, black corduroy skirt. A dingy, flowered headscarf was tied around my head. I cringed when Jacob glanced down at my dusty bare feet standing next to his shiny black clodhoppers. Another reason I hadn't gussied up before I left the house was because white folks didn't like to see us looking too spiffy. One time when I was strutting down Main Street in a bright red dress and matching shoes, a white girl I passed hawked a gob of spit on the tail of my dress. I was so used to holding in my anger, I didn't do or say nothing. But when I got home, I punched my bedroom wall and burned the dress and them shoes.

I sniffed and blinked at Jacob. "Trying to catch up with me for what?" I asked.

"I thought you might like to go out with me sometime. I heard you liked to go fishing. I do too so I was thinking maybe we could go together one of these days." He paused and added, "Real soon."

I loved to fish, but I would have preferred something a little more romantic for a first date. Like a buggy ride, a movie, or a picnic. "I'm going fishing this Sunday after church."

We agreed to meet up at the bank of Carson Lake on Sunday around three o'clock. I was about to head to the cashier when Jacob started talking again. "By the way, a girl like you shouldn't be out here shopping by herself. It ain't fitting. Cute as you are, some old boy might try to take advantage of you. You ought to take a dog with you every time you leave your house."

I laughed. "I ain't got no dog."

Jacob gave me a sideways look. "Then what about your boyfriend?" he asked.

"I ain't got no boyfriend, neither." I got sad and mad when I thought about how James Hardy had dropped me like a bad habit two days ago so he could court one of them no-neck Baxter sisters.

Jacob's eyes got big, and he leaned his head back and gave me the once-over. "Naomi Simmons, you must be the prettiest colored girl in Lexington, Alabama."

I blushed. I didn't agree with him. I thought my eyes was too big and my lips too thin. But I was proud of my honey-colored complexion, high cheekbones, and thick jet-black hair. Boys and grown men had been telling me for years I was pretty, but I still liked hearing it. "Aw shuck it. You think I'm that pretty?"

"Every day. I been wondering how come you ain't married yet . . ."

"I been wondering the same thing myself," I said in a stiff tone. All three of my older sisters and four of my close friendgirls was already married—and one was only fourteen, almost a year and a half younger than me.

Jacob smiled again. "I don't know your family well. But before my uncle Johnny died two months ago, your daddy told him he couldn't wait for you to find a husband so he can concentrate on his lady friend."

I didn't like hearing things was being said about me behind my back, especially by Daddy.

"Humph! That's me and my daddy's business. Why do you care?"

Jacob hunched his shoulders. "Well, I'd like to do you and your daddy a favor, I guess." He laughed. "Anyway, I done heard how dependable, clean, and tolerant you have always been with your daddy and them demanding sisters of yours. A girl with all them good qualities could make me a good wife."

I never expected my first "marriage proposal" to be so vague and out of the blue so I was flabbergasted to say the least. "You don't know much about me, and I don't know much about you." I was lying. The colored folks in Lexington spent more time gossiping and putting everybody's business out in the street, so I knew quite a bit about Jacob. He had started working at the sawmill a few weeks ago. Last year while he was still in the Army, a clumsy soldier accidentally shot him in the foot. He'd been discharged for medical reasons and the government gave him enough money to put a nice down payment on a two-bedroom house. Last month he broke up with a girl he'd been engaged to before joining the Army. A heap of other girls had their eyes on him. If he wasn't good husband material, I didn't know who was.

As for me, I didn't think I was that special. It sounded like he did, though. I was impressed that he went from us going on a fishing date to us getting married.

"You want to get married or not? If you don't, I don't want to waste my time."

"I'll think about it," I said in a firm tone. I didn't like it when men got pushy with me, especially one I wasn't even involved with. It was the first red flag, but I ignored it.

"Oh. Well, if you need to think about it, you must have other eggs in your nest waiting to hatch."

I gave Jacob a tight smile. "Maybe," was all I could think to say.

I didn't have a new boyfriend in sight, but I didn't want him to know that.

I didn't know what to say next, so I excused myself and rushed around to pick up the rest of my groceries. Daddy had gave me a shopping list. It contained only the same things we ate on a regular basis: yams, beans, greens, and a few other boring items. Like on every trip to the market, I snuck in some licorice to gobble up on my way home.

A few seconds after I got in line to pay, Jacob came up behind me and said in a low tone, "I hope you don't take too long to 'think about it.' There is a heap of other pretty girls in Lexington."

Just as I opened my mouth to say something, the scowling cashier hollered, "Keep moving, gal! Y'all need to be out of this store in ten minutes. If you ain't, I'm going to call the sheriff."

Before I could pay for my stuff and make it out the door, a white couple jumped the line in front of Jacob. They immediately started chatting with the cashier about a upcoming church event they was going to attend. I prayed that Jacob would get waited on before our ten minutes was up. If he didn't, he'd have to leave his items on the counter and come back during the colored hours.

CHAPTER 2

IT WAS WARMER THAN USUAL FOR THE MIDDLE OF MAY, BUT WE'D had a bad tornado two weeks before. It blew down one of the two pecan trees in our backyard and shattered every window in the house. Daddy had cussed up a storm when he found out how much it was going to cost to get the windows replaced. He didn't make much money shining shoes downtown and doing handyman work at one of the elementary schools only white kids could attend. My older siblings was married and had decent jobs, so Daddy got money from them when he needed it. I made a few dollars running errands and doing favors for some of our neighbors, but Daddy still gave me a dime allowance every week.

Since the weather was pleasant again, I wanted to enjoy it for as long as I could before the next tornado season, which would be November and December. But tornadoes was fickle so they could also sneak up on us any other time during the year.

It was a nice day, but I didn't have plans to do nothing. I didn't want to spend another weekend being bored. Jacob's clumsy marriage "proposal" had really got my attention. I didn't know if he was serious or not, but I wanted to find out. If James hadn't broke up with me, or if I'd had something better to do, I would have gone home and not gave Jacob another thought. Since I was between boyfriends, a man flirting with me boosted my ego.

Jacob rushed out the market door a few minutes later hugging his bulging grocery bag so tight you would have thought he was scared somebody was going to snatch it away. "That cow gave me a bag with a hole in the bottom. Some of my stuff will spill out before I get to my house!" he complained. "Next time I'll bring something stronger from home like a crocus sack or a pillowcase."

"She put my stuff in a holey bag, too," I said with a heavy sigh. "They do it to me almost every time I shop here."

"Well, they don't do it to me too often, but it burns me up when they do." Jacob pressed his lips together before he heaved out a loud breath. Then he gave me a curious look. "Why you still here? You know this neighborhood ain't safe for us." There was fear in his tone. "You better skedaddle before them crackers have you arrested for loitering. The sentence for that is ten days in jail."

"Um . . . I was counting my change to make sure that lady didn't shortchange me," I lied.

"Well, even if she did, I advise you not to go back in there and call her on it. If you do, she'll call the sheriff and have you arrested for harassing her. The sentence for that is a month and a day in jail."

"Oh. I guess I'll go on home then." We started walking toward the neighborhood where we both lived.

Jacob rearranged the groceries in his bag, but a few green beans slid out anyway. "Dagnabbit! I'll be lucky if they don't charge me with littering," he snarled. He started walking fast, and I did, too.

I was surprised and disappointed Jacob was not trying to flirt with me now. We had almost made it to the end of the block, and he hadn't said nothing else. It was hard to believe he'd had so much to say to me in the store and now he was acting like a cat had his tongue. I decided not to wait for him to bring up marriage again, I did it. "So, you thinking about getting married?"

He looked at me and grinned. "Yep."

"How many girls have you asked?"

"Other than the girl I used to be engaged to before I went in the Army, just you."

"Oh," I sniffed. "Well, like I said, I need to think about it, and I would like to get to know you better."

"All right, then. You know where I live." We went separate ways when we got to the corner.

I only *liked* Jacob. But getting dumped by James had really clobbered my ego. Otherwise, I wouldn't have been so antsy to get another man, and this time a husband. I wanted to be in love with the man I married. It didn't look like I was going to be that lucky off the bat, though. From what my sisters and other married women had been telling me for years, it took more than love to make a good marriage. Security was the most important thing. Love was supposed to develop over time. One of the older ladies I babysat for told me she'd been married to her husband for over ten years and she still wasn't in love with him. She claimed she was happy, though. She also told me the only thing keeping her content was the boyfriend she had on the side. Fidelity was important to me. I was a Christian to the bone and there was no way I'd marry a man and cheat on him.

So far, my luck with men had been bad. I'd had four serious relationships. Neither one had lasted more than a few weeks. Besides, none of them men had decent jobs or was in the church like Jacob. I couldn't get him off my mind. If I didn't take Jacob and run, some other girl would, and there was no telling what frog prince I'd end up marrying. With so many young colored men moving to the North, getting lynched, or joining the Army and never coming back to Lexington, the pickings was real slim.

I took my sweet time walking back to my house. I even stopped along the way and watched some birds building a nest in a big old tree in the middle of our block. I lost track of the time, so I didn't realize how long I'd been gone until I got home. Daddy was standing on our rickety front porch with his hands on his wide hips and a scowl on his coffee-colored, still handsome face. "Didn't I tell you to go to the market and come straight back home? You go yonder to the kitchen and set them groceries down and then drag your tail to the backyard and pluck a switch off one of them trees so I can whup your behind."

"I'm sorry, Daddy. The store was real crowded. One white lady was buying stuff for a party and both cashiers took their time helping her pick out what she wanted. I couldn't ask them to hurry up. You warned me I could get in a heap of trouble if I got uppity with white folks . . ."

Daddy gave me a thoughtful look and scratched his head. "Yeah, I did warn you. You did the right thing by being patient until somebody could wait on you. So, I'll let you slide this time." Daddy snorted and gave me a threatening look. "You might not be so lucky the next time. I'm going to carry Miss Maddie to the movie theater tonight, so you need to get supper ready lickety-split."

After me and Daddy finished eating, he went to go visit Madeline "Maddie" Upshaw, the widow woman he'd been seeing for the past ten years. She lived two streets over from us in a house just as ramshackle as ours and most of the others in our neighborhood.

I stretched out on the living-room couch and thought about everything Jacob had said to me today. He wasn't the first person to tell me my daddy was itching for me to get a job, move out, or get married so he could move on.

I couldn't blame Daddy for feeling the way he did. He'd had such a hard life. He couldn't read or write because he had to drop out of school in first grade and go work in the fields so he could help out at home. Him and Mama had gotten married when he was seventeen and she fifteen. They had thirteen kids, but five died when they was babies. Mama died giving birth to me. Daddy had a real hard time raising eight children. All of my grandparents was dead and all four of Daddy's siblings had passed before I was born. The only help he got raising me and my seven siblings was from our church and the lady friends in and out of his life.

Miss Maddie had already raised her nine kids and sent them on their way. She'd made it clear she didn't want to raise no more—especially me. There was some bad blood between me and her. One of her daughters used to mess around with the same boy I was seeing at the same time. I didn't know about him and her until she cold cocked me after a church picnic last year. She'd caught me and that two-timing boy kissing behind a clump of bushes. I didn't like to fight. But some of my friends was looking and I didn't want to look like a scaredy cat, so I punched her in the stomach—which was holding the boy's baby at the time, but I didn't know.

She lost her baby a few hours later and Miss Maddie had a fit. She stormed into our house and called me all kinds of names and made Daddy whup me right in front of her. She even had the nerve to bring the switch. After my whupping, Daddy and Miss Maddie marched me to her house and I apologized to her daughter. The girl claimed she was so afraid of me. Two days later Miss Maddie put her on a bus and sent her to live with some kinfolks in Massachusetts. Ever since then, Miss Maddie treated me like a dog she didn't like. When Daddy brought her to the house now, I was always respectful to her. I didn't want to jeopardize their relationship because he told me she was the only woman he'd been with since my mama died who made him happy.

CHAPTER 3

RIGHT AFTER I'D STARTED HIGH SCHOOL LAST YEAR, I HEARD from a bunch of folks that Daddy was going around telling people he was anxious for me to be on my own. Just last Sunday while I was at the Baptist church I'd been going to all my life, my preacher came up to me after the morning service. Reverend Sweeney was a head taller than me, so I had to look up at him.

He put his hand on my shoulder and gave me a pitiful look before saying, "Sister Naomi, when are you going to slow down and get married and give your daddy a break?" Reverend Logan Sweeney was only about ten or twelve years older than me. He had taught Sunday school to me and my friends when we was still in elementary school. He had stepped into his current position three years ago when his daddy got too old and sick to continue preaching. I had a lot of respect for him, so his opinion was real important to me.

I forced myself not to stare too hard at his smooth copper-colored dark, muscle-bound body, and shiny black hair. He had a fiancée, but a lot of my friends had crushes on him. I had laughed his comment off and hurried away from him, but on the way home, a moon-faced old lady named Betty Woods who lived two doors down from us, yelled at me as I walked past her house. "Gal, your daddy told me he prays seven days a week for you to get a job or a husband so he can move on. If you don't do it soon, you'll have to settle for the scraps at the bottom of the barrel. I'm going to pray for you, myself. Seven days a week."

"Thank you, Miss Betty."

It seemed like everybody I knew was saying Daddy wanted me to find a husband or a job. He was one of the few who hadn't told me!

I didn't have nothing better to do, so I decided to visit Lula Pittman, my best friend since second grade. She was three months older than me and wasn't a blood relative, but I looked up to her more than I did my own older sisters. Lula would jump in front of a speeding train for me, and I would do the same for her. She lived with her parents and two younger brothers. Her mama was a talented seamstress, and she was teaching Lula all the tricks of the trade so she could do the same kind of work full-time someday. Their house was only two blocks away from ours so it would only take me a few minutes to get there.

It certainly wasn't no walk in the park. In them two blocks, I had to step over a dead lizard stretched out on the sidewalk. I passed by a deserted house where somebody had dumped a old pee-stained mattress in the front yard. The city didn't do much to help the colored neighborhoods look good. Most of the time, it was up to us to haul away our trash and keep the streets clean. A trash can filled with odds and ends had fallen off the back of a truck last week and was still laying in the same spot on the street in front of Lula's house. Somebody had cleaned up most of the junk and rolled the can to the curb.

As soon as I marched up onto the squeaky porch steps at Lula's shabby, brown shingled house, she peeped out the living-room window. Before I could let myself in, she opened the door with a impatient expression on her cute, heart-shaped face. As usual, she wore enough face powder and rouge for two girls. There was blood-red lipstick on her full lips. She had flawless, reddish-brown skin and big brown eyes that always sparkled like new pennies. Today her long thick black hair was in a French twist. She looked like a princess in the pink silk blouse she had made with her own two hands.

"You can't come in right now. I got company." Before I could say anything, she closed the door and came out onto the porch.

"Why can't I come in? I come over all the time when you got company," I said with a pout.

"Because I got Maxwell Rogers sitting in the living room. I think he's fixing to ask me to marry him, and I don't want you to distract him."

I gasped. "What a coincidence! Jacob Purcell proposed to me this morning," I blurted out.

Lula raised her eyebrows and grinned. "My goodness, girl. I'm impressed. Jacob is kind of cute and makes good money at the sawmill. If I was you, I'd snatch him up real quick. One of the Baxter sisters told me she got her eye on him."

It was one of them man-eating Baxter sisters who had stole my last boyfriend. I wasn't about to let nobody in that family take *another* man from me. "I told him I'd think about it."

Lula rolled her eyes and suddenly looked exasperated. "You better get the spirit, sister. What do you need to think about? All the men that *ain't* standing in line to get to you? If you let a golden egg like Jacob slip through your fingers, you need a whupping. Besides, everybody knows your daddy can't wait for you to move out of the house so him and Miss Maddie won't have to worry about you breathing down their necks." Lula glanced at the window. "I need to go back in the house and finish my business with Maxwell before everybody gets back home from fishing and spook him. I'll come over if it ain't too late when he leaves. Now shoo!" Lula skittered back inside and closed the door.

When I got home, I went in through the kitchen door. That's why Daddy and the scheming Miss Maddie didn't know I was in the house. I could hear them talking in the living room and I didn't want to disturb them. On the way to my itty-bitty bedroom on the other side of the kitchen, something Daddy said made me stop in my tracks. "I declare, I'll be so happy when Naomi finds a husband or gets a job. I been taking care of young'uns too long. I . . . I'm tired now."

Miss Maddie started talking like she couldn't wait to get her opinion out of her mean mouth. "I can see that. But I keep telling you to be realistic. You need to admit your gal ain't got a lick of sense in her nappy head, so she don't know how to get a husband. I advise you to do it for her. That's what my folks did for me and every one of my five sisters." Miss Maddie was a nat- ural-born snarky woman, so I didn't need to see her pig face to know what kind of look she had on it.

I couldn't believe what I had just heard. For one thing, I had more than a "lick of sense" in my nappy head. I read the news- paper, books, and magazines on a regular basis. I listened to the radio every day so I could keep up with what was happening in the world, and I got straight A's in school. That heifer had some nerve telling my daddy he had to find a husband for me! I could find one on my own. Didn't she know things had changed since she was my age? Of all the married females my age I knew, I didn't know nary one who had married a man her family picked out for her.

I had a itching to go up to Miss Maddie and tell her one of the most eligible colored men in town had told me today that he thought I'd make him a good wife! I couldn't wait to hear Daddy's response when I told him.

Daddy started talking again in a slow, tired tone. "I'm going to marry her off before Christmas, God willing. The oldest Hawkins boy down the street just broke up with his wife. He is hog-butt ugly, and Naomi is high-and-mighty, so she might put up a fuss when I have him come take a look-see at her."

"And that's another thing. Your girl thinks she's too cute for her own good. Don't let her forget this is your house, and you rule this roost. You always did let her get away with way too much. I'm surprised she ain't even tried to bust me and you up . . ."

Daddy let out such a loud gasp, I was surprised it didn't choke him. "Bite your tongue, Maddie! It took me too long to find a wholesome, Godly woman like you. I ain't going to let nobody bust us up! Not even my own daughter." Daddy paused and cleared his throat. "Naomi ain't going to have no say in it. I'm her daddy and it's my job to look out for her. Me setting her up

with a husband is as much for her good as it is mine. She'll probably kick and scream, but she'll thank me for it later. Regardless
of what she thinks, the Hawkins boy makes a good living, and
got his own place. I'm going to go up to him as soon as I can and
finalize the deal."

I didn't need to hear nothing else. I was going to show Daddy
and Miss Maddie I wasn't something they could unload like a
bale of hay. I went back out the same door I had just come
through and headed to Jacob's house. I didn't know him well
enough to open his door and walk in like I did with folks I knew
real good. But before I could knock, he snatched the door
open. I trembled and yelped when I seen a shotgun in his hand
and a mean look on his face.

"I declare, I thought that roguish deer I been having problems with was back. That critter been using my front porch for a
toilet for a whole month now."

"Can we talk?" As upset as I was about what Daddy and Miss
Maddie was cooking up to get me out of their way, I was still able
to speak in a normal tone. "It's about that conversation we had
at the market."

Jacob's face lit up like a lightning bug. "All right. Come on
in." He waved me into his living room, which was more pleasant to look at than ours. We had a dull brown couch, a gray
easy chair, and a coffee table that used to be a eggplant crate.
Jacob's blue couch had a matching love seat facing it. The dark
wooden coffee table had matching end tables with a kerosene
lamp on each one. He propped the shotgun up in the corner
behind the potbellied stove used to heat the house. It was
larger than the one in our living room, and there was a huge
stack of firewood on the floor behind it. Jacob waved me to the
couch, but I didn't move. "I came to see if you was serious
about wanting to marry me."

He stared at me for a few seconds. "Yeah. I need somebody to
wash and iron my clothes, cook my meals, and keep my house
clean. My mama done told me she is way too tired and old to
keep doing it for me."

I was glad he was being honest, but I wished he had mentioned a few words about "love" and how cute I was. But since time wasn't on my side, I couldn't be too picky. "I can do all them things and more. I chop most of the firewood at my house, and I even know how to fish and hunt," I bragged. "I been doing them things all my life." Jacob had a car, so I decided it was important to throw in, "I know how to drive, too."

He gazed at me from the corner of his eye. "You said you had to think about marrying me. That was just a little while ago."

"Well, I done thought about it. How soon can we go up to Reverend Sweeney and see when he can marry us?"

CHAPTER 4

BEFORE I EVEN MADE IT BACK HOME, I GOT APPREHENSIVE ABOUT visiting Jacob and offering up myself like a sacrificial lamb. But I didn't want to be a old maid and I wanted to make Daddy happy. I had disappointed him so many times. Getting in trouble at school, not coming home when he told me to, and not doing my chores when I was supposed to was a few of the things I did that upset him.

Two days after I'd overheard the conversation between Daddy and Miss Maddie, I told him while having breakfast together that I was going to marry Jacob. At first, he looked at me like I had handed him the key to Heaven's Gate. Then he laid his fork down on his plate and started grinning. "Oh? I didn't know you was thinking about marriage."

I wanted to tell him that I wouldn't have been "thinking about marriage" if him and that witch he was in love with hadn't been thinking about it for me. But I didn't want to cause a ruckus.

Daddy could barely sit still. He shifted in his chair and rubbed his hands together. "God is so good! I am so happy for you! Let me go tell Maddie right now. She's been waiting to hear this news for a long time. I don't want to keep her waiting no longer." Daddy had all kinds of aches and pains, especially in his knees and feet. Sometimes it was hard for him to walk, but he leapt out of his seat and bolted out the front door like a bronco.

Nothing made me happier than to see my poor daddy happy.

Even if it meant giving up my chance to find a man I really did love.

I was sitting at the table gnawing on a piece of ham when Daddy came charging back into the house with Miss Maddie in tow. She made it into the kitchen before he did.

"Praise the Lord, Naomi," she yelled as she goose-stepped up to me and kissed my forehead. Her smile always looked fake when she talked to me, but today it looked even more so. "Willard just told me your good news. Jacob Purcell, huh? I never would have guessed you'd catch such a big fish! What I want to know is *when* will y'all be cutting the cake?"

I forced myself to smile but I had to clear my throat before I could answer. "Um . . . sometime this summer, I think."

Her fake smile disappeared within a split second. "Oh. Not until this summer, huh?" I had never seen such a fake smile. As much as I hated to admit it, Miss Maddie was real pretty for a woman her age. She had peach-colored skin, dimples in her cheeks, and the shiniest black eyes I ever seen. Her body was stout, lumpy, and saggy like most of the other women her age. She hid them defects in nice, loose-fitting frocks, though. This morning she still had on her housecoat and the stocking cap she always slept in. I figured she'd been so happy when Daddy told her I was getting married, she didn't waste no time putting on her regular clothes and fixing her hair. From the way her and Daddy had reacted so far, I realized they was more anxious to get me out of their hair than I first thought. Despite my feelings, or lack of feelings for Jacob, I was glad he was "rescuing" me.

"One of Jacob's aunties in Montgomery is having a operation next week and can't travel for a while. She told him she'd kill him dead if he got married before she could get here."

"Oh," Miss Maddie said again. "Well, summer will be here before you know it."

"I can't believe all my children will have their own homes. I hope you and Jacob start your family before my homegoing," Daddy said. He was standing next to Miss Maddie with his arm around her waist, grinning like he had just found a pot of gold.

Daddy irritated me when he made references to his death.

Whenever he brought it up, chills went up my spine. It was one of the reasons I wanted to do anything I could to let him be happy before it was too late. "Don't you go there again, Daddy. You ain't dying no time soon, so I wish you'd stop bringing it up," I scolded.

I was so pleased when Miss Maddie suddenly remembered the Rawleigh Man was coming to her house to deliver some vanilla extract, face cream for her wrinkles (it didn't work) and chewing gum for her grandkids. Them traveling salesmen only came into the colored neighborhoods once a month before the noon hour. If a customer wasn't home to get their order they had to wait until he came back the next month. Miss Maddie's lips felt like cold raw liver when she kissed my forehead again before she took off.

I was glad Daddy followed her back out the door so I could have some time alone to think about my upcoming wedding.

Three other girls was getting married in a few weeks. I figured that was the reason nobody made a big deal out of my engagement when they got wind of it. Because I wasn't having the fairytale marriage I had dreamed about when I was a little girl. I just wanted to get it over with.

Reverend Sweeney married me and Jacob in Daddy's living room the Saturday after the Fourth of July. About three dozen neighbors, friends, and family members attended. My three sisters and four brothers came with their spouses and all their rowdy young kids, which was half a dozen and two more on the way at the time. I had been babysitting my nieces and nephews since I was eight. Because I was family, my siblings didn't think they should pay me nothing. Every now and then one of my sisters gave me a nickel or some used makeup. Some days when I wasn't in school, I had to juggle them brats and cook and clean for Daddy at the same time. It had got harder and harder for me to have a social life. Getting married was almost like being let out of prison. What my young self didn't know at the time, was that there existed other prisons.

Right after me and Jacob exchanged vows, my eldest sister,

Claudette, came up to me with a stiff look on her face. There was so much nut-brown powder, blood-red rouge, and orange lipstick on her puffy face, she looked like a clown. She was eight months pregnant and had gained so much weight, all she could fit into was drab, homemade dresses big enough to cover half a couch. The one she had on today was a bright yellow and had a white collar, so she didn't look as dowdy as she usually did.

"I guess you won't be able to babysit for me no more, huh?" Claudette sniffed as she adjusted her wide-brimmed white hat. Me and my sisters all had the same honey-colored complexion, high cheekbones, and thick black hair.

"I guess not," I chirped. "I'm going to be too busy taking care of Jacob and the house. And I plan on getting a part-time job cleaning houses or working in the fields until I get pregnant."

"Humph. I hope you don't think marriage is paradise because it ain't. If I didn't have them three young'uns and this one on the way, I'd leave that jackass I married in a heartbeat."

"Well, Reverend Sweeney says marriage is for life. So, I'm going to stay with Jacob until one of us kicks the bucket." I let out a dry laugh.

Claudette gave me a pitying look and it included a little bit of contempt. She was the kind of woman who looked at almost everything from a negative point of view. "Let me tell you something, gal. You'll eat them words someday," she predicted.

I gave her a dismissive wave and moved to the other side of the room. All four of my brothers was tall, dark, and stout like Daddy. They had his thick, liver-colored lips and piercing black eyes. A lot of women found them features right handsome. The only one of my siblings I was close to was my brother Grady. He was only two years older than me. He had married a girl I went to school with two years ago and they had a little boy.

"Naomi, if Jacob ever mistreats you, let me know and I will maul his head," he whispered in my ear.

I slapped the side of his arm. "Hush up! You ain't going to do no such thing because he ain't never going to mistreat me," I snarled. And then we laughed.

My next-to-oldest brother, Dobie, was standing nearby and overheard me and Grady talking. He strutted up to me with a stern look on his face. Before he opened his mouth, he wagged his finger in my face. "Naomi, you know the man is always in charge. The Bible says so. So, you better be good to Jacob." Dobie paused long enough to clear his throat, but his finger was still in my face. "You better obey him, don't never sass him, burn his supper, or cheat on him. If you do, I'm going to maul *your* head." He didn't laugh, but me and Grady did.

Then Daddy walked up to put in his two cents. "Naomi, you ain't got a lick of sense, but I think you made the right decision to marry a man like Jacob instead of one of them teenage scalawags you used to pal around with." Daddy sniffed and dabbed a tear from the corner of his eye. I hugged him before I started mingling with our other guests. Two of the local moonshiners came and brought a huge supply of moonshine. So, the reception got pretty rowdy.

Me and Jacob got a heap of wedding gifts, and everybody had a good time. But I was a little uneasy because it wasn't exactly what I had always wanted. When I was a little girl, I'd always thought I'd have a big church wedding and wear a beautiful white gown. That was when I was still naïve enough to believe I would eventually live a fairy-tale life. Reality kicked me in the butt real quick. Daddy told me up front he hadn't been able to afford something elaborate for my sisters, and he couldn't afford to do it for me. Since I was marrying a man I wasn't madly in love with, I didn't really want a lot of fanfare no how. Besides, the girls I knew who had married for love and had fancy weddings was miserable. One had married a man that couldn't hold a job for more than a few weeks. Another one had married a farm hand who was so lazy and trifling, he only bathed two or three times a week. At least with Jacob I wouldn't have to worry about money, and he was so clean, he would bathe in the morning before he went to work and again when he got home. Other than love, I had everything I wanted . . .

CHAPTER 5

A WEEK AFTER MY WEDDING, WHEN I WENT TO VISIT DADDY, HE told me he was moving in with Miss Maddie. I was shocked and worried. My daddy was so set in his ways and hard to live with, I didn't think he'd ever want to live under the same roof again with anybody else. "Wh-what? I-I don't think that's such a good idea," I stammered.

We was sitting on his living-room couch. Daddy reared his head back and looked at me with his eyes stretched open as wide as they could go and not roll out of the sockets. "How come it ain't? Since when did you start sticking your nose into my business? I don't care if you married and grown now, I'm still your daddy. There's plenty more switches on the chinaberry tree in my backyard."

I rolled my eyes and huffed out a loud breath. "Oh, Daddy. I ain't trying to stick my nose in your business. I just want you to know how I feel about you making such a big decision."

He coughed and rubbed his chest. He had been doing that a lot lately and I was worried about it, too. Daddy thought all doctors was quacks and crooks, so he hadn't been to one in years. But I knew now was not a good time to mention his health.

"Well, me and Maddie think it's a good idea because I spend most of my time at her place anyway. It don't make sense for us to pay light bills and whatnot at two different houses. Besides, I get real lonely now that you ain't here."

Daddy's last sentence threw me for a loop. He was the one who was so anxious to get me out of the house!

"Well, you know Miss Maddie is kind of fickle. What if you give up your house and find out you don't like living with her? Or, what if she don't like living with you and kicks you out? Where will you go?"

"Why don't you mind your own business, gal. You worry about yourself, and I'll worry about me." Daddy gave me a stern look and waved his hands in the air. "Now hush up. I'm through conversating about this." He stomped out of the living room, and I returned to the house I now lived in with Jacob.

When I went to check on Daddy the next morning, most of his clothes was missing. The nosy woman next door told me she'd seen him leaving the house a couple of hours ago with a suitcase. I decided to wait a few days and have Jacob go with me to Miss Maddie's house to check on Daddy. I didn't think he'd threaten to get a switch and whup me in front of my husband. But we didn't have to go to Miss Maddie's house. Four days after I'd seen Daddy, he opened my kitchen door and walked in while I was ironing clothes.

After we hugged, he pulled a chair out from the table and made hisself at home. "Guess what, Naomi?" He didn't give me time to guess. With a crooked grin on his scraggly face, he went on. "Me and Maddie got married yesterday."

I stopped ironing and looked at him with my mouth hanging open. Him courting that battle-axe was one thing; her being my stepmother was such a scary thought, it gave me goose bumps. If she was legally married to Daddy, she'd have access to the money he had saved over the years as well as everything else he owned. If he died, me and my siblings wouldn't have no say-so in making his final arrangements. We had promised Daddy we would bury him next to our mama. Everybody knew that when Miss Maddie's first husband died, she didn't even have a funeral for him because she had made plans to go to Miami on vacation with her sisters that week and didn't want to cancel. She had the undertaker collect her dead husband's body and bury him before most of us even knew the man was dead! "I thought y'all was just going to live together. Y'all been going together for more than ten years. Why did y'all decide to get married?"

"She insisted on it," Daddy claimed. "I declare, I tried my best to get her to agree to us just living together for a while and discussing marriage later. Well, she wanted a serious commitment. She threatened to give me my walking papers and I didn't want to take a chance on losing such a sweet woman and have to start all over and look for a new one." Daddy sighed and massaged his temples. "Lord knows finding a good woman my age wouldn't be easy. Half of the ones I know can barely still walk. Besides, Maddie said if we lived in sin, it would set a bad example for her kids."

"I think it's too late for her to be worrying about setting a bad example," I mumbled.

Daddy raised his eyebrows and stared at me like I'd suddenly sprouted a beard. "I didn't hear you. What did you say?"

I fidgeted in my seat and crossed my legs. "Nothing," I answered in a small voice.

"Anyway, me and Maddie ain't spring chickens. You know my heart ain't too strong, and neither is hers. We ain't got too much time left so we thought we'd tie the knot as soon as we could. She's a big shot in the church, so it wouldn't look right for her to be living with a man she wasn't married to. We didn't tell nobody we was going to get married because we didn't want nobody to try and talk us out of it. I got a lot of plans for me and Maddie!" I couldn't remember the last time Daddy sounded so giddy. He got so slaphappy, he leaped up and danced a jig—and that wasn't easy for a man with severe arthritis throughout most of his body.

I realized now that he was more anxious to move on with his life than I thought. I was sorry I had made him wait so long. The only thing that bothered me was the fact that Miss Maddie took everything she wanted out of the house I had grew up in and sold or gave away everything else. I didn't find out about it until I asked Daddy if I could take the bed and chifforobe out of my old room so me and Jacob could put it in the second bedroom in our house for the kids we'd have someday to use. I was slightly mad because I didn't get that furniture, but I wanted to keep the peace, so I didn't make a fuss.

Me and Daddy took turns visiting each other almost every evening and he couldn't stop talking about how happy he was. Maddie cleaned houses full-time, so with her and Daddy's combined incomes, they was doing all right financially. They didn't sit on the porch for hours on end like so many of the old folks I knew. Every time I turned around, they was going to barbecues, fish fries, and some of the rowdiest parties in town.

Six months after Daddy and Miss Maddie got married, he had a heart attack and died at the kitchen table. I was devastated. But I was pleased he'd got to enjoy some "freedom" before he died. The last time I'd seen him, two days before his death, he was grinning from ear to ear so I knew he had died happy. I was surprised Miss Maddie let me and my siblings help make Daddy's final arrangements. We kept our promise and buried him next to Mama.

A month later, Miss Maddie abruptly disappeared. We found out from her neighbors that she had sold and gave away everything in her house and moved to Springfield, Massachusetts, where two of her kids lived. She hadn't allowed me and my siblings to retrieve none of Daddy's things. We was mad because she disposed of things like our baby pictures, toys, and other knickknacks we could never replace. I knew there was a lot of other evil people in the world like Miss Maddie. That was one of the reasons I promised myself I would try to be as kind and considerate to other folks as I could be.

It wasn't long before there was other major changes in my life. Within a year after Daddy's death, all my siblings had moved away from Lexington to various cities and states. Lula divorced Maxwell and was seeing three other men at the same time so she could decide which one would make a good second husband. However, the biggest change was in Jacob. He started hinting that our money wasn't going as far as it used to so he "suggested"

I get a full-time job. That wasn't so easy to do. Other than working in the fields, running errands for our neighbors, and babysitting, I didn't have no work experience. Besides, I was pregnant and not too many folks wanted to hire a woman in my condition.

As if we didn't have enough things to be worried about in 1918, something else happened that took us all by surprise. The news said it was some kind of deadly virus traveling around the world. When it made its way to Alabama in the fall, it hit hard. Two of my sisters caught the virus and died a week apart in February. My baby was due in September, so I was too scared to go anywhere but to church and the market.

Lula was even more worried than I was because she had two baby boys, and the virus was killing babies left and right. Weeks would go by and the only time I saw her was at church. After so many members of our congregation caught the virus and got real sick or died, me and her decided not to go back to church until things returned to normal. I was glad Jacob felt the same way.

Not only was the virus killing folks, it was also the reason some of the stores, fields, and mills either shut down or slashed their workers' hours. Jacob was still going to work, but only four hours a day, three days a week. The folks who ran the sawmill where he worked didn't want to take no chance and have all the workers get sick at the same time. "This mess better end soon or me and you will end up in the poor house," Jacob told me the week I was supposed to give birth. "And once the baby gets here, you sure as hell better get a job to help out!" he snapped.

"You don't need to keep telling me that!" I snapped back.

"And you better control your mouth, or I'll control it for you," he warned.

"Don't you talk to me like that. I got feelings. It's bad enough you forgot my birthday last week."

Jacob clapped his hands and laughed. "I declare, if I was eighteen and looked as old as you, I wouldn't call attention to myself. You look older than me!" He laughed again. A lot of folks thought I was two or three years younger. But this was just the beginning of Jacob's put-downs. "I don't know what I seen in a loathsome frump like you. No other man would want you. My friends must think I'm crazy—"

I cut him off fast. "I got news for you. Some of your friends told me I was cute, and they wish they had approached me before you did. And to tell you the truth, I wish I had held out for one of them!" I recalled the feeling of dread I had woken up with the day I'd run into that sucker at the market two years ago. Now I believed it had been a bad omen trying to warn me about him. Before I could say anything else, Jacob punched both sides of my face so hard, I seen stars before everything went black.

Chapter 6

WHEN I OPENED MY EYES, I WAS LAYING IN MY BED. THE SAME EL-derly midwife who delivered most of the babies in our neighborhood was sitting next to me. "You got a daughter," she told me as she scratched her hairy chin. I swallowed hard and looked toward the door just as Jacob entered the room with a lopsided smile on his sweaty face.

"Is she all right?" he asked the midwife in a raspy voice.

I was more concerned about my baby. Before the midwife could answer Jacob, I said, "Is my baby all right?" I was going to name her Ethel Mae after the mother I never got to meet.

"Yeah, she's just fine, praise the Lord. She is as plump and strong as a new horse. And she got a set of lungs that would make a wolf jealous. Naomi, you need to be more careful. It's a good thing Jacob was here when you fell. What I don't understand is how you managed to fall and hit *both* sides of your face on your kitchen table leg . . ." The midwife let out a loud sigh and gave me a curious look. "Use an ice pack to make the swelling go down."

Jacob jumped in right away. "This gal has always been as clumsy as an ox. One time she fell off the back porch steps face first and got a knot on the *back* of her head."

"Well, let's pray she don't fall while she's holding this baby and cause her some brain damage before her life even gets started good." The midwife stood up and wiped her hands on one of the damp towels she'd used. "All right now. My work here is over. Jacob, pay me my dollar so I can drag my tail back home."

After the midwife left, Jacob stared at his new daughter for a few seconds, but he didn't say nothing or pick her up. "I didn't mean to hit you so hard, and I declare it won't never happen again. Now give the baby some titty before she gets cranky. I ain't in the mood for no caterwauling."

I knew right then and there that raising Ethel Mae was a job I'd be doing mostly on my own.

Despite how weak I was for the next few days, Jacob didn't help me at all with Ethel Mae. He would hold her and talk baby talk, but as soon as she started crying or needed her diaper changed, he handed her to me. I had to spend so much time taking care of her, it was a challenge to get my other work around the house done. Much of it was caused by Jacob. He left dirty clothes on the floor, hair on the sink in the bathroom, and other messes all over the house.

He complained about the money I spent on movie magazines, smell-goods, and makeup. I didn't want to keep listening to him rant and rave about our finances, so I started baking pies and cakes to sell to our neighbors. That way I only had to ask him for money to pay bills and buy groceries. I mainly shopped at the five-and-dime store and Lula made a lot of clothes for me and Ethel Mae. She had just got a new Singer sewing machine and loved working on it. Almost everything else I bought came from the secondhand store.

Jacob bought his own clothes because he said all my taste was in my mouth. Even with all our money problems, he rarely went near the cheap stores. He had spent more on one pair of shoes than every pair I had put together. The fishing pole I owned was a five-foot-long piece of sapling with a string tied to it and a fish-hook at the end. His was a top-of-the-line bamboo thingamajig. I liked nice things, but I was also practical, thanks to Daddy teaching me the value of a dollar. Jacob usually ran out of money before his payday and often borrowed from me.

It seemed like I was married to a completely different man than the one who had come up to me at the market two years ago. One morning I looked in the mirror and asked myself, "Girl, what did you get yourself into?"

Jacob's bedroom skills was so mediocre, sex with him was just another chore to me. Mopping the kitchen floor gave me more pleasure than he did. If I was tired or not in the mood, he would climb on top of me anyway. I discovered early in our marriage that if I pretended I was having a good time, the quicker he finished. So, I did a lot of moaning and groaning when we went at it.

I griped about having to do all the housework by myself. That didn't faze Jacob, though. The same day I complained about having to let Ethel Mae sleep in a cardboard box because the cribs I liked was so expensive, he went to the woods, chopped down a tree, and made one for her. It looked better and was sturdier than the ones in the store. One time he bought me a box of candy and took me to the movies the same night. Another time he served me breakfast in bed. One evening while we was eating supper he told me, "Naomi, I hit the jackpot by marrying you. I know you will help me straighten myself out so I can be a better man and husband."

That comment sounded so strange coming from Jacob because he rarely admitted his shortcomings, or when he was wrong about something. I told Lula about the nice things he did for me, but she wasn't impressed. She said it was too little, too late. And that no matter how nice he was, it would never be enough to make up for his meanness. She went on to tell me I had to be crazy for not leaving Jacob, or that I should at least bat his head with a skillet like she had done with her husband before she divorced him. I kept telling Lula that whenever Jacob was mean to me, I felt better when I recalled the good times and the nice things he occasionally did for me. She still thought I was crazy for not leaving him then and warned me he was going to get worse before he got better.

*   *   *

By the time Ethel Mae turned a year old, the virus had eased up. But now we was all worried about the first big world war that was still going on. Jacob had done his military duty, so I didn't have to worry about him getting caught up in that mess. One of my previous boyfriends and several boys in my neighborhood had joined the Army. Two never made it back home alive. Their funerals was as sad as the ones for the folks who had died from the virus.

I thanked God every day that me, Ethel Mae, and Jacob was still healthy. When I started looking for work, right off the bat I landed a job doing laundry and ironing for one of the richest white women in Lexington. She paid me decent money, but she was so racist and mean, I knew I wasn't going to work for that witch too much longer. I couldn't afford to pay a babysitter, so I had to take Ethel Mae to work with me. She had to stay in the backyard the whole time with baloney sandwiches and a few sugar tits to gnaw on while I was working. Every time Ethel Mae wandered into the house I got chewed out and sent home.

It was Lula who came to my rescue. She was home all day, so she volunteered to look after Ethel Mae for free. When her mama got sick in September from the virus, Lula had to fill a lot of her seamstress orders. Her mama had been grooming Lula to take over for years, but none of us expected it to happen so soon. Lula could sew even better and faster than her mama, so more folks was giving her their business. Even white folks.

Jacob had promised that he would never hit me again, but he didn't keep it. It happened again on our third wedding anniversary. He took me to a seafood restaurant for supper that evening. It was a place that had finally started letting us eat inside instead of having to get our orders to go. We had just started eating our crab cakes and gumbo when a woman who had recently moved to Lexington from Mississippi came through the front door. She looked around for a few seconds and when she seen us, she pranced over to our table and looked straight at Jacob. "Well! I'm glad to see you ain't dead or laid up at the clinic . . ." She sniffed and ignored me completely. "I was worried when you didn't show up last Saturday night to take me dancing."

"What's going on here, sister-woman? This man is my husband!" I snapped.

She did a double take and looked at me with her eyes blinking hard. "Well, excuuuuuse me. He told me his wife was dead."

Jacob squirmed in his seat before he replied. "Uh, you misunderstood me. I told you my *mama* was dead."

The way the woman was glaring at him, you would have thought she was fixing to slap his face. I wanted to slap him myself, but I didn't want to act a fool in public, especially in a white restaurant. It would give them another reason to put more restrictions on us.

"Jacob, I guess I won't be seeing you no more, huh?" she asked with a wounded look on her face.

I answered her question. "You got that right." I looked from her to him. "Jacob, will you tell your friend bye so we can finish our meal?"

He was sweating so hard, it looked like somebody had poured a bucket of water on his face. He wiped his forehead with his napkin and stood up. "Baby, I'll be right back," he said as he escorted that brazen hussy to another part of the restaurant.

There was a sheepish grin on Jacob's face when he came back to our table and plopped down with a groan. "Sheesh! Some folks can get so confused," he griped as he wiped more sweat off his face.

I folded my arms and glared at him. "Tell me about it. Who was that heifer?"

"Uh . . . uh. Just some old gal I ran into at a friend's house."

"How come she thought you was coming to her house last Saturday to take her dancing?"

"Like I said, she was confused. Don't worry about it. I was just playing with her, so she'd buy me a drink—and she did. That's all that was."

I pushed my plate away and stood up. "Pay the check and let's get in the car. I done lost my appetite."

"Yes, ma'am," he muttered.

We was silent for the first couple of minutes on the way home. But I couldn't hold my tongue no longer. "Jacob, I been hearing gossip about you fooling around with other women."

"I ain't fooling around with nobody! Them busybody gossip-mongers is lying!" he hollered as he slapped the steering wheel. "But if you don't start contenting me, I will start fooling around . . ."

"Contenting you how? I do everything a wife is supposed to do. All them gossipmongers can't be lying. I don't see you doing nothing to content me." Before I could go on, he reached over and mauled my head with his fist so hard, I almost passed out.

From that night on, he didn't even try to hide what he was doing with other women. When we finally got a telephone, six months after our anniversary, the first person to call the house was a woman I'd heard he was messing around with. When I handed the telephone to him, he conversated with her right in front of me. I didn't want to get punched or slapped again, so I didn't say nothing. I had too many other things on my mind that was more important than Jacob. One was struggling with the jobs I had to settle for.

The first week into the new year, I took off two days to look for another job. When I went back to work, that mean-ass cow I worked for had hired another girl to replace me. If that wasn't bad enough, I only got half of my pay for the previous days I'd worked and got cussed out for taking off time without permission.

For the next few years, I worked for several other families. Most of them was nice to me and didn't have a problem with me taking off time so I could look for a better job. All I could find was more part-time work here and there, working two or three days for two and three different families each. I hated having to deal with so many different personalities. That and my relationship with Jacob saddened me, but only for brief periods of time. There was times when I felt so overwhelmed, I wanted to lay down and give up on my marriage. But I'd give it all I had before I did that. Daddy used to tell me that getting bent was part of life and that in the end, only the really strong folks didn't break. At the end of the day, they came out better than they was before. Jacob could bend me; but I was not going to let him—or nobody else—break me.

I figured that so long as I had my church, a healthy child, and friends like Lula, I could be fairly happy for the rest of my life. The only thing was, I didn't want to spend the rest of my days only being *fairly* happy.

CHAPTER 7

THE YEARS WAS FLYING BY TOO FAST FOR ME. I COULDN'T BELIEVE IT was already 1932. The country was still in a economic downfall that had started three years ago. The news called it the Great Depression. Banks collapsed, rich folks lost most of their money, and colored folks had to struggle even more to find work. Things between me and Jacob wasn't too much better, but I was determined to make my marriage work. Sometimes he did things that made me think he was trying to be a better person. Last year, he bought new furniture for the living room and had every room in the house repainted. But he rarely let me drive the slightly used Chrysler he had bought two years ago.

He was still mean to me from time to time, and I kept hearing rumors that he was still fooling around with other women. It didn't do no good to confront him. Every incident I brought up was either a "misunderstanding" or somebody had "mistook him for another man." He could never explain lipstick on his shirt collar and jaw, smell-goods that wasn't mine on his clothes, and him being out all night and sometimes days at a time. For a while he claimed he'd got drunk and passed out on somebody's couch and was too afraid to come home and face me, so he decided to stay a day or two and give me time to cool off. The thing was, Jacob was not the least bit scared of me, so that lie didn't hold no water.

There was a lot of times when I cursed myself for making the decision to marry Jacob. It was the worst one I ever made. I didn't have to get married so Daddy could move on. I could have got a job and moved in with Lula or one of my siblings until I saved up enough money to get my own place. Or, I could have held out for a better husband. Like that Hawkins boy Miss Maddie and Daddy had been scheming to dump me off on. I waited too long, though. A month after I married Jacob, Emmet Hawkins married another girl. He had a good job supervising colored workers at the slaughterhouse. Him and his wife had two beautiful children and she was one of the happiest women I knew. I had never heard no rumors or gossip about him mistreating her.

I still kept up with the news on the radio and in the newspaper, but sometimes them reports depressed me. The first week in March, there was a story about a baby boy in New Jersey who was kidnapped right out of his own crib during the night. The story was big news because the baby's daddy was a famous man named Charles Lindbergh. He flew a airplane all by hisself across the ocean five years ago, which didn't make no sense to me. Him being white and having money, I couldn't understand why he didn't just get on a ship if he wanted to travel that bad.

I wasn't interested in airplanes, but I followed the story about the kidnapping. As a mother, I felt for that baby's family, especially his mama. Mr. Lindbergh paid the ransom, but the kidnapper still didn't return the baby. They found that precious little boy's dead body in May, and the kidnapper was still on the loose. I didn't know what the world was coming to. That story stayed on my mind for weeks. I prayed that me and my loved ones would all die of natural causes.

The week after my thirty-second birthday, a old lady who belonged to my church died. She had cooked for twenty-five years for Reverend Garth Spivey, the most well-known and admired white preacher in Lexington. He was always on the radio preaching up a storm. His family had made their money in cotton and sugar cane. Reverend Spivey and his two older brothers had run the businesses until they got too old and then their sons and other relatives took over. Now all Reverend Spivey did was preach and donate some of that money he had inherited to good causes. He also roamed around town donating clothes and baskets of food to folks that needed help—even colored ones.

It was rare to see white folks at our churches. But nobody was surprised to see Reverend Spivey at his used-to-be cook's funeral. Him and his dowdy, overweight wife, Viola, sat in the last pew in the back of the church with me and Jacob. Ethel Mae had stayed home because she claimed she had a real bad headache. I suspected she was putting on a act because I knew how teenagers' minds worked. She was fourteen now and had more important things to do than go to funerals. I figured she just wanted to stay home and read the latest edition of *Weird Tales* magazine while she gobbled up Moon Pies and Tootsie Rolls. I didn't confront her because I used to do the same thing when I didn't want to go with Daddy to a depressing, boring funeral. I had decided I would let Ethel Mae enjoy her teenage years—but I would still try to keep her out of trouble.

I stopped my mind from wandering when I heard Reverend Spivey speak to me. "Did you know the dearly departed?" he asked, looking at me over the top of his glasses. His beady blue eyes reminded me of marbles. He had a lot of wrinkles on his face, and thin white hair, so I assumed he was in his late seventies or early eighties. His wife looked even older. But she seemed to be a real nice lady. The minute she'd set foot in the church, she went up to two new mothers and hugged and kissed their babies.

Our rinky-dink newspaper often ran articles about Reverend Spivey and all the charity work he did for people in Lexington. Two years ago, a tornado did some damage to our church. When his cook told him that it was her church, he paid to have it repaired.

"Yes, sir. Clarabelle lived in my neighborhood. She used to cook a heap of things for my daddy. Before I got married, she taught me how to cook some real good dishes. Folks even pay me to make pies and cakes for them," I bragged.

"Oh? Well, I would venture to say that anybody who could cook half as good as Clarabelle gets a whole lot of praise from me. Do you know anybody like that? I would like to hire a replacement as soon as possible and I need them full-time, Monday through Friday, and occasionally on weekends at a moment's notice. My wife is too sickly to do much cooking." He leaned his head closer to mine and added in a whisper, "She can't cook worth a damn anyway."

I held my breath to keep from snickering. I had never heard a preacher use a cuss word. "Um . . . I don't know anybody available right now. I wish I was . . ."

Reverend Spivey stared at me as he scratched his chin. "You look a mite young to take on such a high-level position, especially for me. I entertain a lot of important folks. Judge Smoot is my first cousin, and he eats like a hog."

"I ain't young. I turned thirty-two last week. I used to clean for Judge Smoot's family two years ago. When he entertained a big crowd, I helped his cook prepare some of the meals. He raved about my smothered pork chops and biscuits."

Reverend Spivey gasped, took off his glasses, and squinted his eyes. He blinked a few times before he put his glasses back on. "Well, I declare. That was *you?* I used to listen to him and his great big family brag about the backup gal who helped out in the kitchen. I heard you could cook up a storm."

I really knew my way around in the kitchen. My older sisters, Daddy, and other older women had taught me a lot. I'd even created new recipes of my own. I didn't want to sound smug, so I said in a very meek voice, "I was that backup gal, sir."

Reverend Spivey scratched his chin some more. "The Smoots was as sad as could be when you left them to take a better job. Why don't you come to my house at your earliest convenience and whup up a supper for me and my wife." He paused and chuckled. "I don't want to go too many more days eating soupy grits, burnt cornbread, and undercooked black-eyed peas. The job pays twenty dollars a week to start. Benefits include a yearly two-week vacation, sick leave with pay, and bonuses when fitting."

Twenty dollars! I couldn't believe my ears. I had been working my fingers to the bone for years and the most I ever made in a week was ten dollars and had never received no benefits. "How about tomorrow?"

"That'll be fine. Will you be able to take time off from work without a fuss? I'd hate for you to jeopardize any commitments you already have."

"I'm sure it won't be no problem." I was so sick of the family I was working for now; I had been praying for a reason to leave. I didn't like to count chickens before they hatched, but I was convinced that I had this job in the bag.

I had to remind myself that I was at a funeral so I couldn't walk around looking or acting giddy. I even managed to shed a few more tears.

As much trouble as it had been for me to cook several dishes to be served at Clarabelle's funeral, it turned out to be a blessing in disguise. When we all moved to the dining area, Reverend Spivey filled his plate with some of the collard greens, yams, macaroni and cheese, and several different meat dishes that I had cooked. I waited until he started eating before I went up to him. "I'm glad to see you trying some of the dishes I brought," I chirped.

Reverend Spivey's jaws was bloated with food. His eyes got big as he chewed and swallowed real fast. "I declare, this is some of the best home-cooking I've had since . . . well . . . since Clarabelle died! Can you read and write?"

"Sir?"

"Did you go to school? I need somebody who can read labels, pricing information, my extensive shopping list, and what have you, for when they have to do some grocery shopping for my household."

"I went to school, but I dropped out in tenth grade to get married. I was at the top of my class. I can read everything from the ingredients on a gum wrapper to anything in the Bible—even them big words."

Reverend Spivey laughed. "Well, I dropped out in seventh grade. Mother didn't like the curriculum, so she decided to teach me and my siblings at home. I ain't book smart, but I know all the basics of life because I'm God smart and that's a lot more important."

"You're right," I agreed.

Mrs. Spivey was standing right beside Reverend Spivey the whole time, but she was as quiet as a mouse until he nudged her with his elbow. "Viola, do you think this gal will work out for us?"

She swallowed the food in her mouth and looked me over real slow. "You ever been arrested, stole something, sassed or hit a white person?"

"Oh, no, ma'am. I been on the straight and narrow my whole life," I said proudly. "Ask anybody here and they will vouch for me."

"Well, we can give you a trial run. You are doing good so far," Mrs. Spivey chirped.

Reverend Spivey nodded. "Well, my dear, it would be a blessing to have you on my staff—if you live up to my expectations. I'll expect to see you at my house tomorrow morning at eight A.M. sharp." He blinked and raised his finger in the air. "But keep in mind, if you don't suit me at the end of the first week, out the door you go."

"Thank you! Oh, my name is Naomi Purcell."

Reverend Spivey grabbed my hand and shook it. "Naomi, it's a pleasure to make your acquaintance." He rattled off his address and in the same breath asked me to hand him the platter with the hush puppies on it.

That was how I got hired to cook full-time for Reverend Spivey. I wasn't even going back to the job tomorrow that I'd been itching to quit anyway. That woman hadn't paid me in two weeks because she claimed I had tossed out some silverware with the dishwater. I couldn't wait to get home today and call her up. She'd be outdone when I told her I had a new job working for one of the most prominent families in Lexington. Leaving her and her nasty family in a lurch was a good way for me to get back at them for being so mean to me.

CHAPTER 8

JACOB AND ETHEL MAE WAS GLAD I'D LANDED A BETTER JOB. WHEN we got home from the funeral, they stood next to me when I called up my old boss and resigned. She got smart and told me she was glad to get "rid" of me because I was a lousy cook anyway. She said a few cuss words, but when she called me a nigger, I hung up on her.

"What did she say?" Jacob asked.

"She cussed at me and called me a nigger. I hung up while she was still talking." Me and Jacob laughed.

"I hope you spit in everything you cooked for that family," Ethel Mae said.

I gave her one of my sternest looks. "Now you know I would never do nothing like that to nobody."

"I'm sorry, Mama. I hate what you went through, and I hope this preacher is as nice as people say he is."

"Well, if he ain't, I'll get another job," I said with a heavy sigh. My hopes was up real high, and I was going to keep them there until I had a reason not to.

"I'm glad you didn't tell that bitch you quit in person. There ain't no telling what she would have done to you!" Jacob boomed. It was good to see a angry look on his face that was meant for somebody other than me. Then he suddenly started grinning. "You did the right thing. I bet she ain't never had one of us hang up on her. I can't wait to tell my friends my wife got a job working for Reverend Garth Spivey. Oomph! Come here and give me some sugar, sugar."

I was in such a good mood, I kissed Jacob and almost enjoyed it. The rest of the day was real pleasant. But I knew it wouldn't be long before Jacob and Ethel Mae did or said something to bring me down.

I got up early Friday morning to get ready for work. I always wore a drab gray uniform to work, but today I put on one of the ones that still had the price tag on it.

The local buses had finally started serving the colored part of town. But I didn't mind that I had to walk a mile the day after the funeral to get to the bus stop to catch the one that would let me off one block from Reverend Spivey's street.

It had rained during the night, so there was a heap of puddles and slippery sidewalks I had to deal with. I had left the house early so I could take my time. The last thing I wanted to do was slip and fall and get my gray work dress messed up. It was drab enough already.

I was glad Reverend Spivey didn't live close to none of the mean white women I'd worked for. I prayed that none of them witches belonged to his church. If they did, I'd worry day and night about him making a brag about my cooking and one of them mean folks bad-mouthing me—especially the ones I'd quit on without giving notice.

I kept my head down as I walked down the street. When a white person approached me, I made sure I didn't make eye contact with them, and I gave them plenty of space on the sidewalk.

I couldn't imagine living in a nice home like some of the ones I passed. The ones in the colored neighborhoods looked a lot like each other, but these houses didn't look the same. None of the houses on my street had a upstairs. These had two or three floors, and some had attics. The wraparound porches had nice outdoor furniture and there was some of the most beautiful dogwood trees I ever seen in most of the huge front yards. With all the prosperous-looking things the folks in this part of town had—especially since President Hoover hadn't got us out of the economic slump we'd been in for a few years—some white folks still wasn't happy enough to treat colored folks like human beings.

The minute I knocked on the back door at Reverend Spivey's huge off-white house that Friday morning, I knew God had really been looking out for me. An elderly woman with white hair who had the same features as Reverend Spivey opened the door. "Um . . . I'm Naomi Purcell. Reverend Spivey wanted me to start cooking today." The woman just stared at me and didn't say nothing. "Can you let him know I'm here?" The woman still didn't say nothing. Finally, Reverend Spivey strolled in wearing a baby-blue robe and flopped down into a chair at the table. He put on his glasses and looked me up and down before he said anything.

"Morning, Naomi. I see you've met Annie Lou."

"Um . . . yes," I muttered.

Annie Lou smiled and said to Reverend Spivey, "I got a itching to take a stroll."

"You do that, dearie." He spoke to her in the same gentle tone that some folks used to speak to a very young child. "Don't go too far and get lost again. If you do, I'm going to lock you in your room."

Annie Lou sucked on her teeth and stamped her foot. "I know my way back home!" She stuck her tongue out at Reverend Spivey and gave him a dismissive wave and scurried out the door. I assumed she was either retarded or senile. He lowered his voice and said, "She's slipping away from us. Some days her mind is as sharp as a serpent's tooth. Some days it ain't. Try not to upset her. She bites."

I thought the preacher was playing with me until he showed me a faint set of teeth prints on the back of his hand. I exhaled and wrung my hands, wondering if I had stepped into a burning house. "Um . . . I'm sure she's a nice lady."

"And a very capable one, too. She does all the laundry and keeps the house clean."

"Well, if you need me to help out with the housecleaning and laundry, I will."

Reverend Spivey sucked in his breath and sighed. "I'll keep that in mind, but I doubt if it will be necessary or prudent. Each time I mention hiring more help, Annie Lou frets. See, she has nothing else to do, so helping around the house makes her feel useful." He whispered, "Sometimes I make a mess just so she can have something to do."

It was on the tip of my tongue to ask what Miss Viola did around the house to make herself feel useful. Some of the other white women I had worked for didn't do nothing but flounce around the house, shop and meet their friends for lunch, drinks, and only God knew what else they did with their time.

"Annie Lou spends most of her time in her room working on puzzles and reading love story magazines. Some days you'll only see her at mealtimes. Don't go into her room unless she invites you. We put her on the third floor at the end of the hall. For some reason she thinks somebody's been sneaking in and stealing her things." Reverend Spivey shook his head and groaned. "Believe me, there ain't nothing in her room anybody would want. Not even the junkman."

"I'm sure me and Annie Lou will get along just fine." I was beginning to feel awkward, but I kept a smile on my face. "You and her look a lot alike. Y'all twins?"

Before he could answer, Annie Lou came back and stood in the doorway. "Brother, you going to tell Naomi I'm colored?"

Reverend Spivey gasped, sprung out of his chair, shot across the floor and stopped in front of Annie Lou with his hands on his hips. "Your mouth is getting too big for your body, missy! How many times do I have to tell you not to talk about that?"

"We told Clarabelle about me," Annie Lou said with a pout.

"You will stay in your room until I tell you to come out!" Reverend Spivey hollered as he wagged his finger in her face. "Now scat!"

Annie Lou scurried away, and Reverend Spivey sat back down. His face was almost as red as a tomato. And then he let out a loud sigh. "Well, it ain't no secret that a heap of the slave owners used colored women for carnal activity. Me and Annie Lou share the same father. My daddy purchased her mama from a sugar cane farmer while I was still in diapers. Only my family, the dearly departed Clarabelle, and a few close friends know she's got colored blood. She'll pass herself off as a white woman when she goes shopping or wants to eat in a restricted restaurant. I don't condone anything of a deceitful nature but if I was in her shoes, I'd probably do the same thing."

Reverend Spivey gave me a woeful look before he went on. "Now that you know one of my family's deepest, darkest secrets, I strongly advise you to keep it to yourself."

"You ain't got to worry about me blabbing your business, sir. Honest to God."

Reverend Spivey went on to tell me he was nine years old when Lincoln freed the slaves and that most of the ones his family had owned left the plantation right away. Annie Lou's mama had died two years earlier and Annie Lou had nobody else but the Spivey family, so she chose to stay. Reverend Spivey promised his daddy that he would look after her until the day she died. She had never been married or had any children.

There was a heap of elderly, used-to-be slaves still alive. Some of the ones who lived in my neighborhood could pass for white. The ones who was still able to get around would be "white" when they wanted to go to a nice restaurant or shop in a store and be treated like the rest of the white folks. What I didn't like about a few was that they thought because of their skin shade, they was better than us darker folks. I was concerned about this Annie Lou riding on a high horse when I had to deal with her. Other than that, I was convinced that I'd enjoy working for Reverend Spivey.

He let out a loud breath and went on. "The market delivers our groceries, and if there is something special you want to whoop up, let me know and I'll add it to the grocery list I prepare every week. Now let me show you the house."

I had never been so amazed in my life. The kitchen was three times bigger than mine. The Spiveys ate breakfast and lunch at the kitchen table, but they got straight-up formal for supper—even dressed up like they was going to church. The room where they ate their evening meals had a long oak table with enough chairs to seat eight folks. The living room was so big I could set my whole house in it and have room left over. The main front window was so tall and wide I could have drove a car through it and not touch the edges. One thing I could never figure out was why folks with money filled their houses with ugly furniture and outlandish knickknacks. There was a life-size statue of a man dressed in a suit of armor standing in a corner.

Reverend Spivey, his wife, and Annie Lou enjoyed the butter-milk biscuits I made to go with the grits, eggs, and sausages for breakfast my first day on the job. "This is scrumptious! Don't you agree, Mrs. Spivey?"

Miss Viola stopped chomping and looked up from the table as I refilled her glass with buttermilk. "Naomi, I declare, you cook better than Clarabelle. I hope you'll be with us from now on," she told me.

"I hope you'll stay with us, too. I ain't never going to miss none of your meals," Annie Lou said with her mouth full of food. And then she said something in a shy tone that made me feel more relaxed. "I like you, Naomi."

They raved about the hush puppies, lima beans, fried chicken, pecan pie, and potato salad I cooked for supper. Each one had more than one helping. When they left the dining room, they was all beaming like the noon-day sun. I couldn't have been happier if I had struck gold.

When I got home that evening, Jacob's car was gone. The house was quiet until I got close to Ethel Mae's bedroom and heard somebody inside giggling. It sounded like more than one person. "Oooh—that felt good! Do it again!" Ethel Mae squealed. I eased open the door and seen her and a boy sitting up in bed.

"Mama! I—I can explain!" she hollered as she pulled the kivver up to hide her naked bosom.

I couldn't believe my eyes. "What in the world is going on up in here?"

"Mama! We was just . . . we was just talking," Ethel Mae replied in a shaky tone.

"In your bed? Boy, whatever your name is, you better get up out of here before I whup your behind!"

"Yes'm! I'll be leaving." The lanky boy leaped off the bed, put his clothes on, and was out the door in less than two minutes.

Right after I heard the front door slam, I glared at Ethel Mae. "Put your clothes on and go in that backyard and get a switch. And make sure it's a thick one!"

After I gave her whupping, she sat on the side of her bed, boo-hooing and rubbing her legs where I had swatted her. If the switch hadn't broke in two, I would have whupped her longer. I stood in front of her with my arms folded. "Baby, you know what you did was wrong."

"I . . . I . . . I know it was, Mama."

"You ain't but fourteen. You don't need to be letting no boy have his way with you."

She sniffled and gave me a defiant look that had become too familiar to me. That kind of disrespect usually got her a few more licks. But I'd whupped her good enough this time. I was anxious to hear what she had to say next. "Lula told me you and her had two and three boyfriends at the same time when y'all was even younger than me."

I couldn't argue with that. I started fooling around with boys when I was thirteen. But I was a firm believer in the saying, "Do as I say, not as I do."

Ethel Mae went on to justify her actions by telling me it was hard to wait until marriage to have sex. She didn't know what the big deal was because everybody was doing it.

"Sugar, I wanted your first time to be special."

She didn't waste no time responding. "It was, Mama. Last year."

I groaned and shook my head. "Wh-what? How many times have you been pestered?"

Ethel Mae shrugged. "I don't know."

"Well, how many boys?"

"I don't know that, neither. They keep coming at me."

I felt like I had failed as a mother, but I wasn't going to give up on my child. I knew that whuppings didn't make kids behave, but I knew that if I didn't discipline her at all, she'd be even more hog wild.

I looked up at the ceiling and waved my arms. "Lord, help me." And then I shook my finger at Ethel Mae. "Go get another switch off that tree."

CHAPTER 9

I WAS SO DISAPPOINTED IN ETHEL MAE, I DIDN'T KNOW WHAT TO DO or say to her. After I whupped her, we sat down on the couch. Her face was so tight, I could have bounced a dime off it. I put my arm around her shoulder anyway. "Baby, why do you let boys take advantage of you? All they want is to have a good time with you."

Ethel Mae turned and looked at me with her eyes narrowed. "Well, I'm having a good time with them, too. Besides, it's the only way I can make friends," she argued.

I gasped. "Why do you think that's the only way you can make friends?"

Ethel Mae sniffled as fresh tears pooled in her eyes. "Mama, look at me. I'm fat and ugly. I ain't got but two or three friend-girls and they only like me because I do their homework and give them money."

I gasped again. Ethel Mae had Jacob's creamy dark skin and baby face, so no way was she "ugly." "You ain't ugly and you ain't that fat. What about that Williams girl next door? She's fatter than you and uglier than homemade sin. She got a heap of friends, girls and boys. And she's engaged to get married."

"Well, something is wrong with me."

I spent the next hour trying to convince my daughter that she was just as good as anybody else. By the time I finished talking, she had perked up. I was pleased when she promised she wouldn't have sex again until she was married or engaged. I didn't believe she'd keep her promise. All I could do was pray that she wouldn't get hurt or pregnant. She was messing around with more than one boy, so she wouldn't even know which one got her pregnant.

After we got more relaxed, I told Ethel Mae about my first day working for Reverend Spivey and how much I had enjoyed it. The way her face lit up with pride, you never would have guessed that she'd got another whupping a little while ago. "Mama, I am so proud of you. Everybody in town knows what a good man that preacher is. I wish I hadn't ruined the day by letting that boy into the house."

I sighed. "Well, it's over and done with now. The way that rascal hightailed it out of here, I don't think he'll approach you again."

"It wouldn't do him no good if he did. I'm through with his tail."

The Sunday after I caught Ethel Mae in bed with that boy, she reluctantly went to church with me. I thought maybe after the service I could get Reverend Sweeney to say a few words to her that might make a difference in her behavior.

Before the morning service ended, she went to use the outhouse behind the church. After fifteen minutes had passed and she hadn't returned I got worried and went to look for her. I was horrified by what I seen when I got outside. Ethel Mae was backed up against a tree by the side of the outhouse letting a boy who sang in the choir have his way with her.

"Y'all stop that!" I screamed. The boy pulled up his pants and trotted into the woods behind the outhouse. Ethel Mae pulled up her bloomers and stared at me with a blank expression on her face.

"Girl, have you lost your mind? How could you do something so vile on *hallowed* ground?"

"I . . . I . . . I'm sorry, Mama," she whimpered.

"Sorry is right! Come on and let me get your nasty tail home."

We had walked the four blocks to church because Jacob didn't want to come, wouldn't let me use the car, and he'd refused to drive us. I was too disgusted to go back inside the church, so I would have to get Reverend Sweeney to talk to Ethel Mae some other time. I fussed at her all the way home and some more when we got inside. I whupped her again.

Three days later when I was riding the bus home, I seen her and a different boy rush behind a deserted building that used to be a bank before it failed last year. I knew what they was up to, so I didn't even bother to get off the bus and follow them. When she got home a hour after me, I didn't even confront her.

I didn't like to burden other folks with my problems, but I thought it would do me a world of good to talk to somebody about Jacob's and Ethel Mae's antics. Holding it all in had finally took a toll on me. The one person I knew I could always count on to be there for me was Lula. She had divorced her second husband six months ago and had a heap of boyfriends when she was married and between husbands. Talking to her was almost as good as talking to a preacher, so I planned to see her today before it got too late.

Both of Lula's parents had passed and her brothers had married and moved on. She lived with her current boyfriend, Lewis Blackburn, and her two teenage sons. They occupied the same house she had grew up in. As bad as I needed to talk to her, I didn't want to do it while Lewis and the boys was home.

Lula liked to kick up her heels and visit the local moonshiners' houses a few times a month, and every now and then I went with her. I didn't drink, but I liked to listen to music, and I loved to dance. A lot of the men had been trying to be more than friends with me for years. They left me alone when I made it clear to them I was not the cheating type.

Ten minutes after I finished cooking supper, I looked out my living-room window and seen Lula strutting down the street. That sister was dressed to kill in a low-cut black blouse and a tight flowered skirt with a split halfway up her thigh. I ran outside and caught up with her. "I need to talk to you," I panted.

"I'm going to visit one of them moonshiners. I need a drink," she told me. She was walking fast so I had to trot to keep up with her.

"I would love to go with you, but I ain't dressed for no party like you." I had on a pair of black britches and a plain white blouse.

"Pffftt! Girl, you been to them moonshiners' houses enough times to know that some of their guests show up looking like hobos," Lula snickered.

"All right, then. I'll go with you." I was glad she stopped walking so fast.

"What do you need to talk to me about?"

I blew out a loud breath. "Jacob and Ethel Mae are both out of control."

Lula stopped in her tracks and listened with a pitying expression on her face as the words poured from my mouth. "He hits me more often now and he comes home with lipstick on his neck and jaws. Ethel Mae is letting boys pester her left and right. I'm surprised she ain't got pregnant yet. If I don't talk to somebody, I'm going to take a one-way trip to the county nuthouse."

When I stopped talking, Lula gazed at me for quite a few seconds before she said anything. "Girl, I never thought your life was perfect, but I didn't know all that was going on. I will admit that I been hearing about Jacob fooling around for years. I never brought it up to you because I didn't want to upset you. I wish you had said something before now."

"I wish I had, too."

"What you need to do is whup Ethel Mae more often and harder. And you need to fight Jacob back the next time he hits you. You want to borrow my switchblade?"

I shook my head. "I whup Ethel Mae all the time, but it ain't never done no good. The last time Jacob slapped me, I slapped him back." Lula started laughing first and then I chuckled for a few seconds.

She looked up and down the street at the neighbors staring out their windows at us. "This ain't the time and place to talk about them two fools. When you get ready to talk about them again, call me or come to the house. But for tonight, let's go get loose."

There was several moonshiners operating only a few blocks

from where we lived. Most of them owned stills and made their own liquor. But a few bought some from the white bootleggers who passed through our part of town from time to time.

Me and Lula decided to visit the closest moonshiner; a shady man named Elmo Petrie. He made good money, but he was still greedy. He had a "party" going on at his house every day except Sunday and that was only because he was the choir director at our church and had to be present until the evening service ended. By then he was too tired to host a bunch of drunks.

One reason Elmo was the most popular colored moonshiner in Lexington was because he really knew how to show his guests a good time. He served free snacks, and he had a Victrola phonograph and a heap of records so folks could dance all they wanted to. He knew I loved Bessie Smith, so whenever I showed up, he'd put on one of her records and I would dance my tail off.

Elmo's house was at the end of the block he lived on. Like the rest of the homes in the colored part of town, it was shabby and plain on the outside. Inside was a different story. He had painted his walls a bright yellow and the furniture in his living room matched. He had so much company that he built two outhouses in his backyard. The still he used to make his alcohol was in the woods behind the outhouses.

Elmo was standing a few feet from the front door when Lula opened it. "Hello, ladies!" he boomed as we made our way in. "It's always good to see y'all. It's kind of early so I ain't got a good crowd yet."

Elmo was married to one of Lula's cousins, but it was no secret that he was a ladies' man. There was a rumor going around that him and Jacob messed around with some of the same women. I couldn't figure out what women saw in a bug-eyed, tubby, fifty-year-old man like Elmo—not that Jacob looked like a film star.

Lula looked over his shoulder. "What do you mean you ain't got a good crowd? There's enough niggers up in here now to make a Tarzan movie!" Everybody within earshot roared with laughter. Lula snickered and pushed Elmo to the side. "Get out my way and go get me a shot of white lightning and a glass of cider or buttermilk for Naomi."

"All right, then. Y'all come on in and make yourselves at home." Elmo waved us in.

I followed Lula to a couch backed up against the wall. There was a man sitting on one arm, and a woman on the other so there was plenty of room for me and Lula. My butt had just touched the couch when David Burruss, a man from my church, grabbed my hand and pulled me up to dance. I couldn't shimmy and twirl as good as some of the other women, but that didn't stop me from dancing every chance I got.

I really enjoyed myself that night. But it didn't take long for the gloom to return. Jacob was still gone when I got home a few minutes after midnight. He didn't come home until daybreak. I was still awake, but he didn't say nothing to me when he came into the bedroom. All he did was look at me with contempt, shake his head, and give me a dismissive wave.

I thought Ethel Mae was in her room, but before I left for work the next morning, I caught her creeping in through the back door with her shoes in her hand. She had been out all night, too. I looked at her and shook my head. "Before you get ready for school, go get a switch."

CHAPTER 10

T HINGS STAYED PRETTY MUCH THE SAME FOR THE NEXT COUPLE OF years. It was the first Saturday morning in April, 1936. Jacob had went out to get me some ice cream two days ago and I hadn't seen him since. After I ate some bacon and eggs, I decided to stretch out on the couch and listen to the radio for a while. I would have preferred to listen to a comedy program, or a station that played music. But early in the day, the reception was so bad in my neck of the woods, our rickety old radio only got the stations that broadcasted the news.

I sat bolt upright when it was announced that yesterday they had executed the man who had kidnapped the Lindbergh baby four years ago. This was one of the stories I had thought about off and on since it first broke. I ran to the phone and called up Lula. She answered right away, like she usually did.

"They electrocuted the devil who kidnapped and killed the Lindbergh baby," I blurted out.

"I heard it on the news. Anybody that harms children and women need to go straight to hell with the rest of the devils. Speaking of devils, how is Jacob?"

"Beats me. He went to get me some ice cream two days ago and I ain't seen him since."

"Maybe the store he went to is in China," Lula snickered. I didn't think her comment was funny. She realized I didn't because her voice got real serious. "Well, with him gone so much, you must save money on your food bill."

"I save a few pennies here and there. Sometimes I still cook when I know he ain't going to eat with me. I love to cook."

"It's a good thing that's what you do for a living." We chatted for a few more minutes before she had to get off the phone to finish the wedding dress she was making for Judge Smoot's granddaughter.

Cooking for Reverend Spivey wasn't my only job responsibility, though. He counted on me to help him look after his wife and Annie Lou. His memory was still sharp as a tack for a man his age; but most of the time his wife and half sister didn't know if they was coming or going. Miss Viola had a habit of getting up in the middle of the night to get a snack. Almost every time she did that, she'd leave half-eaten food on the kitchen table until the next morning. By the time I got to work the next morning, there'd be flies and gnats swarming all over the place. She'd also leave the water running in the kitchen sink until somebody heard it.

Annie Lou was a even bigger concern. Like me and Lula and several other women I knew, she liked to eat the sticky orange clay off the ground that Alabama was known for in certain areas. The week after the news about the execution of the Lindbergh baby kidnapper, she went for a walk that Thursday evening and scooped up a wad of clay and didn't realize a plum-sized rock was in it. She ate it, too. It was a good thing I was still at the house when she came busting through the kitchen door squalling like a panda. If she had come ten minutes later, she would have been in big trouble because I would have left to go catch my bus. I clapped her on the back, but she couldn't upchuck the rock all the way out of her throat. While she was coughing and screaming bloody murder, Reverend Spivey came home after visiting his lawyer. He heard the commotion in the kitchen and shot in like a bolt of lightning. He stuck his fingers down her throat but couldn't get the rock out, so he rushed Annie Lou to the hospital. Miss Viola was hysterical, so I insisted on staying with her until he got back home.

Annie Lou was lucky she could pass for white. Otherwise, they would not have treated her. The doctor got the rock out, but he told Reverend Spivey that if I hadn't clapped Annie Lou on the back in time, it might have done a lot of damage to her insides, or even killed her.

When Reverend Spivey paid me Friday morning, I was pleased as pie to see a five-dollar bonus included. "Naomi, you're such a blessing to this household, I would be remiss if I didn't show our appreciation." He had just finished scarfing down the lavish pancake breakfast I had cooked, and was still sitting at the table, picking his teeth with a broom straw. Nobody had mentioned it yet, but him, Miss Viola, and Annie Lou had all gained about ten to fifteen pounds since I started cooking for them.

"Thank you, Reverend Spivey. I try my best to stay in . . . in . . . um, God's good grace," I sputtered.

He continued to pick his teeth with a broom straw. "Praise the Lord! It's good to have another righteous soul under my wing. I hope you will be with us until God calls us home."

"I ain't going nowhere," I replied with a chuckle as I smoothed down the sides of my stiff gray work dress. "I wouldn't leave this job to go work for England's King Edward."

His eyebrows rose up in such a sharp way, they looked like hairy horseshoes. "Oh! I see you keep up with the world news. My other colored servants don't even know who our vice president is."

"Well, my daddy wasn't educated, but he was a wise man. He told me that if a person learned a lot about things in general, life would be more enjoyable for them. He encouraged me to read anything I could get my hands on." I paused and chuckled again. "Even *Weird Tales* and *Screenland* magazines."

Reverend Spivey nodded before he responded. "Well, I don't read publications of that nature, but I'm sure they can provide a lot of entertainment. One of my grandsons reads the same magazines because he wants to be a writer someday. The boy claims he gets a lot of creative nourishment from them. It pleases me to know that you are such a well-rounded woman, Naomi. I admire your spunk, intelligence, and willingness to please others—not

to mention them scrumptious meals you prepare. God's got his
eye on you." Reverend Spivey was the first white person to pay
me a compliment. The way Jacob and Ethel Mae had me feeling,
I needed something to make me feel good about myself. Getting
a compliment from a man on his level made me feel so much
better.

One afternoon in late May, Reverend Spivey was sitting at the
kitchen table. He had been sipping from the same cup of coffee
for fifteen minutes. He often drunk it after it had got cold. I was
wiping salt off the table that Annie Lou had spilled. "Naomi,
you've been wiping that same spot for almost half a minute."

My hand froze. "Oh! I guess I got carried away," I said as I
folded the dishrag.

There was a serious look of concern on his face.

"I can read folks well enough to know when something is
bothering them. My dear, you are distressed. And this ain't the
first time I've noticed it." He waved me to the chair facing him.
None of the folks I had worked for had ever allowed me to sit at
their table, even when they wasn't sitting at it. "Tell me what's
wrong and maybe I can provide you with some helpful advice."

I reluctantly sat down. Another thing Daddy had warned me
about when I was growing up was that it wasn't smart to tell
white folks too much of your business. He claimed they didn't
care and would look down on us even more for admitting some
of our weaknesses. I hadn't worked for any other white folks I
felt comfortable enough with to discuss my personal life, but
most of them hadn't showed much interest in what my life was
like outside of their houses anyway. Even when some of my used-
to-be employers tried to act like they cared about me, I didn't
trust them. But I trusted Reverend Spivey enough to confide
in him.

I didn't tell him everything Ethel Mae and Jacob was doing,
but I told him enough. He seemed so interested, I was glad I'd
decided to talk to him instead of my own preacher, Reverend
Sweeney. I had been trying to talk to him, but I only seen him at

church every Sunday. Every time I tried to set up a meeting with him, he wanted to add me to a long waiting list. I was around Reverend Spivey five days a week. I could get advice from him as often as I needed it.

When I finished talking, Reverend Spivey's face looked like it had frozen solid.

"A wayward child is a very serious problem. I raised my young'uns strictly by the Good Book but that ain't no guarantee they'll turn out right. I'm very proud of my two eldest girls. They are both nurses in Atlanta and they have lovely husbands and children. But my baby got the Devil in her. I spent a fortune on her wedding, but within a year she started disrespecting her husband and drinking like a big fish. I do not tolerate insolence from *anybody*, not even my loved ones. Ten years ago, when I found out she was running around with another woman's husband, I told her to straighten up and fly right, or she'd be sorry. Naturally, she pooh-poohed me. The man she chose to consort with is at the bottom of the barrel when it comes to scum—a *bootlegger*. I declare, I couldn't believe a child I'd raised, could throw away her virtue and marriage. I disowned her and we've been estranged ever since. I told her that if she ever set foot in my house again, I'd give her a whupping she'd never forget. Then I'd chase her fornicating tail straight on back to that den of iniquity she chose over the grand home me and Viola gave her as a wedding present."

One thing I knew about white folks was that no matter how much money they had or how well respected they was, their lives had just as many cracks as ours. But I couldn't think of nothing worse than a person giving up on their child—especially a preacher. After all the headaches Ethel Mae had caused me, I didn't think I could ever disown her. "Have you talked to your daughter since she left?"

"She wouldn't want to hear what I had to say, and vice versa. Last I heard, she and that other woman's husband was still carrying on. I think infidelity is one of the gravest sins. I don't tolerate that behavior from nobody, not my family or my staff. Now

you best remember that." Reverend Spivey paused and narrowed his eyes. "I'm sorry to hear that your husband is fornicating with other women. But there is a big difference between a
child and a husband. We expect young'uns to make a whole lot
of foolish mistakes because they are still learning their way
through life. A woman is more obligated to her husband, so she
is duty-bound to be more tolerant where he is concerned."

I didn't like his last sentence and now I regretted telling him
about my personal problems. "But what if—"

Reverend Spivey cut me off by holding up his hand. "Let me
finish making my point." He snorted and steepled his hands on
the table. "I'm sure a God-fearing woman like you knows it's
your burden to honor the choice God made for you. If He saw
fit to send this particular man to you in the first place, you have
an obligation to remain with him until death separates y'all." He
paused again and dipped his head. "Understand?"

I wasn't bold enough to point out that every other preacher I
knew advised us to leave relationships with wicked or evil people. Maybe they didn't mean children, but it had to include bad
husbands. Another reason I didn't want to protest was because I
still thought I could salvage my marriage, at least until Ethel Mae
was on her own. I had grown up with one parent, and it hadn't
been no picnic. Especially since Daddy had to cater to seven
other kids besides me. I didn't want my daughter to experience
the feelings of emptiness I'd endured.

I didn't want to risk upsetting Reverend Spivey by disagreeing
with his beliefs.

"I understand." What I didn't understand was how a man who
was so religious could disown his own flesh and blood daughter.
Daddy had raised me to forgive and forget. He'd had problems
with my siblings, but he believed that a child should be loved unconditionally, no matter what they'd done. I didn't have enough
nerve to point that out to Reverend Spivey, neither. Another thing
Daddy had drummed into me was that I was to *never* question
the motives of a white person. I cleared my throat and went on.
"Reverend Spivey, you ain't got to worry. I ain't going to leave
my husband."

I didn't want to break up my family, but I did want to get more enjoyment out of life. I didn't know how I could do that and still stay with Jacob.

Ethel Mae finished high school in June—something I never expected her to do. In September, the day after her eighteenth birthday, on the twenty-fourth, she called up my brother Grady in Branson one town over from us, and made arrangements to move in with him until she found a job. She'd been saving her baby-sitting money and the few dollars she made working on the farms since she graduated, so she didn't leave home empty-handed. Branson was only one town over from us so it wouldn't be hard for us to visit each other. I didn't even try to talk her out of moving. I loved my daughter, but I needed a break from her and all her shenanigans.

Now all I had to deal with was Jacob. That scoundrel hadn't been home in two days. He finally came home the day after Ethel Mae left. He blamed me for her moving. "If you hadn't whupped that gal so much, she wouldn't have run away."

"She didn't 'run away.' She's a grown woman now and can do whatever she pleases. And I only chastised her so much because you wouldn't do it at all."

"Humph. She would have been on the straight and narrow if you had been the kind of mama mine was to my sisters," he said in a nasty tone.

"Is that why your oldest sister deserted her husband and their five kids? Is that why your youngest sister is in prison for cutting a woman's face?" I shot back.

Jacob gave me a thoughtful look before he busted out laughing. "Well, you got me that time. I'm just going to miss my child."

Despite all the headaches Ethel Mae had gave me by neglecting her chores, sassing me, sneaking out in the middle of the night, and fooling around with a bunch of boys, I was going to miss her, too. She had left behind the potbellied orange cat she'd found on the street and brought home a month before she moved. I let her keep it because I loved animals. We didn't know if the cat was a boy or a girl. Whatever it was, I was going to make out like she was a girl, so I named her Catty. She got attached to me right away because I was the one that fed her on a regular basis, cleaned up after her, and cuddled her every chance I got.

I was glad Ethel Mae had left her pet with me. It was nice to get some respect and affection in my own house, even if it came from a cat. As loveable, friendly, and cuddly as Catty was, Jacob hated her. He hollered at her and swatted her with a switch for no reason at all on a regular basis. Catty hated him, too. One time when he pulled her tail for jumping up onto the couch while he was laying on it, she flew up into his face and scratched him so bad, I had to put a bandage on his chin. There was no telling what he would have done to her if he knew she'd used the bathroom on one of his favorite shirts. After I had a good laugh, I washed the shirt.

I was glad Catty had learned to hide when Jacob was in the house. I let her stay outside while I was at work. When I let her in, if he was present, she'd yowl and crawl up under the couch and stay there until he was no longer a threat.

A week after Ethel Mae moved out, Grady called to let me know she'd found a full-time job cleaning house for the same family he worked for as a handyman. I was glad to hear that she wasn't sitting around twiddling her thumbs. Three days later, Grady called me again. "Ethel Mae moved into a rooming house. I went over there two days in a row, and each time there was a different man visiting her. I guess she ain't never going to stop dropping her bloomers for any and every man who approaches her."

"I guess she ain't," I said with a heavy sigh.

"She sure is her daddy's girl. By the way, who is Jacob running around with these days?"

Grady was the only family member I'd told about Ethel Mae's and Jacob's behavior. When I conversated with any of my other siblings, I twisted the truth to make it sound like I had a wonderful life. The last thing I wanted was for one of my brothers to come to Lexington and beat up Jacob. "I wouldn't know. But don't worry about me. I still got a lot to be thankful for."

"You deserve better, Naomi. I hope that before long, Jacob will change his ways and treat you the way he's supposed to. I been praying for something to happen that would help you enjoy life more while you're still young enough."

"I been praying for the same thing," I said with another heavy sigh.

Me and Grady's prayers was answered a few days after that conversation, the first Sunday in October. His name was Homer Clark.

CHAPTER 11

THE DAY I MET HOMER, I HAD ALMOST GIVEN UP ON EVER KNOWING what it felt like to be truly happy, and that depressed me. I thought it was the reason I got up that morning with the same sense of dread I'd felt when I first got involved with Jacob. I had ignored the dread then and I ignored it this time, especially since it didn't last but about a hour.

It was ironic that I met Homer at the same place where Jacob took me on our first date: the fishing bank of Carson Lake. I didn't know if this coincidence was a bad omen or a good one.

Right after Reverend Sweeney's afternoon sermon that Sunday, I went home and took off my good dress. I put on some raggedy brown britches and one of the plain blouses I wore when I did my housework or went fishing. As usual, Jacob was nowhere in sight and his good suit was not hanging in the closet. He only dressed up when he went to church—which was rare now—or a night out on the town. Catty loved boiled pig ears more than anything else, even grits. When she seen me put a mess in her bowl, she lifted her tail and waved it. Then she rubbed her side against my leg so hard, I seen sparks from her fur. After I fed that spoiled cat, I put her in the backyard.

I collected my fishing gear from the kitchen closet and took off. It was a twenty-minute walk to Carson Lake, but it was a nice sunny day for October, so I didn't mind. I was surprised I didn't see nobody I knew sitting on the bank like I usually did on a

Sunday. There was only one man. He turned to look at me when I plopped down on the ground a few yards from him. He smiled. I had never seen him before, but I smiled back.

"Shoot!" I suddenly exclaimed.

"Ma'am?" the stranger said. He had a nice deep voice and was a sight for my sore eyes. His brown skin was the same shade as molasses and he looked to be a few years older than me. His thick jet-black hair had only a few strands of gray. "Is everything okay?"

I sighed and slapped the side of my thigh. "I left my house in such a hurry I forgot to put my bait can in my bucket. I got to go all the way back home," I complained as I stood back up.

The handsome stranger held up his hand. "Hold on. You ain't got to do that. I got enough bait for both of us." He sprung up like a jackrabbit and came up to me holding a Chase and Sanborn coffee can half filled with healthy looking worms. He was at least a foot taller than me, and he didn't have a bulge around his middle like Jacob. I couldn't take my eyes off his. His peepers was like none I'd ever seen on a man. They was whiskey-brown, narrow, and slanted like the ones on a sleepy wolf. If I never saw this man again, I would always remember them haunting eyes.

While he was putting a fat night crawler on my fishhook, a sexy smile was stretched across his face. When our eyes met again, I flinched like something had jumped up and bit me. I suddenly felt so giddy I wanted to giggle and act coquettish. I used to do that when I encountered a cute boy when I was still in my teens—and before Jacob derailed my life. I didn't want to embarrass myself, so I managed to stay composed. This man had aroused feelings in me I thought was gone forever. I blinked, but I still didn't take my eyes off his.

"Excuse my manners, ma'am. I'm Homer Clark." He shook my hand. His grip was so firm, my hand felt like a wet noodle in his.

"I'm Naomi Purcell," I said shyly. When he handed my pole back to me, I cleared my throat, and we sat back down.

"I got some hog head cheese if you want to nibble on something." He nodded toward a brown paper bag on the ground next to his bucket. "I made it myself."

"Thanks, but I'm fine. I'll eat when I get home," I sniffed. "You must like to cook. Making hog head cheese takes a long time and it is so complicated and messy. I don't know too many men patient enough to deal with all that fuss."

He chuckled. "I like to cook and I'm a patient man." The next thing I knew, he sat down next to me. "You don't mind if I sit closer, do you?"

I thought it was strange that he would ask after he'd already flopped down a few inches from me. "I don't mind." I had to force myself not to stare at this luscious man. I was a virtuous woman, so I had never let thoughts of a sexual nature regarding another man enter my mind. But right now, my mind was all over the place! I even tried to imagine what Homer looked like butt naked. I wondered if I had finally lost my mind . . .

For the next couple of minutes, Homer told me a short version of his life story. He had been born and raised in Toxey, another small country town near us. His wife had died after she got bit by a mad dog four years ago. His teenage son had died in a car wreck two months ago. Homer didn't have no sisters or brothers. The few kinfolks he had left was scattered all over the country. He moved from Toxey to Lexington three days after his son's funeral because it was too painful for him to stay there. The same week Homer arrived in Lexington, he got hired at the lumber mill.

I was glad he was a "patient" man because I couldn't tell him my life story in a couple of minutes. Once I started talking, the words rolled off my tongue like water. I didn't leave no stone unturned. He grimaced when I told him about Jacob and his girlfriends, his violence, and how often he criticized my appearance, cooking, and housekeeping. (I was too shy to include his complaints about my bedroom performance.)

Homer winced when I told him about Ethel Mae's antics. I rattled on for at least twenty minutes. But Homer didn't seem to mind. Even though Lula and Reverend Spivey always lent me their ears when I needed to unload, it was so different with Homer. My body—especially my head—felt like I'd been cleansed. However, I knew that every cleansing was temporary. That was good enough for the time being, though. One reason I told Homer so much was because I didn't think I'd ever see him again. He knew everything there was to know about my family, my friends, my church, and even Catty. I was surprised when he reached over and squeezed my hand.

"Naomi, I am so sorry your man don't respect you. And your daughter should be ashamed of herself. Maybe now that she's on her own, you will have some peace of mind."

"Well, I think I will. But dealing with my husband is much worse than dealing with my daughter."

"A beautiful woman like you should be treated like a queen. I worshiped the ground my wife walked on. I went out of my way to show her how much I appreciated her. I gave her flowers, took her on buggy rides, and served her breakfast in bed every weekend. Thelma Jane—that was her name—was a wonderful woman. She would go without a new dress or shoes so she could use that money to buy smell-goods and other frills for her family and friends. We didn't have much money, but it pleased me to know that Thelma Jane was so considerate and generous to others." A woeful look crossed his face. "I am so lonesome without her."

"I'm sorry to hear that." I didn't want him to get no sadder, so I decided it was time to leave. Besides, I hadn't caught nary a fish. I stood up and brushed grass off the back of my britches. "Um . . . it was nice meeting you. I best be getting back home now."

Homer cracked a weak smile and stood up. "Same here. I'd better skedaddle. I'm having supper with some friends from work, and I need to get home and clean these fish. They'll be part of our supper." He stared into my eyes for a split second before he went on. "If I never see you again, I really enjoyed your company."

"I enjoyed your company too, Homer. I hope you will enjoy your supper, and welcome to Lexington."

"Thank you, Naomi." He smiled and walked away. I fiddled around with my gear until he had made it out to the road. I watched until he was clean out of sight. Homer seemed like such a nice man to conversate with and I hoped to see him again.

CHAPTER 12

HOURS AFTER I GOT HOME, I WAS STILL THINKING ABOUT SOME of the things Homer had said to me, especially the part about a woman like me should be treated like a queen. For the first time in my life, I almost felt like one.

I felt so good the rest of the evening, I hugged Jacob's neck when he walked through the door. I wasn't being frisky, but every now and then I liked to show him a little affection. Sometimes it backfired and he got suspicious. He reared back on his legs and put his hands on my shoulders and gazed at me from the corner of his eye. "What you up to, Naomi?"

"I ain't up to nothing. I'm your wife, remember? Can't I welcome you home when I feel like it?" I still had my arms around his neck.

"Humph. I can't remember the last time you welcomed me home." He squinted his eyes and clinched his jaw. "You must be guilty of something," he accused.

I sighed and moved away from him. Jacob was getting so hard to deal with. It was no wonder I didn't attempt to be nice to him more often. "I ain't done nothing to be guilty of. Supper will be ready soon. Take off them dusty brogans and I'll fill up the foot tub with warm water so you can soak your corns. I got some new lotion you can rub on your feet."

He stared at me with a curious expression on his face. Then he said something I didn't expect to hear. "Thanks for thinking about me. I like it when you show me some love. I wish you would do it a lot more." He stopped talking and caressed his chin. "I guess you ain't such a bad wife. Even though you done lost your shape. We might make it until death do us part after all."

"We might." I wanted to add, "and we might not." But I kept that part to myself.

Reverend Spivey was scheduled to preach a funeral the following Thursday morning. I was surprised to see him standing in the middle of the kitchen floor when I knocked on the door at my usual time.

"Morning, Naomi." His voice sounded raspy and there was a somber expression on his face. "I tried to reach you by telephone this morning, but you'd already left."

My heart immediately started racing. He had never called me at home before. My first thought was that he had called to tell me he was letting me go. That would have depressed me to no end. I would have missed the Spivey family. I had recently met his daughters and a couple of his other relatives when they came to town to attend a wedding. They had been so nice to me, I hated to see them leave. "Oh," I mumbled. "Is something wrong?"

I relaxed because the expression on his face didn't look so serious now. "Quite the contrary." He folded his arms and told me that after the service, he was going to go to the home of the bereaved family so he could console them some more. There would be a lot of food laid out there, so that's where him and Miss Viola was going to eat supper. "Annie Lou hates funerals so she refuses to attend any these days. I've ordered her to remain in her room until we return. She's got enough puzzles to put together and knitting to do, that'll keep her busy."

"What if she leaves the house and gets lost or hit by a car?"

Reverend Spivey shook his head. "That ain't going to happen. She always minds me. I'll bring her a plate, so you don't need to cook nothing today. Go back home and spend your day lollygagging or doing whatever you do when you don't have to work. You'll receive your regular pay for today."

If somebody had told me I'd get a job working for such a kind and generous man, I would have told them they was crazy. A few of the white folks I used to work for had been real nice to me, but none of them came close to being as nice and generous as Reverend Spivey. "Thank you. And I'll be praying for that bereaved family." I let out such a huge sigh of relief, my breath could have blown out a burning bush. I didn't waste no time. I spun around and skittered back to the bus stop.

When I got home, I did a few chores, ate two baloney sandwiches for lunch, and then I listened to the radio for a little while. I was only halfway through the day, and I was getting bored. I was so used to being out of the house every weekday, I didn't know what to do with myself.

I never knew when or if Jacob was going to eat supper at home. I usually cooked enough for both of us anyway. The food he didn't eat I fed to Catty. I got so bored just sitting in the house by myself. I called Lula's house, but she didn't answer her phone and I didn't feel like visiting none of my neighbors. By evening I couldn't stand the boredom no longer.

It didn't take long for me to decide to get out of the house. I got my fishing pole and bucket and headed back to Carson Lake. I never expected to see Homer Clark again. But there he was, squatting in the spot I usually occupied. I didn't say nothing, but as soon as he turned around and saw me, he started grinning like a butcher's dog.

"Naomi! It's so nice to see you again. You look as beautiful as ever." A man who thought I was "beautiful" when I knew I looked like a hobo was a man after my own heart. I knew I wanted to get to know him better . . .

"Thank you. Um . . . I didn't forget to bring bait this time." I held up my bucket.

He laughed. I was so happy to see this handsome stranger again, I forgot all about fishing. He did too because he lifted his line out of the water and laid it next to his bucket on the ground. "The fish ain't biting. But I'd rather sit here and chitchat with you anyway."

I was so taken aback the only thing I could think to say was, "Why?"

His eyebrows furrowed and he gave me a curious look. "Well, I like you and I ain't made many friends here yet. I only got my radio to keep me company. I don't enjoy listening to them silly comedy shows and President Roosevelt's long-winded speeches the way I used to."

I surprised myself that I was bold enough to ask the next question. "Don't you have a woman?" Right after I said that I flinched. I thought I was getting too personal, too soon. To offset that nosy question, I said real quick, "You might not have much fun at one of our churches, but you'll meet some nice people."

There was a wistful look on his face for a few seconds. "I ain't been able to find a church like the one I belonged to in Toxey. I visited two here already, but the spirit didn't come into me at nary one. I have met a few nice ladies through my co-workers, but nothing panned out."

"Well, if you want to have a good time, several moonshiners live in our part of town. They have parties going on at their houses almost every day. You will definitely meet some interesting folks at them places."

"I know about them moonshiners, but I don't drink, and I don't like to be around rowdy folks like the kind alcohol attracts."

Homer was no ordinary man. I couldn't believe that it had took me thirty-six years to stumble across such a fine specimen of a man. Other than the colored preachers in Lexington, I didn't know no colored men who didn't drink. It was a shame his wife had died. That woman had hit the jackpot when she married him. I felt so sorry for Homer. He had so much to offer and nobody to share it with.

Then he said something that really surprised me. "I know you probably get tired of slaving over a hot stove every day, because it's what you do for a living and then you go home and cook for your husband. I would really like to make supper for you some day."

"I declare, that's so nice of you! I'd have to think about that, though."

"You can even bring your husband. I'm shy about making friends in a new town. Maybe me and him can become friends. I hope he likes to play checkers and go fishing."

I gasped so hard I almost swallowed my tongue. Just the thought of a beast like Jacob becoming friends with a charming man like Homer made my head swim. If they became friends, there was no telling where I would fit in. "Oh, good gracious no! If I told him another man invited me to his house for supper, he'd light into me so fast I wouldn't know what hit me."

"All right, then. You been battered enough. I was feeling pretty lost and lonely when I first met you. See, it was also the anniversary of my wife's death." Homer's voice cracked. "Your kindness uplifted me so much, I went home and prayed I'd see you again. I hope me and you can become close. Your husband wouldn't need to know about our friendship."

His last sentence caught me off guard. Even though my marriage was a wreck, my vows meant a lot to me. "I guess we could become close, and my husband never needs to know about us." He frowned when I said, "Um if . . . you seen me out in public with him, I advise you to act like you don't know me. You could speak to me, but don't say nothing else. Jacob would get real ugly when we got home."

I could tell by the way Homer's face tightened up, that I had offended him. "You must have one hell of a marriage if you can't even talk to other men in front of your husband. You ain't even allowed to have no men friends?"

"I'm allowed to have some. Like preachers and my husband's friends. They are all married and ain't the kind of men a husband would have to worry about getting too friendly with his wife." I winced when I thought about Jacob's flabby, homely, slouchy, disheveled friends.

Homer nodded and laughed. "But I am the kind of man he wouldn't want close to his wife?"

I nodded.

"Well, I don't care how your husband feels, I'd really like to have a friend like you, Naomi. I was in a state of despair the day I met you. Talking to you gave my morale a strong shot in the arm, and I ain't never going to forget that." Homer paused and looked at me so long I was about to start squirming. And then out of the blue he said, "You seem like a strong woman. I can't understand why you stay with a man like your husband—especially since your daughter is on her own now."

I raised my eyebrows. "A virtuous woman is duty-bound to stay with her husband," I whimpered, as if that was a good explanation. I was a fool, and I knew it. And I was a fool with no options I wanted to consider. At least not yet . . .

Homer gave me a wistful look. "I declare, you are a Godly woman. You remind me of Hagar in the Bible. She suffered a lot because of a man. But she had her faith and hung in there. You remind me of my sister, too."

I looked at him with my mouth hanging open. "You told me you was a only child." If he was a lying man, he couldn't be as charming as I thought he was . . .

He blinked and replied in a raspy tone. "I had a younger sister. She died from a snake bite when she was only five. Growing up, it seemed like I was a only child. That's what I tell all the new folks I meet because it's too painful to talk about my sister."

Me reminding him of Hagar was one thing, me and her was adult women with things in common. But how could I remind him of a five-year-old girl? I wondered. Homer sounded like he was a complicated man, but he was so interesting, I still wanted to know him better. "Oh. Well, I can understand that."

It had took me all my life to find a man who made me feel special. And I wanted to enjoy it for as long as I could.

CHAPTER 13

I ENJOYED SITTING ON THE RIVERBANK NEXT TO SUCH A CHARMING man. I hadn't caught no fish, but I didn't care. I wanted to stay longer, but it was getting late. I stood up and brushed off my clothes. "I guess I should be going home. It was really nice talking to you again, Homer. Um . . . I'm sorry I was so long-winded when I told you about my situation. I hope I didn't bore you."

He stood up and faced me with the biggest smile I'd seen on his face so far. "Naomi, you didn't bore me at all. I would love to conversate with you again. But not at a grimy place like this riverbank." We laughed.

I looked around. A married couple I knew was walking toward us. They looked at me with curious expressions on their faces. I just smiled and waved at them. After they passed, they turned around and looked some more. "Um, they're from my neighborhood," I explained.

"Well, I hope they don't run their mouths off and get you in trouble with your husband."

"You know how colored folks like to blab. If they do, I'll just tell my husband the truth. I ain't got nothing to hide." I don't know what made me brag about how I'd been married for over twenty years and had never looked at another man in a un-Godly manner.

I was surprised he didn't comment on what I'd said, and I wished I hadn't said it. As holy as I claimed to be, I was still imperfect, so naturally I would eventually backslide at least a few times in my married life. If I was going to let another man pester me in bed, it would be one like Homer. But now that he knew I'd never been unfaithful, I figured he'd never try to make a move on me. It was probably just as well. The last thing I needed to do was start behaving like a loose booty—no matter how much fun I'd have.

"Maybe we can meet up some other place where nobody will see us. I would never forgive myself if I was the reason you got another beating from your husband."

"I don't know no other place we can meet up at where we won't run into somebody I know. This is a small town and these people got long tongues."

"You doing anything this coming Sunday when you get out of church?"

I hunched my shoulders. "After I go home and cook supper, I'll either visit one of my friend-girls, or come back to the lake and fish some more. Why?"

"I'd like to cook supper for you at my place."

The thought of me having supper with such a handsome man made my heart flutter. "You mean like a party with other guests?"

"Well"—he stopped talking and scratched his chin—"if you'd like to bring a friend or two that would be fine with me."

Homer didn't sound too enthusiastic about me bringing somebody with me. I wouldn't do that anyway. "All right. What's your address?" I couldn't believe I was being so bold. He told me where he lived. I was about to leave when he hauled off and hugged my neck. He held me so close, I could actually feel his heart pounding and I could hear it in my ears. I didn't know where our friendship was going, and I couldn't wait to find out. While his arms was still around me, I knew I was going to do something to tune up my dull life. And I'd probably do it with Homer.

When I got home, Jacob was stretched out on the living-room couch snoring like a bull. All he had on was his underwear. His ashy bare feet with their thick, discolored toenails looked like hooves. Compared to Homer, Jacob looked like a overweight, wrinkled gargoyle.

While I was in the kitchen putting my fishing gear away, I heard the front door slam. "Naomi, where you at?" It was Lula's voice. Before I could respond, she joined me in the kitchen. "I came by earlier. Where was you? I came over here twice."

"I went fishing after I cooked supper. But they wasn't biting."

I didn't like the way Lula was gazing at me from the corner of her eye. She usually did that to folks when she suspected they was hiding something. I didn't want to know what she thought I was hiding. If she guessed I was involved with another man, I'd lie. "Then why did you stay all this time?"

"Um, I bumped into some folks I knew. We got to talking and I lost track of the time. You want to stay for supper?"

There was a tired look on her face. Her makeup looked stale, and her hair was in limp braids. "I was so busy today, I'm too wore out to cook. Lewis is taking me out this evening." Lula smiled and batted her eyelashes. "I declare that man is as sweet as syrup!" Watching her swoon embarrassed me. "He's the first one I ever had who'll do anything I tell him to do."

We sat down at the table. "That must be nice. I wish I could say that."

I didn't hear Jacob come into the kitchen until I heard him suck on his teeth. "Wish you could say what?" he asked as he strutted up to the table with his hands on his hips.

"Nothing," I mumbled.

"She wishes she had a man like my Lewis," Lula said with a smirk.

Jacob laughed so hard tears rolled out of his bloodshot eyes. He made a sweeping gesture with his hand. "Just look at her. Who would want her?"

"You must be blind in one eye and can't see out the other one. Naomi is one of the best-looking colored women in this town. The only reason you low rate her so much is because she is so much higher up on the food chain than you." Then Lula made a sweeping gesture wider than the one Jacob had made. "Look at you! You done let yourself go so bad, you got the kind of looks only a preacher or a mother could love." And then she wagged her finger in his face. "A lot of men in this town would love to have a woman like Naomi. I can't wait for her to get rid of you so they can swoop in."

Jacob scrunched his face up so tight, it looked like he had one eyebrow. I held my breath because I didn't know what was going to happen. Lula and Jacob despised each other, but they had never got violent with each other. "You bitch! I don't appreciate you coming up in my house and disrespecting me. Why don't you just go to hell?"

"Why don't you just kiss my stretch-marked ass?"

"I'd prefer not to. It's got too many other lip prints on it already. I might catch something."

I held up both my hands. "Hold on now! Y'all stop that," I pleaded. "Let's talk about something else. Jacob, why don't you go back to sleep? You want a pig foot?"

"Piss on a pig foot and you too, woman!" he boomed.

Before I knew what was happening, he raised his hand to slap me. But Lula grabbed his arm. "You touch her, and I'll teach you a lesson you won't never forget!"

"I'm just playing," Jacob snickered. He threw up his hands and cussed under his breath before he shuffled to our bedroom. When he got there, he slammed the door so hard the glasses in the kitchen cupboard rattled.

Lula stood up and shook her head. "Girl, I don't know how you can put up with that low-down funky black dog."

I blew out a loud breath. "I ask myself that every day."

Lula glanced toward my bedroom and looked at me with a woebegone expression on her face. "I can cancel my date and stay over here to make sure Jacob don't do nothing to you."

"Don't cancel your plans for me. I'll be just fine. Jacob has to go to work tomorrow, so after he gets a good night's sleep, he'll be all right." I gave Lula a hopeful look and spoke in a tone low enough Jacob couldn't hear me in case he had his ear up against the door. "You know, one day I might show that jackass he's wrong about no other men wanting me . . ."

Lula raised her chin and gave me a knowing smile before she said in a low tone, "Why wait for 'one day' when you can do it now, eh? Unless you done already cooked up something."

"I ain't cooked up nothing."

She pursed her lips and winked at me. "Maybe you ain't started cooking it yet, but you got it in a mixing bowl."

"That's close enough." That was all I was going to admit for the time being.

Just as I suspected, Jacob had his ear up against the bedroom door because less than a minute after Lula left, he stormed back into the kitchen. His eyes looked like they was about to go up in flames. "What was y'all mumbling about?"

"Nothing," I answered in the meekest tone I could manage.

"Y'all wouldn't have been mumbling if it wasn't something y'all didn't want me to hear."

"It ain't none of your business; but we was talking about Lula's monthly. It came a week early. She's been bleeding like a stuck pig since last night. Happy?"

Jacob reared back on his legs and glared at me with his fist raised. "Didn't I tell you not to sass me?" Before I knew what hit me, he socked me in the eye.

CHAPTER 14

JACOB DIDN'T HIT ME AS HARD AS HE USUALLY DID. WHEN I WENT TO work Friday morning, my eye wasn't black, but it was puffy. Reverend Spivey was so busy scurrying around getting ready for a big church event on Sunday, he didn't get close enough to notice my face. But Annie Lou did.

"Who hit you?" she asked as soon as she wandered into the kitchen.

It was almost noon, and she was still in her pink bathrobe. Her long white hair was in a single braid. There was a rim of cold cream outlining her face.

I was wiping off the table. "Um, I had a little accident," I explained. "I tripped over my cat and fell against the ice box."

Annie Lou put her hands on her hips and glared at me like I was a naughty child. "You stop that! I told that same lie myself when one of my men hit me. Nobody believed me, and I don't believe you. When I was your age, I had oodles of men. If they was colored, we couldn't be seen together in public because they would have got lynched. White folks assumed I was white. I stopped messing around with colored men because I didn't want to get none of them in trouble."

Annie Lou stopped talking and looked toward the doorway for a split second. When she turned back to me, there was a gleam in her eye I'd never seen before. "Brother don't like for me to talk about the days when I was worldly. Anyway, I fooled around with a heap of white men, too. One proposed to me, but . . ." Annie Lou paused again, and a woeful look spread over her face. "I knew that if I married him and had his baby, it might come out looking colored and it's against the law for colored and white to marry. The white folks would have run me out of town on a rail for deceiving them."

I had to be real careful when I conversated with white folks about their personal lives. I'd got fired from a job five years ago because I'd asked a woman too many questions during a discussion she'd started with me about the man she was seeing behind her husband's back. I held my breath and asked, "Did he know you was colored?"

"Good gracious, no!" A dreamy-eyed look suddenly crossed Annie Lou's face, which was now blushing. "I declare, he was a handsome sport, but he had a mean streak half a mile wide. He used to light into me left and right. I can tell when somebody's been clobbered, so don't lie to me."

"I made my husband angry, and he lost his temper," I confessed.

"Lordy! Why don't you get rid of that beast? Get away from him while you are still young enough to get a man who would treat you good." Before I could respond, Annie Lou snatched a piece of bacon off the platter I'd sat on the table and left the kitchen.

Ten minutes later, Miss Viola came into the kitchen with her arms folded. As plain as she was, she was a vain woman. She had a huge closet that was filled with bulky, outlandish frocks covered with everything from exotic birds to flowers. The one she had on today had little bitty Confederate flags all over it. She never left her bedroom until she had put on all her makeup. Her green eyes was droopy, her nose looked like a beak, and every strand of hair on her head was as white as snow.

"Good morning, Miss Viola. You look as lovely as ever."

"Thank you, Naomi. I wish I could say the same about you."

"Ma'am?"

"Annie Lou tells me you're having problems with your husband," she said in a harsh tone as she plopped down in the chair at the head of the table. "Your right eye looks awful. If it swells up any more, I want you to put some ice on it or go back home. We can't have our neighbors or somebody from the church come here and see you. They'll think we are in danger of being accosted by a colored brute."

I swallowed hard and blinked. I didn't like to lie to a preacher's wife, and I hadn't done it yet. "It was my fault. I said something I shouldn't have said."

"I see. Well, honey-child, no marriage is perfect. We have a troubled married couple in our congregation that the reverend counsels on a regular basis. The husband is hot-tempered, and the wife knows that. She knows what buttons not to push, but she does it anyway. I'll tell you the same thing my husband often tells her, and I know he's told you: marriage is for life, even if you're married to a devil. God brought you and your husband together, and it behooves you to stay with him no matter what. Besides, you are in a much better situation than a lot of other colored women we know."

Miss Viola pulled a white handkerchief from her brassiere and blew her nose before she went on. I was not prepared for the mouthful of ridiculous comments she was about to spew.

"A good example is the woman that cooks for my cousin Clem. Beaulah Townes is the most insolent colored gal I know and she's a lousy cook." Miss Viola talked and shook her finger at the same time. "She wouldn't know her place if it bit her on both sides of her butt. I realize some of you people are too ignorant to know better."

Miss Viola paused like she wanted to make sure her words sunk into my head. They did. I thought she was a straight-up idiot for thinking the way she did. I wondered what white folks taught in their schools and churches. I figured they forgot that we was all equal in the eyes of God.

"I know just what you mean," I tossed in.

My words must have given her more steam because she was real giddy when she continued. Her eyes lit up and she shifted in her seat and crossed her legs. "Now when it comes to inferiors—holy moly—a good example is the Indians. I declare, with all the knowledge and religion the white man brought to this country to put them on the right path, they are still acting and living like savages. However, because of our intervention, your folks fared better—but not much. Praise the Lord my folks felt duty-bound to lead your folks from the jungles in Africa to America where the word of Jesus was waiting. Just imagine how bad off y'all would be if y'all hadn't found Jesus! Still running around half naked, eating monkey meat, and speaking foreign gibberish."

Miss Viola lifted her hands in the air and shook them. Then she smiled and patted my hand. "Naomi, you are such a credit to your race. I want you to know that me and the reverend are so fond of you. You will have a job with us as long as you—I should say *we*—live." She paused again so them words could sink in, too. They did. I wasn't too ignorant to know that I was too smart to believe her *gibberish*. "Am I right?"

"Oh, yes, ma'am! I don't know where we'd be without y'all . . ."

"Well now! Let's move on. Pour me a glass of buttermilk before I dive into them grits."

I didn't dislike this silly, misguided woman. If anything, I felt sorry for her because *she* didn't know no better.

While I was pouring the buttermilk, Reverend Spivey shuffled into the room. "Viola, I heard what you just said. Please choose your words more carefully in the future. The same Lord created us all and every one of us is equal in His eyes," he said, giving his wife a stern look. Miss Viola bowed her head and stuck out her bottom lip like a child who had just got a whupping. Reverend Spivey turned to me and added, "Ignore her comments. She don't mean no harm." He winked at me, and I nodded.

So long as Miss Viola treated me good, I would never get uppity with her about some of the things she said. I had a good thing going and I wanted to keep it that way. I knew that I would never find a better job. That worried me because Reverend Spivey was in his eighties and his wife was just as old. He was still pretty robust, but she was getting weaker and more senile by the day. If Reverend Spivey passed before she did, I didn't know if I'd want to keep working for her. I could tolerate her comments now but only because I knew Reverend Spivey would always say something that would keep me from getting upset. I couldn't stop myself from worrying about what I was going to do when this job ended. When the future of my job wasn't on my mind, the future of my marriage was.

The only thing that kept me from going crazy was the fact that I was going to go to Homer's house in a couple of days to have supper with him.

When I got on my bus to go home, something came over me when I got off. I thought I had finally lost my mind. I turned right when I should have turned left and didn't stop walking until I got to Homer's front door.

His small, green-shingled house didn't look no better or worse than the rest of the ones in the colored part of town. There was a little bitty front porch with a gray glider on it and some potted plants that needed to be watered. Homer's front windows was so murky, I couldn't see in. I knocked but he didn't answer. I was just about to leave when he opened the door.

"Naomi! What a nice surprise!" He waved me into his living room. All he had in it was a lumpy blue couch with a brick in place of a missing leg. He used a empty fifty-pound lard can for a coffee table. Homer's living room was so small, the potbellied stove used to heat his house was in a corner, not in the middle of the floor like most of the other houses I knew. Nothing matched, not even the paper-thin curtains hanging at his two living-room windows.

"I hope you didn't come to tell me you can't come for supper on Sunday," he said to me.

I shook my head and turned to the side so he could see my puffy eye. "Good God!" He wrapped his arms around me and the next thing I knew I was crying like a baby. The harder I cried the tighter Homer hugged me. And I liked it.

CHAPTER 15

HOMER LET ME CRY FOR AS LONG AS I WANTED TO. I FELT SO comfortable wrapped up in his arms, I wanted to stay in them forever. I couldn't figure out what was happening to me.

When I finally stopped crying, Homer led me to his teeny-weeny kitchen and got a wet towel and sopped tears off my face. "Feel better?" he asked as he rubbed my back.

I sniffled and nodded. "I'm sorry for coming over here like this, unexpected. I feel a little better now so I should go on home."

"Do you think it's safe? You can stay here as long as you want. If you want to leave Jacob, you are welcome to move in with me."

"Huh?" was the only word I was able to get out until I thought about what he'd just said for a few moments. Homer was amazing. He barely knew me, but he was willing to let me *move in* with him. "Thank you, but I can't do that. I really should go home now. I'm sure Jacob has cooled off by now. Um . . . we still on for Sunday?"

"I hope to God so. But I don't want you to get into more trouble with Jacob."

"I won't. I just need to watch my mouth. When I come on Sunday, if I see anybody close to your house that I know, I will walk around the block and come back." I exhaled and pulled away.

Homer gave me the strangest look before he said anything else. "I'd like to watch your mouth myself."

"Why?" I asked dumbly.

I almost jumped out of my skin when he pulled me back into his arms and kissed me so long, I almost lost my breath. I was gasping for air when he turned me loose.

"Naomi, we both know where this is going, don't we?"

"I . . . I guess," I answered in a tone too meek and uncertain for a married woman about to go at it for the first time with another man. I coughed to clear my throat so I could speak in a stronger tone, "Go lock your door."

Homer looked like he was fixing to laugh. "I never lock my door."

I chuckled and tapped his crotch. "You want somebody to walk in on us? If they do, the gossips will make mincemeat out of us within twenty-four hours. By the time my husband finished chastising me, there wouldn't be enough meat on my bones to make a sandwich."

Homer chuckled and locked his door. When he took my hand and led me to his small, neat bedroom, I didn't hesitate to follow. "Naomi, if you want me to stop, you better tell me now."

I didn't say nothing, but I was thinking that he picked a fine time to say something like that. I just looked into his eyes and smiled. He started tugging my clothes until I pushed him away. The only reason I done that was because he was tugging too slow. I almost fell trying to get out of my clothes so fast. By the time I was naked, he was, too.

As soon as I laid down in his bed and slid up under the fresh-smelling bed kivver, I felt more like I belonged here than in my own bedroom. He did *everything* a man could do in bed to make a woman feel good. And I wasn't surprised.

I'd had some passionate boyfriends before I married Jacob. Even as teenagers, they knew a lot more about pleasing a woman than he did. I couldn't imagine what he did in bed with his girlfriends that had them acting like fools.

When me and Homer finished, we didn't say nothing for about five minutes. He finally broke the silence. "You seem tense. You all right?" he panted, as he squeezed my hand.

"Uh . . . huh," I purred. Then I gave him the biggest smile I could manage. "Thank you for making me enjoy being a woman again."

"Thank you for letting me show you what a real man is supposed to act like. Now come on, let me help you get cleaned up."

After Homer gave me a gentle bath—yes, he *bathed* me—he helped me into my clothes. We kissed several more times and if I hadn't pushed him away, we would have gone at it some more. I didn't want to press my luck and stay too long or get so carried away that I wouldn't go home at all. "Naomi, you still seem tense. You regret what we done?"

"Nope. It's just that I got on new shoes and I ain't broke them in yet. My feet hurt a little bit from walking over here from the bus stop."

Homer let out a dry laugh and nudged my foot with his. "When you come back on Sunday, the first thing I'm going to do is soak your feet and give them a massage. After that I'm going to dry off and kiss every one of your little piggies."

His comment was so endearing. When I was a little girl, Daddy used to call my toes "little piggies" when he bathed me. Homer said other cute things that made me tingle. He called bloomers "step-ins," like my daddy and other old folks did. He referred to my female parts as "goodies." God was so good to me.

I didn't even feel my feet on the ground as I walked home. I groaned when I saw Jacob's car parked in front of our house. There was another one parked behind him that I didn't recognize. I took a very deep breath before I opened the front door. Jacob was sitting in the chair facing the couch with a jar of moonshine in his hand. Ethel Mae was on the couch. Next to her was a plump young man in a plaid shirt and wrinkled black britches.

"Mama, where you been? We been waiting for you to come home for over two hours," Ethel Mae wanted to know. I hadn't seen her since she moved out. I was disappointed to see she had put on a few more pounds. Every button on the tight red blouse she had on looked like they was about to pop.

"I . . . I was visiting a lady who sings in our choir. She's real sick," I lied. Then I forced myself to smile. "Is this the young goat farmer you wrote about in your last letter?"

"Naw. I had to fire that useless so-and-so. This is Clyde Newsom. He works odd jobs around town," Ethel Mae said. She introduced me to her new "boyfriend" and before he could respond, they got up to leave. "I hate to run. But Clyde borrowed his brother's jalopy, and he told us to have it back in time for him to go to work. He's a night watchman at a logging outfit."

"I'm sorry I didn't come home sooner," I apologized and shifted my weight from one foot to the other. I ignored the tight look on Jacob's face.

Jacob set his jar down on the table and glared at me. "What lady did you go visit?" I didn't like the gruff tone of his voice, so I took my time answering. "You done gone deaf, Naomi. I asked you a question."

"Huh? Oh! This lady just moved here from Tuscaloosa last month, so you don't know her. And who I visit is really none of your business." I gave Jacob a mean look before I went up to Ethel Mae and hugged her neck. "Come see us again soon."

"I will. Bye, Mama. Bye, Daddy."

"Uggh," Jacob growled as he threw up his hands.

Ethel Mae rolled her eyes and gave me a pitying look. "Good luck, Mama. I'm going to pray for you. I'll pray for you, too, Daddy."

"Uggh," he growled again.

I stood in the doorway until they drove away. Before I could turn around, Jacob staggered over to me. He grabbed me by my shoulders and spun me around to face him. "Did that Tuscaloosa woman put this purple mark on your neck?" he asked as he stabbed my neck with his finger.

I felt the tender spot a few inches below my chin where Homer had nibbled. Even though he had been gentle, he had left his mark. "Um . . . a mosquito bit me and I was itching so bad I had to scratch my neck. I guess I scratched too hard." I was amazed at how easy I was able to lie.

"Like hell! You think I'm crazy? Who was you really with? I know a sucker bite when I see one!"

"You *should* know a sucker bite! I'm sure you done left some on quite a few necks." It hurt to say what I said next. "You done told me numerous times that I was a loathsome frump that no other man would want, remember?"

The way Jacob's lips was quivering, I thought he was fixing to laugh. "Well, that's still true today." Suddenly, he gave me a wild-eyed look. "Don't you never sass me in front of my daughter again!" Before I knew what he was doing, he grabbed my arm and held me in place, but not for long. I managed to get loose and run into the kitchen. He was right on my heels. I grabbed the first thing off the counter I could get my hands on. It happened to be a butcher knife.

"You hit me and I'm going to cut your throat!"

Other than slapping Jacob or biting his hand during some of his violent outbursts, threatening him with a knife was the boldest move I'd ever made. It worked because he didn't hit me.

"Aww, to hell with you, you old rag doll." He gave me a dismissive wave and hitched up his britches before he stomped out the front door.

My head was swimming, so I couldn't think straight. I was so antsy, I couldn't stand still. I put the knife back on the counter and ran to the front window. As soon as Jacob drove off, I bolted out the door and started walking in the opposite direction. I trotted all the way back to Homer's house.

CHAPTER 16

I KNOCKED ON HOMER'S DOOR FIRST, AND THE REASON I DIDN'T AT-
tempt to open it and walk in was because I didn't know him well
enough to do that yet. When he didn't answer, I opened the
door and eased in. I called out his name several times as I crept
from his living room to the kitchen, then the bathroom, and finally his bedroom. I even looked out the back window to see if
he was in his backyard chopping firewood or something. He was
nowhere in sight. I would have left him a note, but I didn't have
no pencil in my purse.

Before I left, I peeped out his living-room window to make
sure nobody I knew was around. The coast was clear, so I rushed
to the end of the block. It was a good thing I did because right
after I turned the corner, I saw two women who belonged to my
church. I waved at them. They waved back, but they had curious
expressions on their faces. I took a few more steps and when I
turned around, they was still looking at me. I had become such
a good liar I made up one on the spot in case they asked me who
I was visiting. I would tell them Catty had chased after a squirrel
and I'd come to find her. They didn't ask me, but I'd save the
same lie in case I needed to use it at a later date.

Just before I made it to my house, I suddenly decided to go
visit Lula. She wasn't home, neither. I even let myself into her
house and called her name and searched every room but didn't
see her. I didn't want to talk to nobody else, so I went back home

and plopped down on my couch. Catty peeped from the doorway before she trotted over to the couch. She leapt into my lap and started purring and wallowing around as I stroked her belly.

There was so much on my mind, my head ached off and on, day and night. I didn't like how my life had spiraled even more out of control than it was before. I was glad Ethel Mae seemed to be happy, though. But I was not happy she still needed so many different men to feel good about herself. I figured I had to accept the fact that she was going to continue letting men use her for her body until she couldn't attract them no more.

I don't know what made me decide to go to Elmo's house. But that was what I did next. I wanted something to distract me. If a bunch of rowdy drunks couldn't do that, nothing could.

"Come on in, Naomi. I got plenty of music and not enough women to go around," Elmo said in his gravelly voice as soon as I entered his crowded living room.

I danced twice before I sat down on the arm of the couch. One of my closest friend-girls since first grade, Martha Lou Picket, was sitting on the couch. She had on a tight yellow dress, and a headband and high heels the same color. She looked like a banana with a nut-brown face. There was a gold necklace with a cross on it around her neck. She had on some diamond-shaped gold earrings. Even though we was the same age, she looked five years younger than me. I tried to convince myself that it was because she spent a ton of money on expensive makeup and face cream, but I knew the truth was that stress had aged me before my time. Martha Lou had always been what the old folks called "fast." When we was in school, she cared more about having a good time than learning. She had dropped out when we was in seventh grade.

"Hey, Naomi. I ain't talked to you since that tent revival last month." She grinned and patted my arm.

Martha Lou was a prostitute and didn't care who knew it. She had started working more than fifteen years ago at one of the seedy colored sporting houses. It was in a secluded part of town where the white men could ease in and out and not worry about being seen by the wrong people. Martha Lou had hated splitting her money and taking orders from the shady woman who ran that particular house, so she started doing house calls only. When she wasn't "working," she liked to do the same things me and the rest of my female friends did: shop, cook, go to church, and have a good time at the moonshiners' houses.

I greeted Martha Lou with a one-armed hug around her neck. "I declare, you look mighty prosperous. Business must be real good."

"Every day!" She paused and gave me time to consider her words. I didn't laugh until she did. She lowered her voice and said, "Most of the white men who like dark meat don't want to wait until the Thanksgiving turkey is served to get some." We laughed again.

Martha Lou was from a very nice Christian family. She was the only one that still lived in Lexington. Seventeen years ago, her daddy had got hit and killed by a train he'd tried to outrun. Her mama died of grief two months later. One of her two older brothers had been in prison for the past ten years for robbing the same market where I shopped. Her other brother had died in the first big world war. Her younger sister had moved to New York five years ago and never looked back.

Martha Lou's husband had left her for another woman sixteen years ago and took their two baby girls with him. She had no idea where they was at. I was one of her only real friends. "It's good to see you, Naomi. How are things with that fool you married, about the same?"

I hated it when people asked me about my marriage, but I never lied. "Everything is still about the same," I moaned.

Martha Lou gave me a mournful look. "Damn! Well, you was always too nice to that jackass and everybody else. I remember in school how you used to do other kids' homework and give them part of your lunch. I was the only one who paid you a nickel for doing my homework. Them other kids never done nothing for you. They even blabbed on you for passing notes and chewing gum in class."

"Well, I can't help being nice to folks. That's just the way my daddy raised me."

Martha Lou sniffed and gawked at me, like she was seeing me for the first time. "Girl, they ought to make you a saint for putting up with Jacob." She leaned closer to my face and added, "We all know he ain't never going to stop messing around with other women. You need to give him a dose of his own medicine: find you a spare pecker to fall back on. Just don't get caught. If you treat your spare as nice as you do everybody else, he'll treat you like a queen."

"I would never cheat," I said in a stern tone. Now I was a liar and a hypocrite. Being a goody-two-shoes hadn't done me a lick of good.

"I wouldn't call payback 'cheating' if I was you." Martha Lou looked toward the door and started fidgeting. "Uh-oh! I got to scoot. One of my regular tricks just moseyed in. He'll want to hurry to a motel and do our business so he can get back home to his wife." Martha Lou giggled and said in a low tone, "She thinks he's at the lake bank digging for night crawlers."

I rolled my eyes up and snickered. "Go make your money, honey. But be careful and have fun."

Before Martha Lou stood up, she gave me a knowing look and whispered in my ear. "Girl, you know you can come clean with me."

My heart immediately started beating so hard I could hear it. My voice came out in a whimper. "Huh? W-what do you mean?"

"I know about you and Homer Clark."

I gasped and grabbed her arm. "Who told you?"

"Ain't nobody told me. His next-door neighbor is one of my favorite tricks," she sniffed. "I paid him a visit today. I was still sitting in my car when I seen you go into Homer's house. The walls in my trick's bedroom, and Homer's, is as thin as paper. While me and him was going at it, I could hear you and Homer doing the same. Don't worry, I ain't going to tell nobody. Me and you been friends for a long time, and I wouldn't do nothing to cause trouble for you." Martha Lou stood up and smoothed down the sides of her dress and winked. "You have fun, too. If Homer was a paying man, I'd love to ride on his train."

I was so stunned I could barely breathe. I waited until Martha Lou and her trick left and then I took off. I went straight to Homer's house and let myself in. He was sitting on his couch reading a magazine. "Somebody knows about us!" I blurted out before he could say a word. I scurried across the floor and literally fell down next to him. "She seen me come into your house, and she heard us through your neighbor's bedroom wall."

There was a panicky look on Homer's face as he dropped the magazine and shifted in his seat. "She who?"

"A hoochie-coochie woman named Martha Lou. She . . . uh . . . turns tricks with the man who lives next door to you."

"Oh, that woman. Pffftt." He breathed a sigh of relief and waved his hand. "I wouldn't worry about her. She's pretty cool in my book."

I gave him a suspicious look. "How cool?"

His eyes got so big you would have thought he'd stepped in front of a snake. "Oh, hell no! I wouldn't touch her coochie with a fire poker," he chuckled. "I just meant she ain't the kind to go around blabbing. I done chatted with her several times at the five-and-dime and the market." Homer tapped his lips with his finger. "Now give me some sugar and let's go stretch out in the bed for a spell."

When I opened the door to leave and go home, I looked around to make sure I didn't see nobody else I knew.

I walked fast and took the short cut through the woods, so it didn't take me long to get back home. I was worried about somebody else finding out about me and Homer. I knew I was taking a risk, but he was worth it.

I was in bed when Jacob stumbled home just before midnight. I didn't want to talk to him, so I played possum. He grunted and cussed under his breath as he staggered into the bedroom. I cringed when he sat down on the side next to me, smelling like somebody had doused him with moonshine.

"Wake up, Miss Thing. You got a job to do," he snarled.

I didn't move or say nothing. The next thing I knew he was on top of me, tugging on my gown. I still didn't move or say nothing. I laid there like a dead woman while he had his way with me. It had been several weeks since we'd had sex, and it had been a gruesome experience for me. This time was no different. No passion, no tenderness, no pleasure for me. The way he went at it, you would have thought he was using the toilet.

I got about two hours' sleep that night. I woke up Saturday morning just before dawn. While Jacob was snoring like a buzz saw and grinding his teeth, I slid out of bed. I tiptoed to the bathroom and scrubbed my sore body with enough soap to clean off a mule. I put on one of my cutest white cotton blouses and my favorite pair of britches, which was just tight enough to show my curves. I didn't bother putting on no makeup because I didn't want to use up no more time. After I hugged Catty and filled her food and water bowls, I slunk out the front door.

I didn't know if I had already lost my mind, because I was doing things I didn't think I'd ever do. I went to Homer's house *again* and went straight to his bedroom. He was a light sleeper so as soon as I opened the creaky bedroom door, he sat bolt upright. "Naomi! You all right?" He grabbed my hand and pulled me down to the side of the bed.

"I had a bad night." I took several gulps of air. Homer looked confused as I went on. "Jacob had sex with me while he thought I was asleep."

Homer shuddered. "My Lord! On top of everything else, he's a *ghoul*! Well, you know I'm here for you any time you want to come over, day or night." He paused and scratched his head. "I . . . I don't know how much longer I can stand by and watch you suffer." And then he said with his lips quivering, "Something's got to be done!"

I knew Homer was not a violent man, so I knew he wasn't talking about beating Jacob up. I had told him enough about Jacob for him to know he wasn't the kind of man you could talk some sense into. Even if he did do something that stupid, what reason would he give to Jacob that wouldn't expose our affair? "Like what?"

"Like you leaving him."

I gasped. "Where would I go?"

"What about your daughter? And I'm sure your brother Grady would love to let you move in with him and his family. I'd take the train or bus to visit you as often as you let me."

"Branson wouldn't be far enough away from Jacob. I don't want to give up my job, my friends, and my church."

"Then don't move to another town. Move in with me—"

I drew in a real deep breath. "I told you how Reverend Spivey feels about adultery. If he stopped speaking to his own daughter for cheating on her husband, he sure wouldn't let me slide."

Homer hugged and squeezed me real tight. He offered to let me spend the whole day with him. And if he could borrow his neighbor's car, he'd take me on a long drive, and we would eat lunch at one of them roadhouses. "I know one between here and Mobile that ain't too strict. They serve colored folks the same days and hours as white folks. But we'd have to sit at a table near the white folks' toilet."

I reared my head back and smiled. "I wish I could stay with you today and do all that, but it's too dangerous. Jacob is already suspicious, so I'd better slow down. If he leaves the house today, I'll come back and stay as long as I can. Otherwise, I will see you tomorrow when I get out of church."

Homer kissed me with his arms around me so tight, I thought he'd accidently break my bones if I didn't leave right away. I never wanted to leave him.

It was hard to believe that I'd lost my head over a man I had just met five days ago. But I had.

CHAPTER 17

As SOON AS I GOT INSIDE MY HOUSE, I TOOK OFF MY SHOES. I EX-haled and looked around before I tiptoed to the bedroom and cracked open the door. I was glad Jacob was still snoring. I breathed a sigh of relief and went into the kitchen and started cooking breakfast.

Five minutes after I set the bacon, grits, eggs, toast and coffee on the table, Jacob stumbled in, fully dressed. I gave him a cheer-ful greeting. He glared at me and gave me one of his familiar dis-missive waves and grunted, "I ain't hungry."

"Okay. I'll keep a plate in the oven for you if you change your mind. By the way, can you go to the market and pick up some more grits and bacon? We ran out this morning." I couldn't be-lieve I was able to sound so pleasant after being raped a few hours ago.

"Why can't you go to the market? You ain't crippled—but you will be if you keep disrespecting me the way you done yesterday in front of Ethel Mae and that boy. I got more important things to do than go to that market. Shoot. That's woman's work." Jacob went on to tell me he was going to Mobile in a few min-utes to visit Cousin Sidney. He also told me he hadn't forgot about the purple spot he'd seen on my neck yesterday. He shook his fist in my direction and told me that if he ever found out I was messing around with another man, he'd make me suffer. Then he laughed.

"Jacob, you been making me suffer since we got married. Besides, you told me no other man would want me," I said with a smirk. "So, how come you worried about me messing around?"

He grunted again and gave me another dismissive wave. "Well, you might run into one of them men who's so horny and trifling they don't care who they go at it with. Them kind would pester a snake if they could find its coochie."

"I'm married to one," I said under my breath so he couldn't hear me.

He rattled off a list of things for me to do around the house while he was gone: chop some firewood, shine his shoes, and iron his undershorts. "And you better have them buttons sewed back on my blue shirt before today is over. Bye, ugly."

I didn't leave the kitchen until I heard him slam the front door. A split second later, Catty strolled in and sat down next to my bare feet. "I'm so glad you can't talk. You'd call me a fool for staying with Jacob." Catty jumped up into my lap and laid her paw on my hand. Maybe she couldn't talk, but I was convinced she understood everything I said. She probably thought I was as big a fool as so many other folks thought for still being with Jacob.

I was glad he was out of the house. It gave me time to think about Sunday and how I was going to spend it with Homer. Our plan was for me to leave church early so we could spend at least two or three hours together. Jacob hadn't been to church but a few times this year, so I didn't have to worry about him following me there.

It was evening and Jacob hadn't come back home yet. I cooked some peas and baked some chicken wings for supper. Before I ate, I did all the chores he had told me to do.

I was sitting at the kitchen table leafing through a catalogue when the telephone rang. It was Lula. "Lewis told me he seen Jacob and that bow-legged Dixon woman eating lunch today," she started.

I sighed. "He told me he was going to visit his cousin in Mobile."

"That's where Lewis seen them at. He had to haul some lumber over there for his boss. Jacob didn't see him, so I wouldn't mention it to him if I was you. Lewis don't want to be known as a blabbermouth. Anyway, they was cuddled up at one of them fried chicken places near the bay."

"So, what else is new? As long as he don't do his dirt in my face, I don't care."

"What about them women who call your house? That's almost as bad as him doing his dirt in your face."

"Lula, you should know by now I can't make Jacob behave."

"All right, then. I just thought you'd like to know about what he was up to. I'll see you at church tomorrow. After the service, I'll treat you to some barbecue at the restaurant on Franklin Street. We'll have to leave church early because colored folks have to eat and be up out of there before the evening rush."

"Um . . . thanks, but I'm going to come home and change clothes so I can go fishing for a little while. I heard the blue gills was biting."

"I'll go with you—"

I cut Lula off. "That's all right. I need some time alone so I can do some thinking. The lake bank is more relaxing and private than my house."

"I understand. I declare, only a saint could hold in their pain as good as you do."

Jacob didn't come home until Sunday around 9 A.M. I was in the bedroom getting dressed for church when he strolled in. Not only was his clothes wrinkled, there was plum-colored lipstick on his jaw.

"How was your cousin?" I asked.

"Huh? Oh! H-he's doing just fine. He was glad to see me."

I didn't ask nothing else, but he went on to tell me some cock-and-bull story about how him and his cousin spent time fishing and working on his car. "Um . . . I told him I'd come home and change clothes and come back so we could finish working on his car. I'll probably be gone most of the day . . ."

I smiled. "That's nice. I'm sure he'll appreciate your help, so take all the time you need. If it gets too late, you should spend the night. Them Robinson boys next door got chased by the Klan driving from Mobile the night before last."

"I heard about that. They was lucky. Me, I'm old and can't drive as good as I used to. I doubt if I'd be able to outrun a possum, let alone the Klan."

"Uh-huh. Like I said, you should spend the night in Mobile." I slid my feet into the low-heeled black pumps I always wore to church. "I'll see you whenever you get back. I'm going to attend the morning and afternoon service today. And I might even stay for the evening service so I will probably be there until evening. And . . . um . . . when I leave, I might go fishing for a while." I added the fishing story in case Jacob didn't spend the night in Mobile and got back home before I did.

Jacob rolled his eyes. "If you go fishing, you better take the lantern in case it gets dark. With your clumsy self, you might stumble and fall into the lake." He laughed.

I laughed, too. "I know my way around Carson Lake well enough. But thanks for suggesting I take the lantern. I probably will be gone until it gets dark." I almost felt giddy. If Jacob didn't expect me to come home until after it got dark, that meant I could spend several hours with Homer.

CHAPTER 18

I DIDN'T FEEL THE LEAST BIT GUILTY ABOUT COMMITTING ADULTERY.
I just had to make sure Jacob didn't see no more marks on my
neck or anywhere else on my body in the future.

I wanted to see Homer as often as I could, but it wasn't going
to be easy. I had a lot of scheming to do. I figured I could spend
time with him after church every Sunday, and evenings during
the week when Reverend Spivey let me go home early. I wasn't
sure about Saturday. That was the day I did most of my household chores, marketing, and visiting Lula and some of my neighbors.

I'd squeeze in even more time when Jacob went on another
one of his bogus trips to Mobile. I never knew when he was
going to be gone all night, so I didn't plan on trying to sneak to
Homer's house during them times. I hated to admit to myself
that if I'd known adultery could be so much fun, I would have
done it a long time ago. The only thing was, Homer was the first
man I liked enough to do it with.

On Sunday after Reverend Sweeney's morning sermon, I
went home, changed clothes, and gathered up my fishing gear.
Homer laughed when I opened his door and strolled in with my
fishing pole, a lantern, and a bucket. "You going fishing?"

I chuckled. "Not today. I didn't know if Jacob would beat me
back home. I told him I was going fishing after church so we
could have a lot of time together."

"That's good. I want to spend as much time with you as I can."

I didn't think Homer could make me feel no better than he already had. But he did. After we ate the turnip greens, hot-water cornbread, smothered chicken, and sweet potato pie he had cooked, we made love. He treated my body like it had been served to him on a silver platter. Afterwards, I dozed off and when I opened my eyes, he was staring at me with a lopsided grin on his face. "Don't move. You look so serene laying there. I wish you could spend a whole night with me."

I froze and explained that I could never stay away from home for a whole night. I couldn't think of one excuse in the world I could use to pull that much wool over Jacob's eyes. "I declare, there ain't nothing I'd rather do than spend a night with you, sugar pie. But I don't see how I can do that right now."

"We will figure out a way to make it happen and it's going to be soon. My fortieth birthday is the Saturday after Thanksgiving. My neighbor already told me I can borrow his car so we can go celebrate in Mobile. I know a few restaurants over there with food so good and tender, you don't even need teeth to chew it." We laughed. "But Mobile is a hour-long drive, each way. By the time we finish eating, it'd be too late for us to make the long drive back home at night, so we'd have to get a motel room. Let's pray we can find one that'll rent to colored folks. The Klan's been real busy lately going after colored folks on them dark highways. We need to come up with a good reason for you to be away from home for a couple of days, so we don't have to do no driving at night."

A "good reason" suddenly came to me. "I got it! I might know of a way. A old lady named Sister Chastain who used to live across the street from us moved to Toxey last year. She used to help Daddy take care of me and my siblings when my mama died. She would only charge Daddy fifty cent a day and he did handyman work for her. She took care of me until I was old enough to go to school. Jacob knows she means a lot to me. I call her up from time to time to check on her. She's been sickly for a few years now. I could tell him I want to take the train to go visit her," I said.

"That's a good idea, but what if he offers to drive you to visit this sick lady? And ain't she got no kinfolks in Lexington Jacob might run into? They could spill the beans about you not going to visit her."

"Oh, he hates this lady even more than he does Lula. She told me in front of him on the day we got married that she didn't know what I saw in him. She's been at the top of his piss-list ever since. None of her kinfolks live in Lexington no more, and she told me I was the only person over here who calls her."

"Well, I think we need to go for that. We can leave Friday after work and come home Sunday afternoon, so you'll have plenty of time to go home and get some rest. I don't want you to be too tired to get up and go to work on Monday."

"Thank you for being so considerate, sugar. But I went to work before with just a couple of hours sleep and I was able to do my job. One thing I will do is make sure Thanksgiving is extra special so Jacob will be in a good mood the Friday after. The last thing I want to happen is for him to start an argument before I can get up out of there."

I visited Homer one evening the following week, and the next Sunday after church. I hated going so long between visits, but I had to be real careful. I promised him to visit more often when I could.

The second Monday in November, Reverend Spivey let me off an hour early. He was driving his wife and Annie Lou to visit one of their old friends who lived several miles away. They planned to stay for supper so there was no need for me to cook. I practically skipped to the bus stop.

Homer usually got home from work every day around half past five, and I never knew when or if Jacob was coming home each day. In case he did get home before me today, I had already cooked up a lie about why I was gone. I was going tell him I had been to a baby shower for a woman who sang in our choir. There was always a pregnant woman or two at our church. So, every time I went to the nickel and dime store, I picked up a few baby items to have on hand for the next shower I actually did attend.

I wasn't worried about Jacob asking which one I was going to visit. He wasn't interested in babies, cooking, sewing, shopping, or anything he thought of as "women's issues."

I waited until 6 P.M. I wanted to give Homer enough time to get home and relax a little. My heart sunk when I stepped out of the house just as Jacob was parking.

I groaned when he piled out with his eyebrows raised. "What's this? Where you going?" he barked as he started strutting toward me.

"Um . . . one of the young women at church is expecting. Some of her friends are having a little baby shower for her," I said as I held up a shopping bag with some rattles and bibs. "Supper's ready. I'll be back in a couple of hours or so."

Jacob rolled his eyes and shook his head. "Baby showers! Bah! Damn women!"

I was sorry I couldn't get in touch with Homer to let him know I was coming over. I didn't like to show up unannounced at a man's house even though we was more than just friends now. I did that with my first serious boyfriend, and I walked in on him and another girl. I didn't think I had to worry about that with Homer. I was already grinning when I opened his door. "I apologize for showing up out of the blue. But I got off a little early. I rushed home and got my supper cooked, and, well . . . here I am."

"Baby, I am so glad to see you. You don't never need to apologize for showing up out of the blue. You got a open invitation to come here any time you want." Homer went on to tell me again that he never locked his door, and I could come in whether he was home or not and wait for him. If that didn't make me feel even more special, nothing would. Then he took my hand and led me to his couch and started stroking my thigh.

"I don't think I have time to do nothing," I said shyly. "I really want to, though."

"And that's another thing, I don't want you to think we have to go at it every time we get together." He cocked his head to the side and looked me in the eyes. "Now, how was your day?"

After I told him about my day, we discussed a few more hum-drum subjects. "What do you think about Roosevelt getting re-elected last week?" he asked.

I snickered and waved my hands in the air. I had learned in school how white folks had added some kind of amendment to the Constitution after the war between the North and South ended that allowed colored *men* to vote. Even a constitutional right as a American citizen to vote was pointless and dangerous for us. I only knew a few colored men brave enough to go to the polls when elections came up. The ones who did got harassed, threat-ened, beat up, or kidnapped and killed by the Ku Klux Klan. "If I was allowed to vote, I would have picked him, I guess. But it don't matter what white man is in the White House, things stay the same for colored folks."

"Sure enough," Homer agreed. "Thank God we colored folks look out for each other. You are so lucky you got your church, friends like Lula, and your daughter. I ain't got nobody . . . ex-cept you."

Even though I had told Homer I didn't have enough time to make love, I made time.

CHAPTER 19

ETHEL MAE DIDN'T HAVE NO TELEPHONE YET, SO WE NEVER KNEW ahead of time when she was going to pop in on us. Grady had mentioned to me last week that she'd been talking about coming home to celebrate Thanksgiving with me and Jacob. She hadn't been home since the middle of October. She'd come with a new boyfriend in tow. I didn't even try to get to know her men friends because so far, she'd only brought the same one to the house twice.

I knew Jacob was up to something the night before Thanksgiving. When the telephone rang while we was eating supper, he jumped up to answer it so fast, he almost fell. All he said to whoever was on the other end was, "I'm on my way."

I knew it wouldn't do no good to ask him who had called because if it was one of his lady friends he'd lie about it. But I asked him anyway. He immediately started scratching the side of his head and blinking real hard. "Just one of my co-workers. He lives way out by the swamps. He wants me to come to help him get his car started. He's taking his family to Toxey so they can spend the holiday with some kinfolks."

"That's nice of you to help him with his car. Baby, you be careful out there driving at night on them dark roads."

He drew in his breath and looked at me with a curious expression on his face. "I been meaning to ask you how come you been so goody-goody lately? You ain't gave me no mean looks, sassed me, or nothing like you usually do. I declare, you been walking around looking like a cat let loose in a bird nest. You didn't even flinch yesterday when I said you was getting more unappealing by the day."

I hunched my shoulders and snickered. "I knew you was just trying to get on my nerves. I'm so used to you low rating me; it don't bother me no more. Anyway, I got a lot to thank the Lord for tomorrow."

"Oh. Well, I'll see you in a little bit. Oh! If I can make it to the market on Liberty Street before they stop serving colored folks, I promise I'll buy you one of them big dill pickles you like so much."

"Thank you, Jacob. I'd really love to chomp on a pickle before I go to bed." He hadn't showed me no kindness in a while, so I felt a little better toward him now. He didn't come home at all that night.

When he stumbled through the living-room door at 10 A.M., Thanksgiving morning—without the pickle he'd promised to bring me—I went up to him and hugged his neck. "Happy Thanksgiving," I greeted.

He looked confused. "Same to you, sugar." He paused and scratched the side of his head. "You mad at me?"

"No," was all I said.

Ethel Mae and her latest boyfriend had arrived a hour earlier, and I didn't want to spoil their visit. "Hello, Daddy," she said in a flat tone. She gave me a dry look before she got off the couch and hugged him.

Jacob didn't even acknowledge the boyfriend. "Hi, sugar." He grunted and looked her up and down. "I declare, you look right healthy. I can see you ain't missed no meals since the last time I seen you." Ethel Mae rolled her eyes, but I knew his sly reference to her weight bothered her. She introduced her boyfriend before she sat back down next to him. Jacob didn't acknowledge Arthur Mack. The young man still stood up and attempted to shake Jacob's hand. But Jacob acted like he didn't even see him, so Arthur Mack returned to his seat with a puzzled expression on his face. He smiled when Ethel Mae whispered something in his ear. I assumed she was apologizing for her Daddy's rude behavior.

I was in the chair facing the couch. Jacob plonked down at the other end of the couch, and he had to make another reference to Ethel Mae's weight. "It's mighty crowded on this couch. I hope I don't get squashed to death."

"Jacob, go get a chair from the kitchen," I suggested.

He didn't even look at me or say nothing. Ethel Mae scrunched up her face and gave me a weary look. I stayed quiet while she and Jacob conversated about a few mundane things such as her job, the bright yellow dress she had on, and what she cooked for supper yesterday. I could tell from the blank expression on Jacob's face that he wasn't the least bit interested in none of them things. The whole time they was talking, Arthur Mack didn't say a word, or move nothing on his body except to blink his eyes. Just like me.

Finally, Ethel Mae said what she had probably been dying to say ever since Jacob walked into the living room. "Daddy, don't you think it's time for you to stop beefing with Sister Chastain? It would be nice for you to drive Mama to visit her in Toxey tomorrow, so she won't have to take the train."

Jacob waved his hand and growled, "If your mama wants to waste money on the train to go spend some time with that old battle-axe, I don't care. I got better things to do with my time."

"You better hope you never get sick. I wonder how many folks would get on a train to come visit you," Ethel Mae snapped as she shot Jacob a hot look.

He sat up straighter and looked at Ethel Mae with his eyes narrowed. "Gal, keep sassing me and you will suffer," he warned. "There is a heap of switches left on them trees yonder in the backyard."

"I'm sorry, Daddy," Ethel Mae said. And then she wobbled up off the couch. "Mama, let's get everything on the table so we can eat. Me and Arthur Mack want to get back on the road before it gets dark."

Jacob was a little more pleasant at the table. When Ethel Mae told him how much Arthur Mack liked to fish, Jacob suddenly started paying attention to him. When me and Ethel Mae started cleaning off the table, they was still talking about fishing reels and the best kind of bait.

By the time Ethel Mae and Arthur Mack got up to leave, Jacob was in a real good mood. He even volunteered to take out the trash and chop some firewood.

When me and Jacob went to bed, he went to sleep as soon as his head hit the pillow.

I didn't sleep much that night because I was so excited about spending Friday night, all day Saturday, and part of Sunday with Homer. I wanted to jump out of bed and dance a jig. As much as I tried not to think about it, I was falling in love with him. I was worried because I didn't know how far I could let myself go. I was too mesmerized to care, though. The thought of breaking up with him was as far in the back of my mind as it could go. And that's where I was going to keep it.

CHAPTER 20

I COULDN'T BELIEVE THAT AT MY AGE, I WAS DOING THINGS I HAD never done before I started fooling around with Homer. I'd never been unfaithful to Jacob or even to any of the men I dated before we got married. I'd never spent time in a motel room with a man. I had never lied to a preacher, and lying to Reverend Spivey so I could leave work early on Friday to visit a sick friend in Toxey bothered me. But my head was so high up in the clouds, it was easy for me to justify my actions by reminding myself that I wasn't perfect, and God expected his "imperfect" creations to make mistakes.

I was so excited about spending Homer's birthday with him, I wanted the day to be even more special. On my way home from work on Friday, I got off the bus on Main Street and went into the five-and-dime store at the end of the block to get a card for Homer. This was one of the stores where colored folks could only shop three hours a day, Monday through Saturday. I didn't see no clock and I didn't have a watch, so I had to ask the cashier how much time I had to pick out a card. "You got about one minute," she answered. I was surprised she sounded so pleasant. "What type of card?"

"A birthday card," I answered in a meek tone.

The cashier didn't say nothing else. She came from behind the counter and went up to a rack a few feet away and snatched a card. She rung it up without letting me look at it first.

While I was waiting for my bus, I opened the card and rooted around in my purse until I found a pencil. It didn't take long for me to decide what to write in it. My handwriting looked like a chicken's footprints so I printed to make sure Homer could read every word:

> *My Dearest Homer,*
> *Thank you for breathing new life into my body.*
> *Not to mention other things (smile). You mean the world to me.*
> *Happy birthday, my dearest.*
> *Naomi.*

I sealed the envelope and slid it into my purse between a letter from Grady and a flyer advertising wig-hats. I rushed home so I could get there before Jacob. I had already packed what I was taking on my rendezvous. All I had to do now was change out of my drab gray work uniform, take a bird bath, splash on one of my smell-goods, and put on a cute blouse and skirt. I didn't have no time to waste, and I didn't want to be slowed down by nobody, so I decided to go back to Homer's place through the woods behind our house. Me and my friends used to have fun playing hide-and-seek in them same woods when we was little, but now they wasn't too pleasant. The trees grew so close together, it had to be a struggle for each one to get air. Once I started feeling like I couldn't breathe, I trotted until I got to the road that led to Homer's house.

Homer had told me if I got to his house before he got off work to let myself in and wait for him to pick up the car his neighbor was letting him borrow. Then he'd pick me up and the things he was taking with him. I'd duck down in my seat until we got away from our side of town. I knocked on his door and when he didn't answer, I let myself in and eased down on his living-room couch. I didn't like being in Homer's house alone so I was glad when he got home five minutes later. It only took him a few minutes to get his stuff and lead me by the hand out the door to the car parked in front of his house.

Homer's neighbor's car was a rusty old Ford that didn't look like it could make it to the end of the block, let alone all the way to Mobile. But he told me his neighbor had done a lot of work on it, so we didn't need to worry about car trouble.

"I declare, this is going to be the best birthday I ever had." Homer grinned, with one hand on the steering wheel and his other hand clutching one of mine.

I was so excited, I could barely sit still. I couldn't have sat still even if I wasn't excited. The seats was wore down to the springs so it felt like I was riding on a bed of nails. "Lord knows it'll be the best weekend I had since I was a teenager," I declared.

"Don't worry. When your birthday rolls around next year, we'll do something just as special."

My birthday was almost ten months away. I hadn't allowed myself to think that far ahead. I didn't know how much longer Homer would want to be with me. Now was as good a time as any to bring it up.

My stomach knotted up and I took a deep breath first. "I . . . I just hope we'll still be together then . . ."

Homer blew out a loud breath. "Why wouldn't we be?" He squeezed my hand and gave me a quick glance. The look in his eyes frightened me. He looked like a spooked deer. "Naomi, I love you with all my heart and I want to have a future with you."

My jaw dropped. I was happy to hear him say he loved me, but I was concerned about the part of us having a future together. How long of a future was he talking about? I wondered. It was hard enough now, sneaking around to see him. I knew sooner or later his neighbors would see me going into or leaving his house and get nosy and start blabbing to somebody who might know somebody who knew me. "But I'm a married woman," I reminded him. "What kind of future are you talking about?"

"I want you to be my woman from now on." Homer coughed to clear his throat and went on. "I want you to leave Jacob."

My jaw dropped again. I sucked in a deep breath before I responded. "He might eventually divorce me so he can marry another woman, but he's so spiteful he'd never go through with a divorce if he knew I'd been seeing you. And if he did, he would broadcast it to the whole town, and even tell folks me and you started seeing one another while me and him was still married. My church family would be horrified, and my boss would have a fit if he found out I been deceiving him all this time."

"What about the way your *husband* parades his girlfriends around town? Everybody must know what a hound dog he is."

"They do, but he don't have the saintly reputation I got. Nobody cares about what he's doing. Besides, folks don't judge men the way they do women. We'll just have to keep our relationship a secret . . . um . . . forever."

We didn't talk again for about ten minutes. The whole time, Homer's face was tight, and so was my chest. I could feel the tension, but I didn't say nothing about it. Finally, I said, "I need to get out and go pee. The next time we see some bushes, stop."

"Uh-uh. I ain't going to have my woman squatting down in no bushes. Can you hold it until we get to a filling station? I need to get some gas anyway."

"I can hold it." I was glad he seemed more relaxed now.

Ten minutes later, we got to a filling station. We didn't see no WHITES ONLY sign in the window, so Homer stopped. He got some gas, and we used the outhouse for colored folks behind the station. When we got back in the car and drove on, I gushed about some of my best recipes I wanted to use the next time we had supper at his house. I promised I would do all the cooking and cleaning up afterwards. Homer liked the idea, but it was a awkward conversation.

We still had more than twenty miles to get to Mobile, so I decided to play possum. I laid my head on his shoulder and kept it there until we got to the shabby motel in Mobile at the end of a dirt road.

I could still feel a little tension after we got inside the musty, dreary-looking room, so I suggested we go out to eat as soon as possible. Homer took the two pillows off the bed for us to sit on in the car. Not having them springs sticking in my backside made the ride a lot more comfortable.

I wasn't too familiar with Mobile, but I didn't care what restaurant Homer took me to. I was surprised when he stopped in front of a small place with a big, plastic, grinning chicken perched on top of the roof. He parked in a lot right next to a white couple getting out of their car. They looked at us like we'd stepped on their feet. "Homer, you sure we can eat here?" I asked him as we piled out of the car.

"Yeah. But the waiters ain't too friendly and colored folks have to pay and tip them *before* they get their food. If they serve you something you didn't order, don't complain and ask them to take it back and bring you the right one. If you do, I guarantee you they will hawk spit into your new order."

I sighed. "I am so sick and tired of the way we get treated—as if we ain't paying the same money white folks pay! No wonder so many colored folks move up North."

We both ordered fried chicken dinners and lemonade. I was surprised at how nice and friendly our dark-haired, freckle-faced waitress was. She even smiled and told us she hoped we would enjoy our meal. As soon as she left, I reached into my purse and pulled out the birthday card and handed it to Homer.

When he finished reading what I had wrote, he looked at me with tears in his eyes. "Naomi, you don't know how much this means to me. I been praying for you to fall in love with me."

CHAPTER 21

MY NOTE DIDN'T SAY NOTHING ABOUT ME LOVING HOMER, BUT I did. I decided it was time for me to tell him what he already assumed. "Homer, I love you, too. But—"

He didn't let me finish my sentence. "But you got a husband, and you don't want folks to know you been committing adultery. Well, if you had a chance to move up North so you wouldn't have to face nobody's wrath about being with me, and be done with segregation, would you leave Alabama?"

I pressed my lips together and blinked. "I probably would. But it would have to be something I knew I could count on. I'd have to give it a lot of thought."

Walking away from Jacob was one thing and that would be a giant leap for me. Leaving the only place I'd lived in all my life and starting over in a new state scared me. When it came to work, I didn't know about nothing but catering to white folks' needs in their houses and working in the cotton and sugar cane fields. I had been a small-town country girl all my life. The pictures I'd seen in magazines of some of the cities up North looked exciting. But I didn't think I could get used to them tall buildings, sidewalks filled with folks, and bumper-to-bumper traffic this late in the game.

"I don't know if I could adjust to none of them up-North states," I admitted. "Why did you ask me?"

Homer puffed out his chest and grinned. "Baby, I know a

place up there that is paradise compared to a hole like *Al-abama.*" The harsh way he said the name of my state made me flinch.

Our table wasn't close enough to the white folks' tables, so they couldn't hear us. But we still spoke in low tones. "You ever lived in the North?"

"No, but I been up there a few times. Remember my cousin I mentioned to you a few weeks ago?"

"The one in Michigan who works for the Ford people?"

"Yeah. His name is Fred. He wrote me a letter a couple of weeks ago and told me if I was to move up there, he'd help me get a job working at the Ford Company."

"My Lord. A job with a outfit like Ford would be a dream come true for any colored man. You thinking about going?"

"Yup. And I want you to come with me."

My head started swimming right away. Homer was the first man to treat me so special, and I was still getting used to it. The thought of letting him turn my life completely upside down by relocating was something I never expected.

I gave Homer a pensive look. "I don't know. Leaving behind the only life I ever knew would be a mighty big step for me. From what I done read about life in a place like Michigan, it would be like me moving to a foreign country. I'd be like a fish out of water."

Homer shocked me when he furrowed his eyebrows and started talking in a angry tone. "Dagnabbit, Naomi! Ain't you tired of that jackass beating you and flaunting his lady friends in your face?"

"I ain't never actually *seen* him with no woman so I don't know if I would say he was 'flaunting' them in my face."

"But you do know he's fooling around, or you wouldn't have mentioned it to me or to that preacher you work for, right?"

"Right," I agreed. "Let's stop talking about me leaving Jacob and enjoy ourselves for the time being. It might be a real long time before I can get away again to spend more than a few hours with you."

"All right, then. But I am serious about getting you away from Jacob before he hurts, or kills, you."

Them words gave me a chill. I didn't know if Jacob was capable of killing me, but I believed he could do it by accident. He'd clobbered me a few times and knocked me down and I'd hit my head on something hard. Any one of them times could have been fatal. It was just a matter of time before he hit me again. "If Jacob kills me, it would be a accident. He only means to scare me when he gets violent."

"Hogwash! And John Wilkes Booth only meant to 'scare' President Lincoln."

"You're scaring me now. Stop talking about violence."

Homer apologized for bringing up such a grim subject and scaring me. We didn't discuss nothing else but our jobs, the weather, and I shared a few funny stories somebody had told me.

By the time we got our food, I had lost my appetite. The food was delicious, but I had to force myself to finish everything on my plate. Since Homer had paid and tipped our waitress up front, we didn't have to wait on the check. When we got in the car we only talked about the beautiful scenery, and other mundane subjects.

I was glad when we got back to our motel room. I had never been in one before, so I wanted to enjoy the experience. I admired the fluffy white towels in the bathroom. There was a big boxy radio on the dresser facing the bed. We listened to a comedy show while we was making love. When we finished, Homer fell asleep right away. It took me a while to get to sleep because so many thoughts was swimming around in my head. He was offering me a chance to start a new life. I knew that women my age didn't get too many chances to do that.

When we got up Saturday morning, we went back to the same restaurant for breakfast. After stuffing ourselves with bacon, grits, eggs, and toast, we left and drove around until we came to a park with benches. Before Homer could find a place to park, I seen a WHITE FOLKS ONLY sign on a tree.

"I'm so sick of this damn segregation, I could scream!" I complained.

"I told you, you wouldn't have to deal with it in Michigan," Homer reminded me. "Can you imagine what it would feel like to have white folks treat you like you was one of them?"

"Reverend Spivey treats me like that," I said with a sniff.

"And how many other Reverend Spiveys have you met?"

"None," I admitted with a defeated sigh.

We picked up some snacks and went downtown. I didn't even care what stores we could or couldn't shop at because I didn't plan on buying nothing. When we got to a flower shop, Homer insisted on going in. I didn't see no WHITES ONLY sign in the window, so I followed him. The pretty young redheaded lady who waited on us was real nice and friendly. She even helped Homer pick out the huge red rose he gave me and told us to come back again.

When we got back to the motel, he wrapped his arms around me and pulled me down on the bed. After staring into my eyes for several seconds he said, "I'm luckier than a rabbit with five feet."

I laughed. "I ain't never heard nobody say that."

"Well, it's because you ain't never met a man who was as happy with you as I am."

Homer always said and did things that made me feel good about myself. All of the times he had seen me naked, he never mentioned the stretch marks on my slightly pot belly. When I brought them up, he kissed them. Whenever Jacob seen me naked, he made mean comments about my body from the few strands of gray hair on my head to my flat feet. I had never criticized Jacob's pot belly, bad breath, gas, receding hairline or anything else. I knew if I did, it'd give him another reason to hit me or say things even more hurtful.

I used to read a lot of fairy tales when I was in elementary school, and I always wondered what it would be like to have a Prince Charming of my own. Now I knew.

"Homer, I'm so glad I make you happy. Losing your wife and your son, and not being close to your family must be real hard."

"It was until I met you."

We spent the next hour talking about a heap of different things. I was glad he kept up with the news as much as I did so we discussed a lot of events happening in other parts of the world. He told me interesting stories about his experience in the Army. I cried when he told me how much he missed his son and how he'd been so overwhelmed with grief, he'd fainted at his boy's funeral.

I enjoyed conversating with Homer. He laughed when I told him I cooked pig ears for supper three or four times a week because it was Catty's favorite meal. He mentioned movies he wanted to take me to see and us going on picnics when the weather got warm again. I couldn't count the number of times he told me he didn't know what he would have done if he hadn't met me. That comment made me shed a few more tears. My head felt like it had swole up so big, I was surprised my neck was still able to support it.

I slept like a baby that night, wrapped in Homer's arms. I didn't dream as often as some of the folks I knew. When I did, it was usually a nightmare about Jacob hurting me real bad. But I'd had a few good dreams. In them, I was as happy as pie. I had convinced myself that I could only be completely happy in my dreams. Well, now I was living my dreams.

When I woke up during the night, Homer was sitting up in bed staring at me like I was something good to eat.

CHAPTER 22

EVEN THOUGH WE WAS CELEBRATING HOMER'S BIRTHDAY, HE WAS pampering me more than I was him. He got out of bed before me on Sunday morning and impressed me again. That sweet man had already laid out the dress I was going to wear, my underwear, and a bottle of one of my favorite smell-goods that he had gave me. When I complained about my back being stiff after I took a bath, he gently eased me face down on the bed and gave me a massage before we went to breakfast. By the time he got through with me, I felt like I had a brand-new back.

I was getting so spoiled, I didn't know what to do with myself. I wanted him to keep on spoiling me. Making me happy made him happy. The more time I spent with Homer, the younger I felt. It was like he had gave me back the youth I had wasted on Jacob.

It bothered Homer that the nice rooms at the front of the motel was for white folks only. There was mold on the walls in our room, the gummy linoleum floor had a big black stain in front of the door, the mattress on the bed was lumpy and hard, the kivver was stiff and dingy. But we still cuddled and smooched like we was laying on a bed of rose-scented feathers. "Naomi, I wish we could always be like this," he whispered in my ear as we lay wrapped in each other's arms.

"I wish we could, too," I replied.

Homer knew I loved Tarzan movies. When he found out the

latest one was playing at a theater on the outskirts of Mobile, he insisted on us going to see it. As bad as I wanted to go, I had to turn him down. It was already Sunday afternoon, and the movie wasn't going to start until evening. I had told Jacob I'd be back home Sunday before it got dark.

Another reason I couldn't stay in Mobile longer was because I was worried about being away from Catty for too long. I hadn't asked Lula to babysit her because I didn't want her to ask me no questions about the "sick lady" I was going to visit. Lula gossiped with a lot of folks, so I had to always stay on my toes when me and her conversated. I wanted to tell her about Homer so bad, but I knew I couldn't. Even if she didn't mean to blab other folks' business, her lips got loose when she drank. She'd told me embarrassing things about people after she had promised them she wouldn't. So, for now I had to keep my business to myself. When and if the time was right, I'd tell her everything.

I had left enough food and water for Catty on the back porch, and I knew she would stay outside until I got back. I was concerned about her being chased into the street by some of the unruly kids in our neighborhood and getting run over by a car. I wasn't concerned about her running away, though. She was too attached to me to do that. Almost every day when I came home from work, Catty would be sitting or lying on the ground in front of my house waiting for me. As soon as she spotted me, she would lift her tail in the air and wave it. Then she would trot up to me and rub against my leg. Catty was as close as I'd get to having another child, so she meant the world to me.

Homer was going to drop me off as close to my house as he could so I wouldn't have to walk too far to get home. And we had to do it by a certain time. Jacob expected me to take the bus from the train station to our neighborhood and them buses stopped serving our area at 6:00 P.M.

When we got back to Lexington, Homer parked behind a deserted building three blocks from my house. "Can you come over tomorrow after you get off work?" he asked, with a smile.

"I ain't sure. If Jacob ain't home, I might be able to come for a little while. Otherwise, I can't see you again until next Sunday after church. But if I'm lucky and get let off work early during the week, I'll come then."

Homer's smile disappeared and a weary expression crossed his face. "All right, then." He gazed at me for so long, I got nervous. I was just about to say something, but he beat me to it. "Naomi, I think of you as *my* woman now. I ball up inside when I think about Jacob making love to you."

I agreed with Homer that I was his woman, but I was still Jacob's wife. He didn't say nothing else. He just kissed me real hard.

It was a miserable walk home. A wasp tried to land on my face, and I had to dodge a mean dog because it had already bit me before. Right after I chased him away, I seen Elmo Petrie strolling in my direction. His house was in the opposite direction but some older folks with problems getting around wasn't able to go to his house to drink moonshine so sometimes he brought it to them. I ducked behind a tree so he wouldn't see me. Each day I felt like a bigger fool than the day before. But I would do whatever I had to do to continue seeing Homer and keep Jacob in the dark.

I was in no hurry to get home, but I figured it would be better to face Jacob right away and get it over with. I prayed he would not be in a frisky mood. The thought of having sex with him after my passionate weekend with Homer almost made me sick to my stomach. I put the thought out of my head as fast as I could.

I was a few yards from my house when Catty shot out of nowhere and started running toward me. I scooped her up into my arms and carried her all the way back to the house, with her waving her tail against my face.

When I made it to my front room, I could hear Jacob talking to somebody on the telephone in the kitchen. Catty jumped out of my arms and disappeared toward Ethel Mae's old bedroom. It was one of the places she holed up in when she wanted to hide from Jacob.

I took a deep breath before I headed toward the kitchen. When Jacob seen me in the doorway, he abruptly hung up. "Naomi! Welcome home! How was the old hag?" He plonked down at the table.

I was glad he didn't do nothing to "welcome" me home, like hug and kiss me. It was bad enough he did it when he pestered me in bed. I set the bag with my clothes in it on the floor and sat down in the seat across from him.

"She was looking and feeling pretty bad when I got there. But by the time I left, she was doing much better." I sniffed and gave Jacob a tight look. "Who was you talking to on the telephone?"

He blinked and snorted before he answered. "Oh, it was a wrong number."

I knew he was lying. But I'd had such a good weekend, I wanted to stay in the good mood I was in so I didn't confront him. He didn't ask about my train ride or nothing else. As far as he was concerned it was business as usual and he didn't waste no time letting me know that. "Before you go to bed, darn them socks I laid out on the dresser. I spilled some molasses on the floor behind you and it's done got hard and sticky, so you need to mop it up before it gets moldy."

"I will after I check on Catty. And then I'm going to rest for a little while."

Jacob looked my face over with a frown on his. "You sure do need to get some rest. You look like you ain't slept in days. Um . . . I'm going to go out for a spell. I declare, it's good to see you." He was out the door in a flash, and I couldn't have been happier.

I was glad to be alone so I could think about how wonderful Homer had been to me. Now, each time I thought about him, my heart felt like it was skipping every other beat. If he'd had a telephone, I would have called him every chance I got. He was one of the few people I knew who could afford a telephone but didn't want one. His reason was that he only liked to converate with people he could see. He had gave the folks at the mill where he worked his neighbor's telephone number to leave messages for him if necessary.

I didn't know how I was going to wait until next Sunday to see Homer again. It would be a while before I felt comfortable enough to ask Reverend Spivey if I could get off early again. So, I had no choice but to wait.

CHAPTER 23

THE WEEK AFTER ME AND HOMER GOT BACK FROM MOBILE, SEEMED like it was never going to end. By the time that Sunday arrived, I was ready to climb a wall. When I attempted to get out of bed around 7 A.M., Jacob sat up, pressed his finger against my lip, and growled in my ear. "Be good now!" I groaned because I knew what was about to happen. He was panting like a dog in heat when he slid my nightgown up to my bosom, tugged off my bloomers, and did his business. The only good thing about his lovemaking episodes was they never lasted more than four or five minutes.

I went to church right after me and Jacob ate breakfast. Lula came up to me as soon as I stepped inside. We sat down in a pew in the last row. "What's this I hear about you taking the train to visit old lady Chastain in Toxey?" she asked, looking at me from the corner of her eye.

"So, Jacob told you, huh?"

"Yup, but I wish I had heard it from you. When did you start keeping secrets from *me*?"

People started giving us fisheyes, so we lowered our voices. "It wasn't no secret. I called your house to tell you, but you didn't answer your phone. And it was a last-minute decision."

Lula stared at me with her eyes narrowed so tight, they looked like slits. "Naomi, you up to no good?"

My face got piping hot before I pushed the latest lie out of my mouth. "N-no, I ain't up to no good."

Lula's eyes was wide now. "In a pig's eye you ain't. You been acting mighty mellow lately. I declare, if any woman in this town *should* be up to no good, it's you. Whatever you're doing, I advise you to enjoy it for as long as you can." Lula shook her finger in my face and continued talking. "But be careful. I don't want you to slide into something that'll cause you more pain than you are already going through with Jacob."

I looked down because I didn't want to look Lula in the eyes and lie to her. "Like I told you, I ain't up to no good." I sniffed and opened my hymnbook, and she started gossiping with the woman sitting on her other side. I was glad Reverend Sweeney started the morning service a few moments later so we all had to hush up.

Lula had to leave early because she and Lewis was going to go have supper with his sister in Branson. I had a few short conversations with a couple of other women I was friends with. Everybody knew Jacob was cheating and beating on me, so they didn't bring up his name. One of the women I heard he was fooling around with was sitting across the aisle. When she seen me looking at her, she moved to another pew. As soon as the morning service ended, I eased out the door and headed to Homer's house.

A man who left church at the same time offered me a ride home, but I turned him down. To stop anybody else from offering me a ride, I turned down a dead-end street. But I had to go through some woods to get to the road that led to Homer's house. It was cold so I was glad I had my thickest wool shawl wrapped around my shoulders. I snagged my stockings on a bush and had to beat off a bat, but I didn't care. I would have walked through fire to be with Homer. He had me acting like a fool and I couldn't stop. If somebody had told me I'd be doing some of the things I was doing to see Homer, I would have told them they was crazy.

Homer gave me a bear hug as soon as I walked through his door. He was so anxious to get his hands on me, we didn't even make it to the bedroom. He kissed me real hard and carried me to the couch. We made love for so long, I had to come up for air. "Let's cool off for a little while," I suggested. "We got at least three or four hours before I have to go home."

"We'll cool off . . . in a minute," he panted. "I'm so happy to have you back in my arms. I want the whole world to know what a good woman I found. I declare, I don't know what I'm going to do if we have to stay in Lexington and keep sneaking around like this."

I didn't know what to say about what he'd just said, so I kept quiet. I just laid there and let him do whatever he wanted to do to my body.

Things went on as usual for the next few days. I didn't even get mad when Jacob called out another woman's name in his sleep two nights in a row.

I was thirty-six-years-old, but I felt like a teenager, and I was acting like one. I was trying to make up for all the years I had missed out on enjoying my life before I married Jacob. He did things with me I hadn't done since I was a teenager. We had pillow fights and waded in the lake when it wasn't too cold. When he was real frisky, he gave me piggyback rides or carried me over his shoulder like a caveman to his bedroom. One evening he borrowed his neighbor's car so he could take me for a ride. He drove to Carson Lake and parked in a secluded spot. We got out and walked hand in hand along the river bank for about twenty minutes. He leaned me up against a tree and kissed me long and hard and told me he was going to love me until the day he died. I didn't want him to think I wasn't as committed as he was, so I told him the same thing. A few days later, he took me for my first buggy ride, and I enjoyed it so much that afterwards, I kissed the jaw of the horse that had pulled our buggy. Before I left Homer's house that day, he told me, "You done made me so happy, I don't care if I die tomorrow." His comment brought tears to my eyes.

I visited Homer the first two Sundays in December after church, and a few times on weekdays when Reverend Spivey sent me home early. On the third Sunday, Homer offered to meet me at church for the morning service. "Baby, I want us to feel the Holy Spirit at the same time, in the same place." I couldn't describe how happy his words made me. I was convinced there wasn't nothing this wonderful man wouldn't do to make me happy.

I got to church first and sat down in one of the pews close to the front. Homer arrived five minutes later. We had agreed not to sit together so he flopped down in a pew in the row directly behind me. Every few minutes, I turned around and gazed at him. Each time our eyes met he licked his lips and winked. After Reverend Sweeney ended his long-winded sermon, he asked if there was anybody who had been recently blessed. If so, he invited them to share their good news with the congregation.

I almost slid off the pew when Homer sprung up, marched up to the pulpit, and leaned his face so close to the microphone his lips almost touched it. He introduced hisself, hugged Reverend Sweeney's neck, and thanked the congregation for making him feel so welcome. I held my breath and squirmed because I had no idea what he was fixing to say next. It was the last thing I expected.

"Brothers and sisters, I appreciate the opportunity to stand before y'all today and share my blessed news." Homer gazed up at the ceiling. "Dear Heavenly Father, I know you will always keep your eyes on me and continue to guide me and her. Thank you for leading me to this glorious house of worship today." Then he gave me a sly glance. "I feel like I'm so close to the Rapture, I'm about to bust open. I been blessed with the woman I'd been praying for all my life. The Lord knew she wasn't perfect, but He knew she was perfect for me and that's why He led me to her. I believe that by serving the Lord together, me and her both will reach perfection."

I had never heard such a profound testimony in my life. I exhaled and started fanning my face with my hymnbook. I couldn't believe a living, breathing, handsome man could praise me so high. Like him, I felt so close to the Rapture *I* was about to bust open, too. It was a struggle for me not to sashay up to the podium and reveal to the church that it was *me* Homer was talking about. I had never been the type to make a brag, so even when me and Homer could let the world know about our relationship, I would still be the same humble woman I'd always been. I knew that if I let the cat out of the bag too soon, the scandal it would cause would be of epic proportions only seen during Biblical times.

"Bless your soul, Brother Clark. I can tell you are a righteous man to the bone." Reverend Sweeney grinned as he rubbed Homer's back. "Would you like to tell us the name of your beloved?"

Homer grinned before he answered in one of the sweetest tones I ever heard him speak in. "Well, since I ain't officially asked her to marry me, I don't want to give out her name." He dipped his head for a few seconds and added, "In case she turns me down." He laughed and after a split second, the church laughed, too.

Then the busybodies got loose. "She must be ugly if he don't want to tell us who she is," a husky-voiced woman in the pew in front of me said to the woman sitting next to her.

"Humph. An ugly woman couldn't catch a juicy-butt man like him with a bear trap," her friend said with a snicker. She went on to add, "He's new in town, but he don't get out much. I ain't seen him at nary one of the moonshiners' places, no house parties, no cookouts, or no place else. He must be shy."

"Hmmm. Maybe he's hiding something," the first gossip suggested. "Because if he don't get out much, when and where did he meet this mystery woman?"

I was so glad Lula had stayed home today. When it came to gossip, her tongue was as sharp as a sword. She would have had a field day trying to get the goods on Homer. I didn't want to wait for the busybodies to say something that would make me mad, so I got up and left.

I was glad Homer had already left. I didn't want him to come up to me because every eye in the room would have tripled in size. No matter what they heard him say to me, they would have turned it into a full-length drama.

When I got to Homer's house, he was sitting at his kitchen table with a big smile on his face and his arms outstretched. I ran up to him and plonked down into his lap.

"Baby, I appreciate what you said at church today. If you don't slow down with all them praises, you will have my head so big I'll need to walk around with it in a harness."

He laughed and started stroking the side of my arm. "Well, sweet thing, I feel so blessed, I had to share it with somebody."

After I gave him a quick peck on his jaw I told him, "I wouldn't trade you for five other men."

I was not looking forward to Christmas next week because I didn't think I'd be able to spend any of it with Homer. He was disappointed when I told him so on my last visit, but he understood. Before I left his house he declared, "Naomi, as long as I got you, every day is Christmas to me."

CHAPTER 24

I WAS ON PINS AND NEEDLES WAITING FOR CHRISTMAS BECAUSE I DIDN'T know what mood Jacob would be in. I had almost crossed his name off my gift list because of the way he had behaved last year. I had bought him a new leather belt and he claimed he liked it. A few hours later, he used the same belt to swat my legs because I had backtalked to him when he complained about the meal I had cooked. I bought him some socks this year from the five-and-dime.

Me and Homer had exchanged gifts five days before the holiday. I gave him some fancy pomade for his hair, a new shirt, and a quilt Lula had made (I'd told her I was going to send it to a bedridden woman in Mobile who used to live next door to me). He gave me three bottles of my favorite smell-goods and a see-through nightgown to wear only when I visited him. I'd used some of my pocket change to pay for Jacob's gift. I'd spent a whole week's pay on Homer's.

Grady had paid for Ethel Mae to have a telephone installed for her Christmas present. I was the first person she called on Christmas Eve. She rambled on for two minutes about how happy she was to finally be able to call me up and how she couldn't wait to see me and Jacob again. But in the next breath she said, "Mama, I'm sorry I won't be spending the holiday with you and Daddy. My new boyfriend wants me to celebrate it with him and his family. We'll celebrate next Christmas with you."

"Baby, that's fine. You go on and have a good time with your boyfriend's family. Come see us when you can." I was a little disappointed that Ethel Mae didn't want to come home for Christmas, but all I cared about was her being happy.

With Jacob being so unpredictable, and the fact that I didn't want to entertain no company, I told him and everybody else I was not going to cook no big holiday meal like I usually did.

Lula called me up on Christmas morning and invited me and Jacob to eat supper with her and her family. I had just hung up the telephone when he strolled into the kitchen. "Lula invited us to eat supper at her house this evening." I cringed at the thought of spending such an important holiday with him now.

I breathed a sigh of relief when he rolled his eyes and gave me a dismissive wave before he plopped down at the kitchen table. "Pffftt! I wouldn't eat supper at that trollop's table on the Lord's birthday, even if He was the guest of honor," he snickered. "Shoot! I bet she ain't even clean. If I was to eat something she cooked, there ain't no telling what kind of germs and yuckity-yuck I'd be putting in my stomach."

"Then keep your tail home—or go visit one of your floozies. I'm going."

Jacob shot me a look that was so hot, my flesh actually crawled. "Dagnabbit! You ain't going no place! You are going to keep your behind here with me and cook for me like you are supposed to. I'm your husband. Shoot!"

"Maybe if you acted more like my husband, I'd want to spend the holiday with you."

He leapt up out of his chair and stumbled across the room to slap me. This time I ducked, and he fell flat on his face. When he wobbled up off the floor, he charged at me like a wild bull and clobbered me with both fists. When he stopped, I had a busted lip, a bloody nose, and my whole head was throbbing. But I'd put a few battle scars on him, too. I had fought him back before, but this time I was making up for the times when I hadn't. I bit his hand so hard, I felt the bone and blood gushed out. I clawed the side of his face and left three long bloody scratches. He looked at me like he couldn't believe I was fighting so hard. But I wasn't through yet. When I slammed my knee between his thighs, he grabbed his crotch and screamed like a banshee. That was the end of the fight.

"Lord almighty! I ain't going to forget what you just did to me! If I don't leave this house now, I might kill you! You ain't worth going to jail for!" Jacob hollered.

"You ain't, neither! This time I hope you stay gone!" I hollered back.

He hobbled out to his car and took off like a bat flying out of hell.

I didn't go to Lula's house to share the lavish feast she had prepared. I called her up and told her I didn't feel well. When she showed up later with a plate for me and seen my face, she knew what had happened. I was glad Jacob still hadn't come back because if he had set Lula off, I'd have a bloodbath to clean up. And most of the blood would be his.

"Girl, I don't know what it's going to take for you to leave him! Don't you care about yourself?" Lula put some spit on the tip of her finger and slid it across a bruise on my chin. I pushed her away when she tried to get me to go home with her and spend the night.

"Jacob told me I couldn't go to your house. I don't want to go and have him come get me. The last thing I want is to cause a kerfuffle at your house on the Lord's birthday."

Lula looked like she wanted to laugh. "Girl, you know better. He's a jackass, but he ain't crazy enough to cause a ruckus at *my* house. If he ever does, the undertaker will have a hard time making him look presentable."

I shook my head. "Lula, you know I don't want you to get in trouble with the law."

She waved her hand. "Pffftt! I been sewing for Sheriff Zachary's family for years. He tells me every time I see him how grateful he is I keep his elderly mama happy with new shawls, pillowcases, and housecoats every few months. He'd probably give me a medal for rubbing out a colored man like Jacob because it would be one less for the Klan to worry about."

I looked at the floor because I didn't want Lula to see my eyes. "I'm . . . there is something—" I caught myself before I said something I'd regret. As bad as I wanted to tell her about me and Homer, I still couldn't bring myself to do it. Four days ago, she got a little drunk and let it slip that her favorite cousin Maisie Wheeler was cheating on her husband. If she could blab on a blood relative, she could tell on me, too. She said Maisie's actions was justified because she was planning to divorce her husband. Therefore, she was only "married" on paper. I hadn't told nobody, but two other people said to me that Lula had told them the same thing about Maisie. I couldn't say nothing about Lula's convoluted logic because mine was as bad as hers since I'd got involved with Homer.

When I looked up, she was gawking at me with her eyebrows raised and her arms folded. "You trying to tell me something?"

"Um, thanks for bringing me a plate. But I still don't feel good, so I think I'll eat and go to bed. If I don't see you tomorrow, I'll see you at church on Sunday." Before Lula left, she shook her head and gave me a pitying look.

I heard Jacob's heavy footsteps stomp into the bedroom around midnight. "Wake up, pigface. You going to give me one more Christmas present," he slurred. He climbed over to my side of the bed, lifted the tail of my nightgown, and laughed. "All that meat and no potatoes. But you'll do for tonight. Just don't crush me to death with them thunder thighs." He slapped my rump so hard it felt like I'd been stung by a wasp.

I weighed a hundred and thirty-five pounds, the same weight I'd been for the past ten years. Jacob weighed twice as much. He'd put on fifty of them pounds in the last two years. I was tempted to point that out to him, but I knew it wouldn't do no good.

He flopped around on top of me like a fish out of water, and I just laid there like I had been doing for years. He rolled off me three minutes later. When he tried to kiss me, I flinched because my busted lip was still sore. He didn't protest when I told him I had to use the slop jar, which I kept by the side of the dresser in case we didn't feel like going all the way to the bathroom in the middle of the night. By the time I finished emptying my bladder and got back in bed, he was snoring like a moose. I covered his naked body and went to sleep.

Jacob was gone when I woke up Saturday morning. It was dark when he came home. He was blind drunk, so he just staggered past me on the couch, didn't say nothing, and went to bed.

He woke up Sunday morning with such a mean hangover, I had to serve him his breakfast in bed. "You going to church with me today? I'm sure Reverend Sweeney would love to see you. He's always asking me about you," I said as I handed him the tray.

He gave me a thoughtful look. "Hmmm. I should. Some spiritual nourishment would do me a world of good." And then his face got real tight. "But you know I can't stand that sissified, jackleg preacher Reverend Sweeney! And all them high-and-mighty muckety-mucks in his congregation!" he snarled. His voice got soft, and he scratched the side of his face. "Um . . . if you stay home today, we can have some more fun. I declare, you still know how to please me. I enjoyed myself with you Christmas night. I guess you ain't the sow's ear I thought you was after all, because you still got *it.*"

"You still got it, too," I forced myself to say as I opened the curtains and gazed out the window. I was glad my back was to him so he couldn't see the sneer on my face.

It made me feel a little better about him when he complimented me, which he rarely did. However, his compliments always had a second part. "It would have been even better if you was still small. Making love to a stout woman is like making love to a Guernsey."

I didn't know which was worse: being compared to a cow, or a mule like the last time he made a reference to my weight. "I guess I better start watching how much I eat," I muttered as I rubbed the almost flat stomach I was so proud of.

"You better! Otherwise, I'll stop pleasuring you at all. How would you like that?"

"I wouldn't." I couldn't understand what kind of enjoyment he got out of putting me down. I had to press my lips together to keep from laughing. In a few hours, Homer would give me all the pleasure I could stand.

Before I left to go to church, I told Jacob I was going to stay for the morning and afternoon service, and then I planned to visit some of the church's shut-in folks. He didn't bat a eye when I told him I probably wouldn't get back home until evening.

CHAPTER 25

As much as I loved going to church, this Sunday it was torture. I was fidgeting in my seat like them fussy little kids who got dragged in by their folks kicking and screaming. Somehow, I managed to make it through Reverend Sweeney's morning sermon without dozing off. Instead of staying for at least part of the afternoon session, I left church like it was on fire.

I let myself into Homer's house and he immediately embraced me like he usually did. "I already cooked some greens and a rump roast. We can eat whenever you want to," he told me.

"Okay." We kissed a few times before we sat down to eat. Before we could get real cozy, somebody knocked on the door and yelled out Homer's name.

His eyes got big and he whispered, "Hell's bells. That's my next-door neighbor. His tongue is as long as my leg. He'll be in gossip heaven if he sees you up in here."

I had never seen Homer's neighbor on none of my visits, but I recognized his voice. It was a troublemaking lout named Vinnie Dawson. Him and my oldest brother used to go hunting and fishing together. "I know your neighbor," I said in a low tone. I got so panicky, I started shaking. "Can't you act like you ain't home and don't answer the door?"

"You know I don't lock my door. If I don't let him in, he'll let hisself in. Go yonder in the pantry and stay there until I come get you."

"What?" I rolled my neck and looked at Homer like he had lost his mind. "I don't want to hide in no pantry," I said with a pout.

When I heard the squeaky door start to open, I didn't say nothing else. I darted across the floor to the small pantry next to the kitchen.

I was in that musty, cramped room for the longest time before Homer opened the door. "Baby, Vinnie went home to get some tools he borrowed from me. He'll be back in a little while."

"Well, I can't spend another minute in this pantry. A spider crawled up my leg and I saw some bugs as big as hen eggs," I griped. "I'm going to leave now but I'll try and come back to-morrow after work. Reverend Spivey said he might go visit one of his choir members. She recently had a baby and wants him to come bless the child and eat supper with her family."

"Okay, sugar. But you better hurry and get out of here before Vinnie gets back. I hope you can come again tomorrow eve-ning."

"I hope I can, too," I said with a heavy sigh.

I took my time walking home. I groaned when I got closer to my house and seen Jacob's car parked out front. I reluctantly let myself in the front door. The house was so quiet, I assumed he was in the backyard chopping firewood, or taking a nap. I crept up to our bedroom, eased the door open and peered in. What I saw horrified me beyond belief. Jacob was on top of a woman going at it like a wild rabbit!

"OH, HELL NO!" I was more disgusted about him doing his dirt in *our* bed than I was about him being on top of another woman. I gasped and stumbled back a few steps. Words shot out of my mouth like arrows. "Jacob, how could you disrespect me like this?" He glared at me like I was a thief who had broken into his house. What little bit of hair he had left was sticking up on his head like quills. The woman turned her face toward the wall so I couldn't see who she was. But her reddish-brown wig-hat with a blonde streak was on the nightstand. "Aw shuck it! I didn't want you to find out this way!" he yelled, with one hand up in the air.

"I been knowing all along you was a low-down, funky black hound from hell!" I yelled back. "I never thought I'd see you with my own eyes—doing your dirty business in *my* bed!"

"Correction; *our* bed." He shooed me away with his hand like I was a fly. "Now close the door and scat. We can discuss this later."

I was so dumbfounded, I couldn't think straight. I whirled around and ran out the kitchen door. I decided it was probably too soon to go back to Homer's house, so I went and sat on the back porch with Catty. I didn't know how much time passed before I heard Jacob and the woman talking. They was in the living room so I couldn't make out everything they was saying, but I did hear him say, "Don't worry about Naomi. She ain't going to do nothing to you. I'll see you in a day or so. Now give me some sugar and skedaddle before she comes back."

If I had agreed to run off with Homer, I would have packed my things and moved into a rooming house before nightfall. I was a fool for not moving out already.

I sat on the porch for another ten minutes before I went back inside. Jacob was standing at the kitchen counter going through his fishing tackle box. "Hey, sugar pie." There was a sheepish grin on his face like all he'd done was steal a cookie from the cookie jar. "Um . . . I think I'll go see if I can catch a few blue gills."

I gently closed the door and brushed past him. If he wasn't going to say nothing about being in bed with one of his women, I wasn't. It didn't matter no more what he did—and hadn't for a long time. "I'm going to go for a walk. I'll cook supper when I get back." I didn't even wait for him to respond. I rushed out the front door as fast as I could. Catty tried to follow me, but I scolded her and carried her to the backyard.

When I got back out to the sidewalk, I started trotting. Before I made it to the end of the block, a shiny black Chrysler pulled up next to me. It was Martha Lou. She parked and leaned toward the passenger side and rolled down the window. "You look like you in a hurry," she hollered.

"I am," I said in a tired voice.

She stared at me for a few seconds before she said anything. "You want a ride?"

I nodded. I didn't care if somebody seen me talking to a prostitute. I liked Martha Lou and what she did was none of my business. At least she was upfront about it. I knew other women who slept with men for money, but they wasn't as friendly with other women like Martha Lou was.

"You look mad."

I told her I'd had another blowup with Jacob. But I couldn't bring myself to tell her I'd caught him in bed with another woman. "I ain't surprised. Get in and I'll give you a ride to Homer's house."

"Shhhh!" I looked around. "You want somebody to hear you?"

Martha Lou snickered. "I'm sorry. I know you got a reputation to protect."

I froze. "And how do you know where I'm going?"

She rolled her eyes and snickered. "Girl, please."

I sighed. "I'm going to Homer's house."

She lowered her tone. "I'm going to make a house call to his neighbor. I can let you out behind the empty building at the end of his block."

"I can walk," I insisted.

"Girl, you look so frantic. The sooner you get to Homer, the better you'll feel. Now get in this car before I change my mind."

I looked around again before I got into the car that one of Martha Lou's rich white tricks had bought her for her birthday four years ago.

"You want to talk?" she asked as she pulled away from the curb.

"I guess so, but not about me. What else you been up to besides . . ."

"Besides turning tricks?" Martha Lou guffawed. She was one of the most jovial people I knew. I could always count on her to put me in a good mood. "I declare, I ain't got time to be up to nothing else. See, this time of year is always busy for me. My best tricks can't wait to get away from their wives, kids, and in-laws and all the merrymaking that goes along with the holiday season. Me with my greedy self, I got them idiots lined up back-to-back." We laughed.

I sighed and looked upside Martha Lou's head. She had on a new wig-hat with dark brown curls dangling down both sides of her head. There was a purple scarf around her neck that matched her tight purple silk dress. I didn't know what kind of money she made, but she sure put it to good use. I'd been to her house several times and it was always decked out like a display in a magazine. She was generous, too. She didn't attend church too often, but when she did, she always put a mess of money in the offering plate. Reverend Sweeney knew she was a prostitute, but he treated her with as much dignity as he did me.

"Martha Lou, you do what you have to do and don't get mad if folks mean-mouth about you. You ain't the only colored woman in Lexington turning tricks."

"Pffftt! Girl, the only thing folks could do to make me mad is steal my purse." We laughed again. The more I laughed, the better I felt. Martha Lou let me out two blocks from Homer's house and I walked the rest of the way.

Before I walked up his porch steps, I looked behind me and on both sides to make sure I didn't see nobody I knew. If I did, I was going to act like somebody had gave me the wrong address for a new hairdresser.

When I put my ear against his front door, I didn't hear him talking to nobody, so I assumed his company had left. I let myself in. He looked surprised but happy to see me again. "I'm going to go to Michigan with you," I blurted out.

CHAPTER 26

HOMER LEANED HIS HEAD BACK AND STARED INTO MY EYES. "Baby, are you sure?"

"Sure, I'm sure!" I exclaimed.

"Praise the Lord!" he hollered. He led me to the couch, pulled me into his lap, and started rubbing my thigh. Before he could get too excited, I pushed his hand away. I had to take a deep breath before I could tell him I'd caught Jacob in bed with another woman.

Homer's face froze. "My Lord, Naomi! I was wondering how much more mess you was going to take from Jacob. You should have hauled ass a long time ago. If you let him get away with pestering a woman in the same bed he sleeps in with you, you need to get your head examined. I done heard some really wild stories about weak women—"

I cut him off. "Hold on now. I been a fool since I married Jacob, but I ain't never been weak. I just said that I was going to Michigan with you. Does that sound like a 'weak' woman? I stayed with Jacob because I thought that's what a virtuous woman was supposed to do. My preacher, and the preacher I work for, and everybody else keeps telling me the same thing. The only one who don't tell me that is Lula. I deserve everything Jacob does to me if I don't leave him."

"I'm sorry for calling you weak." Homer held my hands in his and kissed the tips of my fingers. "I just want the best for you. I'll write my cousin a letter tonight and let him know we'll be coming. He'll let us stay with him until we get a place of our own. Let's get up out of this one-horse town as soon as possible before that nut hurts you. Or brings another woman to bed with you already in it!"

"I agree with you about leaving as soon as we can." I was so mad, my blood was about to boil over. Jacob had pushed me too far this time. "It was a good thing I closed the bedroom door when I did. If I hadn't, I probably would have boiled some water and scalded him and that brazen hussy. That was what Lula did when she caught her first husband in bed with another woman. She almost burnt that nasty buzzard's pecker off."

Homer scrunched up his face and shuddered. "Good God! Please don't maim Jacob, even though he deserves it. We done come too far for you to wind up in jail for God only knows how long. Just thinking about that gives me goose bumps."

"All right, then. I done put up with him this long, I can go a little longer."

Homer gave me a sympathetic look as he raked his fingers through my hair. "My poor baby. I hope Jacob won't ruin the rest of this year for you."

The longer we talked, the better I felt. Homer assured me I'd love Michigan and I believed him. Lula and most of my friends had visited other states in the North and had a good time. "I ain't been no farther than Mobile."

"Let's take the train instead of the bus," Homer suggested. That way we'd get there sooner, and the train would be a lot more comfortable."

"That's wonderful," I chirped. "I can't wait to see what life is like outside of Alabama."

Homer's body suddenly tensed up. His arm went around my neck so tight, I squirmed. What he said next made me gasp. "Let's take off next month."

My mouth dropped open. *"January?* I got some loose ends I need to tie up and I can't do it all by then. Reverend Spivey gets real busy the first couple of weeks in January hosting suppers for some of his congregation. He'll need me to do a lot of cooking. He's been so good to me; I'd like to give him at least a week or two notice so he'll have time to find another cook."

Homer didn't try to hide his disappointment. For a moment, there was a childish pout on his face. Despite the fact that he was everything I wanted in a man, he did have a few flaws. They wasn't too serious so I didn't mention them. But that was something in the back of my mind I couldn't brush aside. "Well, if you can't leave in January, when can you leave?" I was glad he'd replaced his pout with a smile.

I didn't answer right away because I had no idea when would be the best time for me to take off. I'd have to pray day and night that I'd be able to adjust to such a drastic new lifestyle. Another concern I had was that I didn't have a backup plan if I didn't like Michigan and wanted to leave. I couldn't come back to Jacob, and I sure didn't want to move in with Ethel Mae. As much as I loved Lula, I didn't want to move in with her and her man. Because Homer was putting pressure on me, I wished I had waited until I had cooled off before I agreed to such a major upheaval in my life. But it was too late. I wanted to please Homer because he was the only one who could get me out of the marriage from hell.

I would have to pack up and leave on a weekday while Jacob was at work. Before I left, I'd get in touch with Ethel Mae and let her know. She'd be fit to be tied when I told her I was leaving her daddy for a man I'd only been seeing for a few months. Especially since I'd chastised her so many times for being a floozy. I wasn't going to worry about that. I had spent my whole life catering to everybody else. It was high time for me to cater to myself now.

I wouldn't tell Lula until I was packed up and ready to go. I knew that when she heard I had been planning to run off with a man I had just met in October, she'd try her best to talk some sense into my head. Even though she'd been urging me to leave Jacob, I knew she wouldn't approve of the way I was finally doing it. I had to let Grady and the rest of my out-of-town kinfolks know, but I wouldn't notify them until me and Homer had made it to Michigan. Even though I was approaching middle age, I was still the baby of the family, so I knew my siblings wouldn't like what I was doing.

"Why are you sitting here staring upside the wall?" Homer snapped his fingers in front of my face.

"Huh? Oh, I was just thinking about a few things. I'm sorry, sugar. Um, I think we should leave in March."

I couldn't believe the profound puppy-dog expression on Homer's face now. It was twice as bad as the pout I'd seen a little while ago.

"Baby, if we have to wait until March, I'll go crazy. Can't you tie up your loose ends before then?"

I gave him a thoughtful look as I scratched my head. "Hmmm. I guess March is a long way off. All right, then. We'll leave by the end of February. I'll give notice to Reverend Spivey the first week in the month. By then, he'll be done hosting all of them early year suppers. I . . . I . . . ain't going to tell him I'm leaving Jacob for another man because it would disappoint him too much. He holds me in the highest level of regard. Even though I won't be around, I'd hate for him to think I was like the daughter he'd disowned. I'm only going to tell him that I'm moving north to live with a cousin."

Homer suddenly got so giddy he couldn't sit still. "That's good enough and it's almost true because once we get married, my cousin will be your cousin. Okay, then it's the end of February. I'm going to hold you to that."

I nodded. "That'll also give us more time to save a heap of money so we won't have to live with your cousin for too long," I pointed out. "I want you to know I plan to get a job and pull my load."

"Uh-uh! I'll be making enough at Ford; you won't have to work. You done worked long enough. You're going to sit on the porch and enjoy life."

I was flattered but I was concerned about Homer making decisions for me. "I'm too young to retire. Besides, sitting on the porch is what them real old folks do. I want to do something that'll make me feel useful."

"That's fine. You can go fishing and when we get our own place, you'll have enough work to do around the house to keep yourself busy." He chuckled.

"Let's change the subject."

"Okay. We'll discuss whether or not you get a job when we arrive in Michigan." Homer tickled my chin and went on. "It's a shame you can't bring Catty, but I know you'll think about her every time you cook pig ears."

I wanted to laugh but a sad feeling came over me. Catty was another issue. As much as I loved my pet, I had to choose the man I loved over her. The white folks balked when we rode on the train; there was no way they'd let us board with a cat. "When I tell Lula I'm leaving, I'll have her take Catty in. She's got two cats, so being around them will make it easier for Catty to forget me."

"We'll find you another cat when we move into our own place, and you can feed it all the pig ears you want. Better yet, when I get us a car, we'll drive back down here to get Catty."

"Sure enough?" I got so giddy I almost lost my breath. "Sugar, you mean it? I know Lula would be good to Catty, but I know she will miss me so much, she might grieve herself to death. That's what happened when my oldest brother left his dog with a friend when he went to the Army."

Homer chuckled and kissed me. "I declare, I mean it. I know how much your kitty cat means to you. Okay, then. Instead of waiting until we get a car, I'll borrow my cousin's and we'll come get Catty within a couple of weeks after we get to Michigan. I want you to be happy forever. Without you, I wouldn't want to go on."

"I feel the same way."

CHAPTER 27

I HAD READ A HEAP OF ROMANCE MAGAZINES AND WAS AMAZED AT how some of the women characters let love take over their lives. I never thought it could happen in real life, especially to somebody like me. Because of my relationship with Homer, I felt like another woman had took over my body, and I didn't miss the woman I used to be. I didn't know that being in love could transform a woman the way it had done me. But I still had to act like my old self in front of Jacob and everybody else. The new me was only for Homer to enjoy.

That Homer. No matter how much time I spent with him, it was never enough for him. Sometimes he got depressed when I had to leave his house. One of the reasons he didn't want me to go home was because he hated the fact that I would be alone with Jacob. Even though I had told him weeks ago that me and Jacob rarely had sex anymore, it didn't do much good. He would remind me that I was his woman now and he didn't like sharing me, even with my husband. It warmed my heart to hear him refer to me as *his* woman.

When I left Homer's house Monday evening, I took my time walking home. About a block before I got there, Jacob's car cruised by me. The same woman I'd caught him in bed with was driving. She had on the same reddish-brown wig-hat with a blonde streak that I'd seen laying on my nightstand the day she and Jacob went at it in our bed. I knew she seen me because she had the nerve to honk the horn. I was fuming by the time I got

inside my house. I went directly to the telephone and called up
Lula. She answered on the first ring. "Boogie?"

"It's me," I told her.

"Oh. I was expecting a call from my son." Lula's two grown
sons had moved to Mobile when they finished high school.
Their daddy lived there, and he'd helped them get jobs and
places of their own. They called up Lula a lot, but they didn't
visit her that often. I figured it was because she spent so much
time talking about what a dog their daddy was.

"Can you talk?"

"Yeah, but only for a minute because I can't tie up the line.
That boy of mine is such a bonehead, if he can't reach me, there
ain't no telling when he'll call me back. I need to talk to him
and his brother to see if they are coming to the New Year's Eve
party me and Lewis got planned. They spent Christmas with
their daddy and that heifer he left me for. The nasty dog!" Lula
spent the next two minutes bad-mouthing her used-to-be husband. I had to cut her off and remind her that we couldn't tie
up the line too long in case one of her sons tried to call. I started
talking real fast.

I told her about seeing Jacob and his girlfriend driving down
my street, and her honking the horn at me and how mad it had
made me.

Lula heaved out a disgusted breath. "Naomi, don't sweat over
that. That wench just wanted to needle you."

I closed my eyes for a moment and shook my head as Lula's
words sunk in. I had headaches so often I couldn't tell when one
ended and a new one started. Right now it felt like somebody
was running back and forth on my brain. "I know, I know. I declare, Jacob is going to drive me stone crazy."

"Humph. If you ask me, he's already done it."

I suddenly wished I hadn't called Lula. She spent another two
minutes telling me what a fool I was. I didn't even attempt to
shut her up until she told me Jacob's girlfriend was going
around town telling folks he was going to divorce me and marry
her because she was so young and pretty. The types of women in

Jacob's life bothered me. I'd only seen one so far, but from what I'd been hearing from the gossips, he didn't mess with no woman over the age of twenty-five. And they had to be slim and pretty. Well, I knew I could never compete with them kind of women no more, but Homer made me feel young and pretty enough. What I couldn't figure out was what young, pretty women seen in a dried-up geezer like Jacob. When I mentioned that to Lula, she laughed and agreed with me.

"It's a damn shame you wasted up all of your youngest and prettiest years on him," she added. Them words felt like rocks slamming against my ears.

I didn't want to hear them kind of comments, especially from my best friend. I felt even worse by the time we ended our conversation. Then something popped into my mind that made me feel better. If Jacob was planning to divorce me, maybe I wouldn't have to leave town after all. The thought didn't stay with me long. Even if he filed for a divorce before me and Homer left, and we would be free to let everybody know about our relationship, I still thought I'd be better off in a new location. Besides, Homer was determined to get out of the South and the more I thought about it, I was, too. Even though I'd dealt with segregation and racism my whole life, it had finally taken a toll on me. The last time I went to the market, the manager ordered me to let every white customer in the store get ahead of me in line, eight in all. When it was my turn to check out, the cashier gave me a icy cold look and told me time was up for colored customers. Me and two of my neighbors had to set our baskets on the counter and leave.

I had cooled off by the time Jacob got back home. I was in the kitchen at the table folding napkins when he strolled in and stopped right next to me. Before he said anything, he looked at the pans on the stove and sniffed. "Whatever that is, it smells like you really put your foot in it! You keep this up, you'll be as good of a cook as my mama." He had the nerve to smile at me.

I smiled back. "It's been a while since I cooked some of your favorite meals. Supper will be ready in about ten minutes," I gently said. I didn't say nothing about how often he criticized my cooking, or the plum-colored lipstick on his jaw.

Jacob gave me a confused look. "Woman, what you up to?"

"Who, me? I ain't up to nothing. Why?"

He looked even more confused. "You ain't mad at me?"

I shook my head.

"Good! I knew when I married you that you was the kind of understanding woman who wouldn't take things literal. What you seen in our bedroom, ain't what you thought it was."

I wanted to scream at him that if I didn't see him having sex with another woman in our bed, what did I see? But Jacob's logic was so off-kilter, arguing with him was a waste of time. I didn't waste my time bringing up his girlfriend driving his car and honking at me. He walked over to the stove and lifted the lid off one of the pans and smacked his lips. "Sweet Jesus. You finally decided to cook some black-eyed peas." When he turned back to me, he was grinning like a hyena. But then suddenly he furrowed his eyebrows and gave me a suspicious look. "You probably put something in this food to kill me!" he accused.

I made sure I responded in a gentle tone. "Jacob, why would I want to kill you?" I went up to the stove with a spoon. I dipped it into the pan, scooped out some peas and ate them. He looked at the pan of yams I had cooked. I ate some of them, too. I did the same thing with the macaroni and cheese and the cornbread. When I didn't keel over, he shrugged his shoulders and flopped down at the table and ate like he was at the Last Supper.

My mind was so focused on Homer, I actually enjoyed my food as much as Jacob did.

After a mighty belch, Jacob rubbed his belly and grinned at me. "Oomph! I declare, that scrumptious meal really hit the spot." He picked his teeth with the tip of his fingernail and stared at me for a few seconds. "You ain't all washed up yet. Hurry up and clean up the dishes and put the rest of the food away. I'm going to take you to get a ice cream cone and then to the movie house to see that new Shirley Temple flick. And as soon as the next Tarzan movie comes out, I'm taking you to see it, too."

Chapter 28

HOMER HAD BOUGHT ME SOME ICE CREAM AND TOOK ME TO SEE Shirley Temple's movie last week. But I went with Jacob anyway. He slept through most of it. The first place we went to for ice cream, they refused to serve us. We went to two more before we found one that would serve colored folks so late in the day.

"Ain't it nice we still enjoy the little things in life," he said when we got back home.

"Yeah," I mumbled as I eased down on the living-room couch. I could hear Catty purring from her hiding place under the couch. "Thank you."

"Um . . . I think I'll go out for a spell," Jacob said, already moving toward the door.

I didn't even respond. As soon as he left, I lured Catty from under the couch and we sat quietly and listened to the radio for the next hour. I had a lot of thinking to do. The most important thing on my mind was that this was the last year I'd have to put up with Jacob. When I went to bed, I slept like a baby.

Jacob didn't come home until the next evening. I had visited Homer for a couple of hours when I got off work, and then I'd rushed home and cooked supper. I was dicing some boiled pig ears for Catty when I heard Jacob slam the front door. "Naomi, I'm home!"

I groaned. "I'm in the kitchen." There was pans on the stove with some of his favorite dishes: cornbread, collard greens, mashed potatoes and gravy, fried pig ears, and yams.

"How come you smiling like your jaws done locked up?" Jacob asked when he shuffled in and got up close to me.

"I got a lot to smile about," I replied as I added more bacon grease to the greens. "I got a beautiful house full of nice furniture, my health, a wonderful daughter, my church, and some wonderful friends." I had to stop talking and brace myself because the next words I pushed out of my mouth felt like vomit. "And I got a husband who provides for me and keeps my back warm when we go to bed at night." My next sentence made Jacob puff out his chest. "I bet there is a heap of women in Lexington who would love to be in my shoes."

"And that's a fact. But I advise you to keep them shoes on your feet unless I tell you to take them off." He laughed. "Anyway, it's better to see you smiling than to see you walking around with a face as long as a stalk of sugar cane."

Jacob made several cruder remarks to me that evening. He criticized the purple dress I had on and said I looked like a eggplant in it. I didn't bother to remind him he'd gave me the dress for my birthday two years ago.

He fixed hisself a mighty big plate and ate everything on it, despite the fact he claimed the mashed potatoes was too lumpy, the cornbread didn't have enough salt, and the pig ears was overcooked. He reminded me again that his mama's cooking was ten times better than mine. He howled with laughter until I reminded him that I made a good living cooking for a very prominent family. He told me white folks was so dense when it came to good food, they would swoon over a bowl of mud if a colored woman served it to them.

After he let out a belch that almost sounded like thunder, he stood up. "I'm going back out for a while. You want me to bring you some Moon Pies?"

"No, I been eating too many of them things lately. Enjoy the rest of the evening, baby." I started cleaning off the table. "Uh . . . I'm glad it got a little warmer today. I might go fishing for a little while before it gets too much darker."

"Good! I heard the catfish was biting. Make sure you take

the lantern so you can see them snakes in the grass before they see you."

I waited until Jacob had been gone for ten minutes before I fixed a plate for Homer and put it in a big brown bag. After I put Catty in the backyard with her bowl of pig ears, I grabbed my fishing pole, and a bucket, and took off.

Homer was sitting on his couch soaking his corns when I let myself into his house. His eyes lit up like light bulbs as soon as he seen me. "Hello, sugar! I wasn't expecting you. But I'm so glad to see you again."

I set my fishing gear on the floor. Homer listened with a grim expression on his face as I told him about all the mean and nasty things Jacob had said to me. "He took off right after he ate supper, and I was too antsy to stay in the house. I told him I was going fishing. Did you eat yet?"

"I had a big lunch."

"Well, I brought you something you can eat later today or tomorrow."

Homer lifted his feet out of the foot tub and wiped them with a towel. He smacked his lips and rubbed his palms together when I took the plate out of the bag and set it on the coffee table. I went into the kitchen and came back with a fork and a spoon and set them on the table. But instead of eating, he pulled me into his arms and led me to the bedroom.

I didn't like making spur-of-the-moment trips to Homer's house. I never knew how long I could stay. I knew the "going fishing" story I told Jacob was only good for about a hour or so because it was already starting to get dark. I could have got more out of the lie if I had remembered to bring a lantern with me. When I attempted to get out of bed, Homer pulled me down on top of him.

"Baby, don't go yet," he pleaded.

"I wish I could stay longer, but you know how bad things are at my house," I explained.

He stayed silent for a few moments. Then he asked something I didn't like. "Do you enjoy making love with him?"

I looked at him like he'd lost his mind. "The answer is no, and I done told you we only go at it every once in a blue moon."

"Do you act like you enjoy it?"

I was getting exasperated. "I don't know why you brought up this subject, but let's drop it." I got up and started putting my clothes on.

Homer took my hand and covered it with hungry little kisses. That softened me up. "I'm sorry, Naomi." He promised he wouldn't bring up my sex life with Jacob no more, even after we got to Michigan.

He wrapped a sheet around his naked body and escorted me to the door. He looked so sad when I walked out, it almost made me cry. Never in my wildest imagination did I think I'd end up with a loving, kindhearted, passionate man like Homer.

My body was still tingling when I got home. Jacob was in the living room fiddling around with the radio. "You catch any fish?" he asked without even looking up.

"Um . . . no, they wasn't biting." I put my pole and bucket back in the kitchen closet and then I went outside to chop some firewood.

Lula had invited us to her New Year's Eve party. As much as Jacob hated her, he seemed mildly interested until I told him Sister Chastain might be there. She was the only woman he disliked more than Lula. "You mean the old witch you went to visit day after Thanksgiving last month is going to be at the party?"

"Uh-huh."

"If she is sickly, how is she able to come to a party?"

"She ain't *that* sick," I said.

Jacob went on to tell me that he'd been invited to three other parties and would go to one of them instead. He even suggested I bypass Lula's and go with him. I explained that she was counting on me to help serve drinks and snacks to her guests.

I had promised Lula that I would attend her party, but I couldn't stay long. I couldn't stand the thought of poor Homer ringing in the New Year alone. "Can you stay until the New Year gets here?" she asked when I got there a few minutes before 10 P.M.

"Um . . . I wish I could. But Jacob's been real nice to me today. I'd like to go to one of them parties he got invited to so we could ring in the New Year together. I think he's fixing to turn over a new leaf." I already had a lie prepared in case Lula or somebody else told Jacob I'd left Lula's party to go find him. I'd tell him I searched at all three house parties and they was so crowded I couldn't find him. So, I went to ring in the New Year with an elderly neighbor who lived alone. She was so senile she wouldn't know me from Moses, and if Jacob tried to confirm my story with her, he wouldn't have no luck.

"Pffftt! Jacob has been dogging you all year and you think he's fixing to turn over a new leaf on the *last* day?" Lula guffawed. "Honey child, you done read too many Mother Goose tales. Let me get another drink so I can wash that down."

One of the guests had overheard me and Lula. She knew the reason I needed to leave early. Martha Lou came up to me right after Lula walked off. "I know you'll enjoy the other party you're going to," she whispered. Like always, she was dressed to kill. She had on a bright green dress, a wide-brimmed red hat, and black shoes. A red and green striped shawl Lula had made was draped around her shoulders.

I looked around to make sure Lula and everybody else was out of earshot before I responded. I gave Martha Lou a sheepish look. "You know I will." I sniffed and glanced around again. "I didn't expect to see you here tonight. I thought you'd be . . . uh . . . busy."

"I was supposed to be. But the fool had to reschedule because his in-laws showed up out of the blue. He stayed home to keep his wife off his back. But I got another appointment tonight to make up for him. That's why I have to leave in a few minutes myself. I'm going your way, so I'll give you a ride. Let's tell everybody bye."

I was glad Martha Lou gave me a ride. It was cold outside, and

I didn't like walking in the dark by myself. She let me out at the corner of Homer's block, and I walked the rest of the way.

When I opened his front door, he dashed across the floor and scooped me up into his arms. I had no idea it would be so much fun to ring in the New Year with him.

I had only a few weeks to go before I started my new life and that's what I was focusing on.

CHAPTER 29

As much as I enjoyed listening to the radio, I got tired of all the news stories about Roosevelt's second inauguration coming up in two weeks on the twentieth of the month. It was big news because he would be the first one of our presidents to be sworn into office in January.

The week after the inauguration, the Ohio River flooded. It was a big concern to a lot of folks I knew because some of their relatives had moved to that area. One of Lula's uncles lived there, so she was worried sick until she found out his family was all right. "Girl, ain't you glad the Lord is looking out for me and you? I admit that I thought Jacob would have either hurt you real bad by now or left you for another woman."

"I ain't worried about Jacob no more. This is going to be a very good year," I announced in a firm tone. *Especially for me.* We was sitting on Lula's living-room couch drinking cider that Saturday afternoon. The surprised look on her face rattled me.

"Since when can you tell the future, Madame Know-It-All?"

"I just know," I insisted. I knew it was time to leave before she got too nosy.

I abruptly left and I avoided Lula for the next few days.

I hoped Jacob had a steady girlfriend when I left so he wouldn't be alone, not that I cared that much. I was probably flattering myself by thinking he would miss me. If anything, he'd more than likely be mad that I'd pulled one over on him.

The closer it got to February, the more jubilant I felt. I had to force myself not to act too giddy because I didn't want to draw no more attention to myself than I already had since I'd started seeing Homer.

Ethel Mae came to visit the first week in February. This was one of the few times she didn't bring a man with her, but she bragged about the one she had met a week ago. "Mama, Eugene is the most handsome man I ever latched onto. I'd marry him in a heartbeat if he was to propose."

Me and her was sitting on my back porch steps. Catty was at the foot of the steps lapping up the grits I had put in her bowl. Every few seconds she looked up at me and blinked, probably wondering when I was going to serve her pig ears again. "Ethel Mae, how do you keep up with your men friends? What happened to the one you brought to the house last month? I liked him."

"Pfffttt!" She rolled her eyes and waved her hand. "He went back to his wife. I wish I hadn't loaned him them two dollars he asked me for. Something tells me I ain't never going to get my money back."

I reached over and stroked her arm, which was a lot bigger than it was when she moved out last year. I was glad I had hid the tea cakes I had cooked before she got to the house. If I hadn't, she would have ate them all up by now.

"Baby, you should never lend money to a man and expect it back." I sighed. "I'll be so glad when you settle down with just one. I worry about you and so does your uncle Grady. He told me he ain't seen you with the same man twice since you moved over there. The last time I talked to him, he told me he's sorry he let you move to Branson. He's convinced you're going to get involved with the wrong man."

"I could get involved with the 'wrong man' in heaven, Mama." Ethel Mae sniffed and rubbed her nose. "And anyway, Uncle Grady ain't got no room to talk. His wife spends more time visiting the moonshiners and juke joints than she spends at home. I been hearing all kinds of rumors about how friendly she gets with the men in them places. The next time he brings up my name, ask him how his marriage is going."

"I got my own marriage to worry about."

Ethel Mae gave me a pensive look. "Mama, I love my daddy, but he ain't got a smidgen of respect for you. I heard about you coming home from church early and catching him in bed with a woman."

I shook my head and exhaled. "Did Lula tell you about that? She's the only one I told." I had told Homer, but I knew he hadn't told nobody.

"No, she didn't tell me. You know how fast and far gossip travels among colored folks. Somebody from Lexington was visiting somebody in Branson and a gossip chain got started. That's how it reached me. I heard that the woman you caught in your bed was going around town bragging about it and calling you a pushover and a fool because you didn't even try to jump her. Lord! I don't know nary other woman who wouldn't have beat the dog doo-doo out of her."

"You know I don't believe in violence."

Ethel Mae laughed. "Since when? I seen you clobber Daddy a heap of times when he jumped on you."

"That was different. He hit me first."

"I declare, you must pray a lot more than you used to. Daddy is getting more brazen by the day, and it don't even seem to bother you." Ethel Mae paused and looked at me from the corner of her eye. "You cooking up something?" Now she sounded like Lula.

"I ain't cooking up nothing. I don't have to because I put everything in God's hands."

I hadn't decided how I was going to tell Ethel Mae about me and Homer. When I did, I would explain to her why I couldn't say nothing before I got clean away from Lexington. I was convinced that when I told her how good he was to me, she'd support me. One thing I would make her promise me was that she wouldn't tell Jacob where to find me. He'd find out soon enough when I filed for divorce. Meanwhile, I was going to enjoy every moment I spent with Homer until we left.

The second week in February, I started counting the days to the twenty-eighth. By now, Homer had got so passionate, the minute I walked into his house, he pulled up the tail of my dress and started tugging my bloomers. One day when I showed up in britches, he unzipped them so fast, he broke the zipper. Homer did so many other things that kept me feeling special.

That Saturday, he borrowed his neighbor's car and took me to the same restaurant in Mobile where we'd ate at back in November on his birthday. After we ate some gumbo, he looked at me with a huge smile on his face. "I know we are trying to save our money for our move, but I bought you a present," he told me in a shy tone. I couldn't believe the look of love in his eyes when he reached into his pocket and pulled out a small, white box. It was the kind rings came in. My jaw dropped when he opened it. "I didn't see no reason not to give you a engagement ring now."

The ring had a teeny-weeny diamond, but it wouldn't have impressed me more if it had been three times as big. The diamond was a shade of gold that looked white when I held it up to the light.

Tears rolled down my cheeks as Homer slid the ring onto my finger. Even though Jacob was still tied around my neck like a anchor, I already felt like a free woman. "There ain't nothing else you can do to make me happier," I sniffled. "But you know I can't wear this until we leave." I took the ring off and handed it back to him.

"I know. But I want you to know how serious I am about you. I'll keep it, but the minute we get on that train, it's going back on your finger."

It was going to be hard for me to keep a grip on myself until the end of February. I tried to stay busy so I wouldn't spend too much time dwelling on my upcoming "escape." Homer's cousin had sent him a letter to let him know that he had spoken to his boss on Homer's behalf and that a job at Ford was waiting for him. The cousin had even paid the first month's rent for an apartment we could move into as soon as we got to Michigan. My pot of gold at the end of a rainbow was bigger than I expected!

CHAPTER 30

I PLANNED TO TELL REVEREND SPIVEY ON FEBRUARY 21 THAT I WAS quitting. It was one of my days off and I wanted to break the news to him over the telephone. I had told him how much I hated segregation, so I thought he'd be real supportive of me moving to the North "to live with my cousin" who had left Alabama years ago.

One reason I wanted to tell him over the telephone was because if he started asking too many questions, I could claim somebody walked in and I had to hang up. It was bad enough I had already lied to a preacher, and I felt guilty about it. But I figured it would be easier to do it again if I didn't do it to his face.

The week before I planned to give notice, I went to Homer's house that Saturday around noon, ten minutes after Jacob went to help a friend "work on his car." Me and Homer ate some fried chicken gizzards and buttermilk biscuits for lunch. While I was in the kitchen washing the dishes, I turned around and he was standing in the doorway with a wide smile on his face. And he was buck naked.

After we finished making love, I whispered in his ear, "You make me feel so good. I hope it'll always be like this."

"It will be, sugar. Once we get situated in Michigan, I promise to be the best husband in the world. I declare, I ain't never going to even glance at another woman!"

Homer abruptly stopped talking and stared at me with a

deadpan expression on his face for so long, it looked like he had
been hypnotized. Nobody had ever looked at me with so much
intensity—not even him—and it made me uneasy. Before I could
say anything, he went on. "We'll find a good church home and
attend service every Sunday. I will never hit you or use a cuss
word in your presence. I will help you do the cooking, housecleaning, laundry, and I'll serve you breakfast in bed every weekend. You did all that on your own long enough, so it's time for
you to live a easy life." The last sentence of his wordy speech
made me so emotional, I had to blink hard to hold back my
tears. I didn't know how to react to what he said next. *"I ain't
never going to let you go . . ."*

I couldn't figure out why, but them words gave me a chill. Because I had become such a love-struck fool, I didn't just turn *a*
blind eye to red flags, I turned *both* eyes.

When I went home a hour later, I was so lightheaded, I could
barely feel the ground up under my feet. The moment I turned
onto my street, I had to rub my eyes and blink several times and
make sure I was seeing what I thought I was. There was a *hearse*
driving away from my house!

I stopped in my tracks and rubbed my eyes again to make sure
they wasn't playing tricks on me. My first thought was that a
frisky ole gal or a jealous husband had killed Jacob. I gulped in
so much air, I thought my lungs was going to explode.

Jacob's car was parked in front of our house. Several of our
neighbors was on our porch. They all looked at me with wild-
eyed expressions on their faces. "Here she comes!" somebody
yelled as I approached. Before I could ask what had happened,
Lula rushed out my front door and grabbed my hand.

"Lula, what's going on? Where is Jacob? Why was that hearse . . ."
I couldn't even finish my sentence. I looked into her eyes and
knew she was fixing to tell me something real bad.

And she did. "We think Jacob had a stroke."

"Oh Lord!" I hollered. Despite how mean Jacob had been to
me, I didn't harbor no ill will against him. If he was as miserable
as he made it seem like, being married to me, I wanted him to

settle down with a woman who could make him happy after I left. I hoped that some day when the dust settled, we could at least be friends from afar. "Is he going to be all right?"

"I don't know. I called the Fuller Brothers funeral home and told them to bring their hearse and come take Jacob to the colored clinic. He was still conscious when they got here." Lula sniffled and dabbed a tear off her face. "I got the keys to his car. You don't look like you can drive so I'll take you there. Come on."

I followed Lula to Jacob's car, and we shot off down the street. The hospital in Lexington was for white folks only. Whenever colored folks had a medical situation, we had to get in touch with one of our colored undertakers. They would come with their hearse and transport the sick or dead person to the colored clinic or their funeral home.

During the short ride, Lula told me as much as she knew. Jacob had brought one of his floozies to our house again. Before he could get her inside, he collapsed on the porch. As nosy as our neighbors was, half a dozen seen him go down and they ran to see what was wrong. The woman who had been with Jacob got spooked and took off before the hearse arrived.

"Lula, do . . . do you think he'll make it?" I asked. Under the circumstances, it seemed like the most appropriate thing for me to say.

"Well, he might, and he might not. Lewis's grandpa had a stroke ten years ago and he recovered. He lived another five years, good as new. But one of the white ladies I sew for had one last year and passed two weeks later."

My house was only eight blocks from the small clinic. It was a dreary place, inside and out. The furnishings was drab and the whole place smelled like liniment every time I went there. Some of the staff members was rushing about with agitated expressions on their faces. It was hard to believe that I had been with Homer less than a hour ago enjoying bliss and now I was in the only place I feared more than the colored cemetery, which was less than half a mile away.

Jacob hadn't been situated in a room yet, so we couldn't see him. Me and Lula sat in the waiting room for over an hour before a tall, dark man with a wide face and deep-set eyes walked in. He had on a white hospital coat, so I figured he was a doctor. I was in such a daze, it took me a few seconds to realize it was Dr. Miller, a member of my church. There was a grim expression on his face, so I prepared myself for the worst.

He plopped down in the empty chair next to me and picked up my hand and squeezed it. "I'm so sorry, Sister Naomi. I used to go fishing with Jacob when we was young'uns . . ."

"Jacob died, didn't he?" Lula blurted out.

"No, he didn't die. But . . ." Dr. Miller paused, scratched his neck, and gave me a hopeless look.

"But what?" Lula hollered as she waved her arms.

"It's too soon to tell how much damage was done. He was conscious for a few minutes after they brought him in, but now he's unconscious." Dr. Miller cleared his throat and looked at the floor. "We do as much as we can for our folks, but y'all know we are very limited in every way. I declare, we are short on equipment, nurses, food, and medication so—"

I cut him off as fast as I could. "We know all that, so just tell me about my husband, please," I said sharply.

"Well, Jacob had a massive stroke. He's paralyzed from the neck down."

My whole body felt like it had froze up solid. I couldn't move or speak so I let Lula do the talking. "Is it bad?" That seemed like a dumb question for her to ask. How could being paralyzed from the neck down not be "bad"?

The rest of their conversation sounded like gibberish to me, so I didn't know what they was saying. A nurse with a frantic look on her face suddenly rushed into the room and told Dr. Miller he was urgently needed somewhere else. He excused hisself and trotted out with the nurse.

I could barely breathe. The wooden chair I was sitting in felt as hard as steel. I had so many thoughts floating around inside my head, I couldn't tell where one ended and the next one started. My legs felt so weak I was surprised I was still able to stand up. I had to use the toilet, so I wobbled up and went to look for one.

A nurse spotted me teetering down the hall. She thought I

was one of the patients until I told her who I was and asked where the visitors' toilet was. She apologized and pointed to a door at the end of the hall.

Once I got outside, there was a well-used pathway that led to two small side-by-side outhouses only a few feet from the clinic. One door had a sign that said WOMEN, the other one said MEN. The women's room was occupied. I was too impatient to wait so I went into the men's. When I came out, a fidgety old man was standing in front of the door with a scowl on his face. "Can't you read, gal?" he barked.

I ignored him and kept walking. I was so worried I'd break down and become one of the patients for real.

CHAPTER 31

WHEN I GOT BACK TO THE WAITING ROOM, LULA PUT HER ARM around my shoulder and guided me back to the same chair I'd been sitting in. I flopped down so hard, it almost tipped over. "You have to stay strong, Naomi. Everything is going to be all right. You know I'm here for you. You hungry? You want something to drink? I can go to that little stand down the road to get us some snacks."

I shook my head. "I can't eat or drink nothing until I find out how Jacob is doing." My voice was so low I could barely hear myself.

I was in such a state of shock and disbelief, I had trouble breathing. By the time Dr. Miller returned, which was about a hour later, I was breathing through my mouth.

My legs felt like jelly, but I was able to stand up. Dr. Miller waved me back to my chair and he sat down next to me.

"I have good news for you." He stopped talking and looked from me to Lula. "Jacob is conscious now. That's a good sign. It's too soon to tell if his paralysis is permanent. We'll know more after we run some tests in a little while. Give me a call tomorrow and I may have more news for you."

"That's the 'good news' you have for me?" I asked with my voice trembling.

"Well, it could be a lot worse. Another one of my patients had a stroke a year ago and he hasn't come to yet. The fact that

Jacob has, means he's made some progress since y'all brought him in." The doctor paused again and stared up at the ceiling before he looked back at me. There was a expression on his face I would never forget. His eyebrows was scrunched up and it looked like all the blood had suddenly drained from his face. "Naomi, I don't have time to beat around the bush, so I'm going to give it to you short and simple. If Jacob remains the same despite our efforts, you'll have to take him home and make him as comfortable as possible."

"You ain't got no more good news to tell me?" I whimpered.

"Well, I do have something positive to share and I think it's pretty hopeful under the circumstances. With good, full-time care, Jacob could live another twenty or thirty years. Maybe even longer."

I was tempted to cover my ears with my hands. I didn't want to listen as Dr. Miller babbled on about how "lucky" Jacob was that he didn't have his stroke while he was driving or in the house alone. He admitted that if we hadn't brought him in when we did, he probably would have died.

After patting my shoulder, the doctor advised Lula to take me home. He walked us to the door and the last thing he said to me was, "If I don't call you by noon tomorrow, y'all come back before evening. I'll know by then when I can release Jacob. Meanwhile, you go home and get the bed ready. Now you'll have to keep a heap of towels nearby. He's been puking a lot. Poor Jacob. Unless he recovers, he'll need to be bathed, diapered, dressed, and fed like a baby for the rest of his life."

Me and Lula didn't say nothing for the first few minutes on the way home. Finally, I said, "How am I going to get through this? I'll have to quit my job and stay home to look after Jacob. His life is over, and so is mine."

"You hush up. I'm going to help you as much as I can. Now that Jacob won't be able to go back to work, you'll need your job more than ever. I can come to your house and use your sewing machine to get my work done. And I can do it every day."

"I can't pay you that—"

"Girl, I ain't said nothing about you paying me. I watched Ethel Mae when she was a baby so you could work, and didn't charge you nothing. I'll do the same thing again."

I stared at the side of Lula's head. "You heard Dr. Miller. Jacob will have to be looked after just like a baby."

"I don't care. Taking care of babies ain't no big deal to me. I want you to get some nightclothes and spend the night at my house. You don't need to be by yourself tonight."

"No, I want to sleep in my own bed," I insisted.

When I walked into my house, Catty was stretched out on the couch, sleeping like a baby. She jerked her head up when I slammed the front door shut. When she seen it was me and not Jacob, she got off the couch and followed me into the kitchen, purring up a storm.

I didn't know what to do so I just walked from room to room with my head pounding and Catty was right beside me every step of the way. When I finally sat down on the couch, she climbed up into my lap. "Well, sugar, you ain't got to worry about hiding from Jacob no more," I said as I stroked her belly. My imagination was all over the place because I could have swore Catty smiled.

I couldn't call Homer to let him know what was going on and I didn't feel like walking to his house in the dark. I could have drove Jacob's car, but I was still too shaky.

I didn't sleep a wink when I went to bed. As soon as it was daylight, I called up Ethel Mae. I knew she was probably still sleeping and wouldn't answer right away. She picked up on the tenth ring. "It's me," I muttered as soon as I heard her groggy voice. "Sugar, I'm sorry for calling so early in the morning, but I got some bad news about your daddy."

"Uh-oh. What did he do this time; finally move in with another woman?"

"No, but I wish you was right." When I told her what had happened, she started crying. She cried even harder when I told her he would have to be looked after like a baby for the rest of his life. She offered to come to Lexington as soon as possible, but I told her not to do that until I had more information about her daddy's condition.

What Ethel Mae said next really bothered me. "I told Daddy one time that God was going to make him suffer some day for treating you so bad. Look at him now. But I guess the good Lord is showing him some mercy because he could have died."

"If Dr. Miller is right, he'll be with us for another twenty or thirty years." I hated them words. They tasted like poison in my mouth. Why would *anybody* think it was a good thing for Jacob to live that much longer in his condition?

"Mama, you ain't got to carry this burden by yourself. You got me, Lula, neighbors, and the church to help you. So, it won't be so bad, right?"

I agreed with Ethel Mae, but I had to wonder if God was punishing me for being unfaithful. If that was the case, it was unfair. I wasn't no angel, and I knew adultery was a major sin, but Lula and a lot of my other married female acquaintances had committed adultery *a heap of times* and nothing bad had happened to them! Lula had been unfaithful to both of her two husbands with oodles of men! I'd been faithful to Jacob for twenty years, so my punishment didn't fit my crime. Especially since I'd only done it with *one* man.

For the first time, I wondered if it was worth it for me to keep on living. I shuddered when I realized what I was thinking. I had never heard of a colored person committing suicide. The thought that it would even enter my mind scared me to death. Suicide was worse than adultery and murder put together because every preacher I knew condemned it. Reverend Sweeney and Reverend Spivey had even told me that it was the only sin God would never forgive.

The bottom line was, I was trapped in a miserable situation, and I had no choice but to make the best of it.

CHAPTER 32

WHEN ME AND ETHEL MAE ENDED OUR CONVERSATION, I JUST stared at the telephone I was still holding so long, my hand got numb. I had planned to call Reverend Spivey this morning to tell him I was resigning and moving out of the state. It was a good thing I hadn't told him sooner because now I was going to need my job more than ever. Now I had to let him know about Jacob.

Annie Lou answered when I called around 8 A.M. "He's in the parlor laying hands on a sick baby. The boy's mama was banging on the front door before we even got out the bed this morning. Why do you need to talk to him?"

"Um . . . it's a personal matter. Tell him I called, and I'll call again later."

Ten minutes after I hung up the telephone, Reverend Spivey called me. As soon as I heard his voice, I started crying. I could barely get the words out, but I managed to let him know everything I knew about Jacob's condition and the doctor's grim prognosis.

"Naomi, everything happens for a reason. Jacob's misfortune is no doubt a blessing in disguise. I declare, it could be the conduit God is using to get his attention and lead him to salvation," he told me in the same gentle tone he used when he had to counsel one of his troubled parishioners on the telephone. "As his wife, his burden is your burden. I'm going to pray for you."

"Thank you." My voice was so raspy it sounded like everything from the inside of my mouth down to the bottom of my throat was bone-dry.

I had a headache that wouldn't go away, my stomach felt like it was tied up in knots, and all the pills I swallowed didn't help much. It was times like these that I wished I was a drinking woman. If I was, I would run to one of the moonshiners' houses and have as many drinks as it took to dull my pain. But I knew that when I sobered up, the pain would return.

I was feeling so lightheaded, I almost forgot who I was talking to until Reverend Spivey said something again. "Don't worry about us. We won't starve to death before you are able to return. You can take off all next week if you need to. Don't worry about your pay for them days. I got you."

"I don't know when the doctor is going to release Jacob. It'll probably be in the next few days. When we bring him home, Lula said she'd take care of him during the day, so I don't need to take off all next week."

"Bless your soul. You're going to have a tough row to hoe." Reverend Spivey continued in a voice full of sadness, "My dear mother had a stroke many years ago. Viola, Annie Lou, and the two housekeepers I employed at the time, couldn't handle all the necessary responsibilities required for her care. I hired a live-in nurse who provided excellent care. She was with us until the day Mother died, twenty-five years after her stroke. I know you know your Bible so I'm sure you remember what Job went through. What you're facing is a patty cake compared to what he endured. So, when you get the blues, think about Job."

I knew folks was trying to make me feel better, but it seemed like everything they was telling me was only making me feel even more doomed.

Reverend Spivey quoted a few scriptures before he hung up. I sat down at the kitchen table and just stared at the wall for so long, I started to see spots in front of my eyes. I was glad the telephone rang when it did. It jolted me back to reality.

It was Dr. Underwood calling. He worked the day shift at the clinic. He was one of my used-to-be classmates. "Naomi, Dr. Miller and I discussed Jacob's case in depth." He sounded as tired as I felt. "Unfortunately, his condition hasn't changed since you were here. I wish we could keep him here longer, but we need the bed for the more serious patients."

I gasped. "'More serious'? What could be more serious than a stroke?"

"Well, we admitted some burn victims who got caught up in a barn fire out on Springer Road last night. And just a little while ago, they hauled in a teenage boy with a slew of injuries. He got hit by a truck."

"I see," I mumbled. "Is Jacob conscious?"

"Yes, but he can't speak. He can move his eyes, though. He can hear, so you'll be able to ask him yes and no questions. Tell him to blink three times for yes and twice for no." Dr. Underwood blew out a loud breath and continued. "He can stay here tonight, but you need to make arrangements to pick him up tomorrow. The earlier the better. Once you get him home, if there is any change in his condition, you let me or Dr. Miller know."

It seemed like the world was caving in on me. I knew I had to talk to Homer soon. The support I was getting from Lula and everybody else wasn't enough. I took a bath and put on some fresh clothes. I didn't bother to put on makeup or fix up my hair the way Homer liked it. I covered my head with a scarf. I didn't rush to get to his house the way I usually did. I moved so slow down the street, you would have thought I had one leg. When I got to his front door, I took a real deep breath before I let myself in.

"Baby, come on in!" he hollered as I shuffled into his living room. "You are right on time. I'm almost done cooking breakfast. You want me to make some gravy to go with the grits?"

I held up both my hands. "Homer, I don't want no breakfast."

"All right, then. If you change your mind, let me know and I'll fix you a plate. Did you call Reverend Spivey?"

I nodded.

"I know he'll miss you, but there must be dozens of other

good cooks in Lexington he can choose from." Homer laughed.
"But I doubt if they'll cook as good as you." He snorted and
looked me up and down, but he didn't say nothing about my
dowdy appearance. "Come here and give me some sugar."

I went up to him and we kissed. I didn't know how eager he
would be to kiss me when he heard what I had to say, so I kissed
him longer than usual. I was surprised he didn't comment on
how chapped my lips was. He wanted to kiss some more—and I
did, too—but I pulled away from him because he was grinding
into me, so I knew he wanted us to hop into bed. But he couldn't
have turned me on with a wrench. I pulled away from him.
"Honey-pie, I need to tell you something. But I think you should
sit down first."

Homer's face started getting tight as he eased down on the
couch. I stood in front of him, wringing my hands and shifting
my weight from one foot to the other. I was still in a state of
shock, but it wasn't as bad as it had been yesterday. I wished I
had come to see him before I went to bed last night. Him being
so sensitive and caring, I knew he would have gave me the emotional support I needed. That would have helped me get some
sleep.

I was so dead tired on my feet now I was surprised I hadn't
keeled over. I took the deepest breath I ever took and told
Homer everything that had happened since I left his house yesterday. He grimaced when I said I'd have to take care of Jacob
like a baby for the rest of his life and, because of that, I couldn't
move to Michigan with him now. In the gentlest voice I could
manage, I also told Homer that I would always love him, but I
had to put my husband first. By the time I stopped talking his
face was so tight, I was surprised his skin didn't crack. Instead of
pulling me into his arms and comforting me like I expected him
to do, he stood and put his hands on his hips.

The room was so quiet, I thought I'd suddenly gone deaf. He
narrowed his eyes into slits and then words started shooting out
of his mouth like arrows. *"After all I done for you, you choosing the
same man over me who's been treating you like a mangy dog for years?
You ain't going to get away with this!"*

CHAPTER 33

My JAW DROPPED. I COULDN'T BELIEVE WHAT I HAD JUST HEARD. Homer had never raised his voice to me. My ears had to be playing tricks on me. I soon found out they wasn't. The only men I'd ever been scared of was Daddy and Jacob. But now I was more scared of Homer than the two of them put together.

I braced myself for what he was going to say next. "I done gave notice at my job and they already found somebody to replace me. I told my landlord I was moving so he expects me to be up out of here by the end of this month. I went next door last night to use the phone to call up my cousin last night to let him know what time to meet us at the train station next Sunday. You breaking up with me? Do you think I'm going to let you throw me aside like a old shoe and go on with your life like I never existed?"

"I . . . I didn't say I was breaking up with you." My mind was in a tizzy, but I was still able to recall all the good times I'd had with Homer and all the wonderful things he'd said to me. He was a mild-mannered, caring man who loved me. I tried to imagine how humble he'd be when he calmed down and apologized. That's what kept me from running out the door. "Once I get Jacob home and settled, you and me can go on like before," I offered with a weak smile.

"LIKE HELL. You low-down, selfish bitch!" he shrieked.

My mouth dropped open, my eyes got big, and I almost jumped out of my skin. This was the first time I'd heard him use cuss words. The ugly, twisted expression on his face now sent shivers up my spine. My hands was shaking and my heart racing. It was hard to believe this was the same man who had played with my toes and called them "little piggies." I wished I could go back out the door, come back in, start all over, and tell him in a gentler way. But I had already told him in a gentle way.

My mind was all over the place. Not only was Homer scaring me, but he also confused me. One of the things he loved about me was that I was so caring and compassionate. If I had told him about Jacob and run off with him as planned and left Ethel Mae holding the bag, would that make him change his opinion of me? I wondered. I sure would have changed my opinion of myself if I'd been that callous. I wouldn't be able to live with myself if I turned my back on Jacob. And I couldn't put such a heavy burden on Ethel Mae's shoulders.

I finally said, "Calm down, honey-baby."

Homer balled up his fist, shook it in my face, and started talking in a raspy voice I almost didn't recognize. "Calm down my foot. *Every* woman I let into my life made a fool out of me." I wanted to say something, but I didn't know what. I was so flabbergasted, I couldn't think of nothing to say that wouldn't make him madder than he already was. I moved away a few steps from him. He moved a few steps closer to me and started talking again. "All my life women done milked me like a cow, taking all the love I had to give."

He paused and a woebegone look crossed his face. For a split second I thought he was fixing to apologize and take me in his arms and tell me everything was going to be all right. I was wrong. His face twisted up like a fright mask and his tone got even more hostile. "After I built up all my women's self-esteem and spent money on you wenches, I *still* got mistreated and tossed aside! Well, I'm through fattening frogs for snakes! I treated you like a queen, and this is how you repay me?" Homer was looking at me like he wanted to wring my neck. "Nooooo! This is the worst I ever been betrayed!"

I was glad to still be near the door in case I had to bolt. Homer moved closer to me. "B-but Jacob is my husband," I whimpered.

In the back of my mind—and even though I felt bad about Jacob's situation—I realized that because of him, I was still going to be miserable. And this time it would be more profound and probably a lot longer. I wished he had left me for one of his girlfriends before he had his stroke. It would have been easier for me to take off because whoever she was, he would have been her problem. While my mind was wandering, the scowl on Homer's face got so severe, he looked like a gargoyle.

"He was your husband when you crawled your butt into my bed! He was your husband when you told me you was in love with me, and would divorce him so we could get married! He was your husband when you went against your religion and lied to a preacher so you could spend more time with me. What do you expect me to do now? Without you, my life is over!" His voice cracked and tears pooled in his eyes. Now he was wagging his finger in my face. "Y-you think you can ruin my life and get away with it? HELL NO!"

"How can you be so self-centered?"

"*I'm* self-centered?" he roared. "You made your choice without even talking it over with me. If that ain't proof you was only thinking about yourself, I don't know what is!"

I held up my hands and shook my head. Now I was almost as angry as he was. "Look, I got enough mess on my hands right now I don't need no more. I'm going to have to deal with the biggest burden I ever faced in my life, and I thought you'd have some sympathy for me and offer me some comfort. That's what I need right now."

The way Homer was twitching, trembling, and drooling, I thought he was about to have a stroke, too. He wiped his wet lips with the back of his hand. "You ain't getting no sympathy from me. I done told you that I wouldn't be able to go on without you. Now my life ain't worth no more than Jacob's is. Shame, shame, shame on you, Naomi!"

I figured it was time for me to leave. I said in a voice so gentle, you would have thought I was praying. "Um . . . I'm going to leave so you can cool off. I'll come back in a day or so and we can talk some more. I don't want—"

Homer slammed his fist into his palm and cut me off and said something that chilled me to the bone. "I ain't never going to 'cool off' so don't bother bringing your pig-ear cooking, cheesy black ass to my house again, bitch! GET OUT OF MY SIGHT!" He paused long enough to catch his breath. Then he stabbed my chest with his finger. "And another thing: *I'm going to make your life a living hell until the day you die!*"

I didn't wait to hear nothing else. I whirled around, snatched open the door, and bolted like a caught thief. I didn't care if Vinnie next door seen me galloping down the street. The heels of my shoes was clip-clopping on the sidewalk like a tap dancer. When I got to the corner, I had to stop and lean against a tree because I was out of breath. As soon as I got my second wind, I trotted all the way back home.

My mind was mush so it was hard to recall everything Homer had said in order and then process it. On top of having to take care of Jacob, now I had to worry about Homer's threat. I felt like crawling into bed and staying there for the rest of my life so I wouldn't be responsible for nobody, not even myself.

While I was pacing back and forth in my living room, Lula walked in. "How are you doing?" she asked as she plopped down on the couch.

"The same as yesterday," I lied. I was feeling ten times worse than I'd felt yesterday.

"Well, you look like the life done been sucked out of you. But I done told you, I'm here for you. Do you know when they are going to release Jacob?"

"Tomorrow. They said the sooner I pick him up, the better. They need the bed for another patient. Will you go with me?"

"You know I will. We'll make a pallet in the bed of Lewis's truck where we can lay Jacob when we fetch him from the clinic. Lewis can load him up and carry him into your house when we get back. Now you get some rest. You're going to need it." I didn't sleep at all when I went to bed.

* * *

Jacob looked like a dead man when me and Lula made it to his room the next morning. The only difference was his eyes was wide-open. It was hard to believe he was the same man who had bullied and beat me for so many years. I knew he couldn't have lost much weight since the clinic admitted him, but he looked so small and frail, my eyes burned when I stared down at him.

The clinic didn't have a extra wheelchair for us to use, so a big burly orderly helped Lewis put him on a stretcher and carry him out to the truck. After they got Jacob situated in the truck's bed, I climbed in and sat next to him. I held his hand all the way to our house. When we got there, Lewis got the wheelbarrow from our backyard shed. After he loaded Jacob into it, he wheeled him to the bedroom, lifted him out, and laid him on the bed. I was shaking so hard, Lula had to be the one to tuck him in.

I was so tired mentally and physically, I wanted to scream bloody murder. But I didn't want to break down and put even more of a burden on poor Lula. She and Lewis had a church program to get to so they couldn't stay no longer. She promised that she'd come back before she went to bed, though.

It was so hard to believe that all Jacob could do was blink his eyes. I sat down on the bed and held his hand again. "Jacob, you ain't got to worry about nothing. I'll be here for you until the very end. Do you understand me?"

He blinked three times for yes, and then a great big tear rolled out. I cried too, and not just about Jacob's condition. Homer's threat was still ringing in my ears, but I had to push that to the back of my mind. I'd had similar experiences with two other disgruntled boyfriends before I married Jacob. Both of them had threatened me, but nothing happened. One proposed to another girl a month after I quit him and even invited me to the wedding.

My mind was so overloaded with thoughts, I didn't know what I was going to think about next. I was glad Reverend Spivey told me to take some time off, but I only planned to stay home Monday and maybe Tuesday.

In the meantime, I was going to do all I could to put Homer out of my mind. That was not going to be easy. I still loved him, but because of what he'd said to me yesterday, I knew our relationship was over. Since he'd gave notice at his job and told his landlord he was moving, I had a feeling he would go on to Michigan anyway. He didn't have no reason to stay on in Lexington now. That was why I wasn't going to worry about him. Besides, what could he do to make my life a living hell? The worst he could do was tell Jacob about our affair. But what good would that do now with the shape Jacob was in?

When Lula showed up Monday morning around 6 A.M., reality hit me like a ton of bricks. "How is he?" she asked.

I tried to answer, but I couldn't get no words out. I just led her to the bedroom. "Do you think the two of us can get him out of bed and sit him on the slop jar or the toilet? We can't let him go all day until Lewis gets off work."

"I don't want to try because we might drop him. Maybe we'll eventually figure out a way to lift him and not have to wait on Lewis or one of the neighbor men to help us. Until then, we'll have to rip up some sheets to use for diapers."

"You can have some of my old sheets, so you won't have to do laundry every day. I'll collect as many as I can from the neighbors. I'll be talking to Reverend Sweeney later today and have him get the congregation to donate all they can." Lula smiled. How she was able to do that was a mystery to me. I couldn't even feel my lips, so I didn't know when I'd be able to smile again.

"Lula, I don't know what I'd do without you." Them words made my head swim. I couldn't count the number of times Homer had told me he didn't know what he'd do without me.

She rubbed my back and smiled some more. "I know all this is a lot for you to deal with, but be thankful it ain't something worse."

If somebody told me again to be glad things wasn't "worse," I was going to scream. *What* could be worse than the mess I had on my hands? I wondered. I would find out in a few months . . .

CHAPTER 34

GETTING THROUGH THE FIRST WEEK WAS HARD. THE FOLLOWING Sunday, which was the same day me and Homer was supposed to leave, I felt so overwhelmed, I left Jacob alone and went to the back porch with a towel. I cried until I couldn't cry no more. I felt as sorry as I could for Jacob, but I was also mad at him. He was going to stop me from having a happy life *again*. But I had to admit that maybe his stroke was a blessing in disguise. I'd seen a side of Homer that scared the heebie-jeebies out of me. There was no telling how he would have treated me if I had run off with him. That gave me a lot to think about.

By the time I left the porch, the towel I had brought with me was soaked through and through with my tears. Shortly after I got back inside, Lula, a bunch of folks from church, and several of my neighbors came to the house. Some brought food so I wouldn't have to do no cooking. Even though I tried to keep Jacob clean, there was a few times when he had accidents before I could pin a fresh wrapping on his private parts. That alone almost pushed me over the edge.

Martha Lou stuffed all the soiled sheets into a bag so she could take them to her house and wash them. I was especially impressed at how helpful she was being. I knew that in her line of work, time was money and here she was spending so much of her time helping me. "Naomi, you got my phone number. Call me anytime you want."

"I really appreciate you doing so much. I didn't expect—"

She held up her hand. "Look, you always treat me real nice, which is something I can't say about a lot of them old peahens we know." There was a few of them old "peahens" still in the house. I put my finger up to my lips to shush Martha Lou, but she ignored me. "Humph! Let them hear me. I bet a lot of these heifers around here do the same thing I do for a living. They just hide it."

After everybody had gone back to their own homes, I felt unbearably sad and lonely. Before I joined Jacob in the bedroom, I sat on the couch and read the Bible first. That didn't help much. The bedroom had become the most dreaded part of the house. Even with the lamp on, it seemed dim and dreary. I knew that was because my mood was so dark.

When I finally decided to go back into the bedroom, I had to force myself to look at Jacob laying there, more dead than alive. Despite how mean and violent he had been, I felt so much pity for him. I didn't want to see a mad dog suffer the way he was. What was the point of living if all you could do was blink your eyes? I wondered. I scolded myself for having such a morbid thought. Life was life, and even people in Jacob's condition deserved to live.

His eyes lit up on Sunday when Lula and Lewis helped me lift him into the wheelbarrow and haul him to the bed of Lewis's truck so we could take him to church. Jacob looked so uncomfortable when I laid some pillows in the pew and Lewis propped him up, next to me and Lula. I was glad we had only agreed to stay for the morning service. Before Reverend Sweeney started preaching, he had the congregation say a special prayer for Jacob.

After we got him home and back to bed, Lula and Lewis left. I stood over the bed gazing at Jacob, wondering what was going through his mind now. When he sighed and closed his eyes, I pulled the covers up to his neck. I didn't want to leave him by hisself yet, so I sat down at the foot of the bed and cried again. Catty wandered in and rubbed against my thigh, like she was trying to comfort me.

There was a few nights I couldn't stand to sleep in the same bed with Jacob. It felt like I was sleeping next to a corpse. If I outlived him, one morning I would wake up in bed with a corpse. I didn't want to sleep in Ethel Mae's old room because it was at the back of the house and was too cold this time of year, so some nights I stretched out on the couch with Catty snoozing in my arms.

I couldn't wait for morning to come so I could go to work. Lula always arrived early, so we could drink some coffee before I left. When she showed up Monday morning, I hugged her so tight she squirmed. "Hold on now. My man don't wrap me up like that." She laughed.

"I'm sorry. I'm just so glad you're here."

She gave me a puzzled look. "I spend half of my time here these days and I'm going to continue to do so. I told you I ain't letting you go through this by yourself. If Lewis had a stroke, I know you'd be there to help me."

"Lula, I just feel so guilty about you giving up your time for me and Jacob. But I couldn't go on if you didn't." All of my relatives lived out of town now, but they called every chance they got. My sister Claudette offered to come for a visit, but she'd recently had a heart attack herself and hadn't fully recovered yet. I didn't need two folks in bad health in the same house.

"Lula, I . . . I hope you never move away from Lexington or get tired of taking care of Jacob. If you do, I'd be in a barrel of pickles," I whined.

"You ain't got to worry about that happening. The only place I'll leave my hometown for is Heaven." We laughed. It felt good to enjoy some humor.

By the middle of March, I had a routine. Me and Lula was able to load Jacob into the wheelbarrow, wheel him to the car, and lay him on the back seat. That way we didn't have to depend on Lewis and his truck all the time.

Ethel Mae and her boyfriend(s) came as often as they could to help out, and I didn't care if she brought a different one each time. I was glad my child was happy, but I still didn't like how she was living her life. One evening before she left to go back to Branson, I took her aside and told her, "Baby, I got enough to worry about. Please try to find one man and settle down. Your lifestyle ain't healthy or Christian." There was times when I said something that was so hypocritical, I wanted to bite my tongue right after I said it. This was one of them times. What could be more hypocritical than me getting involved with Homer and making plans to run off with him?

"Oh, Mama. You don't need to keep worrying about me. I'm enjoying life and you should be, too. Why don't you put on some rouge and a low-cut blouse and go to one of them moonshiners' houses and have a good time? Lula can babysit Daddy." Ethel Mae winked at me and added, "Now that he can't do his bedroom job no more, you need to find a man who can . . ."

I dropped my head. My sex life was the last thing I wanted to discuss with my child. I couldn't think of a good response, so I said, "Hush up! You ought to be ashamed of yourself talking to me like that! I'm a married woman."

Ethel Mae looked like she wanted to laugh. "Yeah, but that's a moot point now. You ain't the one paralyzed, so you need to do something for yourself. I bet if Daddy could talk, he would tell you the same thing and give you his blessing. There ain't nothing wrong with getting pleasured."

I gave Ethel Mae a hot look. "And you would know!" I snapped. "Now you stop talking nasty stuff to me. That's disrespectful."

"I will. But I have to say one more thing: you are so behind the times. You ought to be more like Lula."

I wished I could be more like Lula, but I'd never admit that to Ethel Mae, or even to Lula. God had made me a certain way and I wasn't about to try and change this late in the game. I knew now that I couldn't have been the same woman I'd been all my life, if I had married Homer. I would have had to make some changes to accommodate him. I had never thought much about it before, but he had got too attached to me so soon. I thought about the times he'd told me that he didn't know what he'd do without me. That wasn't normal. I'd been living in such a dream world back then, I couldn't see or think straight. In a strange way, I was glad something had happened to prevent me from running away with Homer. I wished it could have been something other than Jacob having a stroke.

"Mama, you look like somebody in a trance," Ethel Mae said, waving her hand in front of my face.

"Huh? Oh! I was just thinking." I cleared my throat. "Anyway, I appreciate you being concerned about me, sugar. But I ain't going to go find a boyfriend. I'm going to let things stay as is. Now you and your friend better start heading back to Branson before it gets too dark."

As much as I loved my daughter's company, I was anxious for her to leave before she said something that would upset me even more than I already was.

CHAPTER 35

*S*PRING WAS MY FAVORITE SEASON. EVEN THOUGH IT RAINED A LOT, the weather never got too warm or too cool. It was also when I planted vegetables in our backyard. One of the many things me and Homer had agreed on was that when we got our place in Michigan it had to have enough room in the back so I could plant a garden.

"What if we move into a place that ain't got no backyard?" I'd asked him.

His answer pleased me. "Then I will work a second job so we can rent a plot out in the country. You can garden all you want there. I'm going to do everything I can to keep you happy, Naomi."

I couldn't believe all the good things Homer had told me. He'd even said that if we was lucky enough to be blessed with a child, he'd help change diapers, burp, cuddle, and feed him or her. Now, I couldn't believe all the mean things he had said to me when I broke up with him. I had to blink hard to hold back my tears. I had probably shed enough already to fill a jug and I was getting tired of crying over two men—or *devils* I should say—who had impacted my life in such a negative way.

I hated to see night come because I was alone in the house with Jacob. As if that wasn't bad enough, I also felt conflicted about the way me and Homer had ended. One night after Jacob had gone to sleep, I decided to take a drive over to Homer's street. I hadn't been near his place since I told him about

Jacob's stroke. I covered my head with a scarf and pulled one of Jacob's old work caps down over it. I scrunched down in the seat as I cruised past Homer's house. The lights was on, but I didn't know if he still lived there, or if a new tenant had moved in. I . drove to the end of the block and turned around. This time I seen a good-looking woman come out the front door. I wondered if she was the new tenant or if Homer had found hisself another woman and forgot about me. By the time I got home, I had convinced myself that the woman was Homer's new girlfriend. Being the passionate, attentive man he was, I knew he would spend his time pampering her just like he had done with me. Because I hadn't heard from him, I also convinced myself that I didn't have to worry about them threats he'd made.

The last Monday in March, I got up to go to work like I usually did. Lula had arrived and even fixed breakfast for me and Jacob. I had my appetite back, so I had put back on the few pounds I had lost.

"You want me to cook supper for you today?" Lula asked as I was about to leave.

"I can cook when I get home. You already do too much for me."

"I don't mind. Besides, that crazy cat of yours been giving me the fisheye, so I better cook her some pig ears soon." We laughed. Despite everything I was going through, I was glad to be able to laugh again.

I was in a good mood as I walked to the bus stop. I bumped into a couple of folks I knew on the way and briefly conversated with them. By the time my bus arrived, I almost felt like my old self.

Colored folks had to sit in the back of the bus, so I passed up a lot of empty seats to get to the crowded colored section where there was only a few seats available. I looked toward the last row and seen something that almost made me faint: Homer. I gasped and stumbled. When our eyes met, he looked at me like he wanted to cut my throat. My heart started beating so hard, I thought it was going to bust out of my chest. I sat down next to a man reading a newspaper.

Two stops later, Homer got up and walked toward the exit.

Before he got off, he turned around and gave me another mean look. I was so nervous when I got to work, I couldn't concentrate on nothing I was doing. I burnt the grits and dropped some jelly on the floor. I had time to cook more grits and clean up the floor before the Spiveys came to eat breakfast. Once they got seated, I spilled coffee on Annie Lou's shoulder. She yelped so loud, you would have thought I'd shot her.

"I declare, Naomi. You been acting real jumpy this morning," she complained.

"Have you been drinking?" Miss Viola asked. With a smirk she added, "Or is it something worse?"

I was glad Reverend Spivey jumped in. "Naomi does not drink. She's carrying such a heavy load these days I'm surprised she is still able to walk." He sighed and looked up at me with his face scrunched up. He gently asked, "How is your husband doing, my dear?"

"About the same," I muttered.

"Well, you keep doing your job as a obedient, tolerant, Godly wife and you will be blessed. Pass the biscuits please."

Right after Reverend Spivey finished eating breakfast, he left to go pray for another sick person at their house. It seemed like half the folks in his congregation had health issues these days and he spent half of his time with them.

Miss Viola had told me once that she didn't like being left alone so much, especially at night. "I know I'm old, but I'm still a woman and I got needs," she also told me. Me and her was in the kitchen alone. She was reared back in a chair at the table; I was sitting on a stool at the counter shelling the peas I was going to cook for supper. I knew better than to ask a white woman, especially one in her position, what she meant. Miss Viola went on to tell me anyway. "See, I have a urinary condition that makes it messy and cumbersome for me and Garth to be intimate." She rolled her neck and swooned. "Bless my soul, I miss it so bad. And I know Garth does, too. Poor thing."

Reverend Spivey was at his church that day organizing a upcoming program and Annie Lou was in her room working on a new puzzle.

"I'm sorry to hear about your condition," I muttered.

"You people are so lucky."

"Ma'am?"

Miss Viola glanced at the doorway and lowered her voice. "Let me tell you something I've never told a soul. Before I got married, I spent a summer in New Orleans with some family friends. Well, I went to a party with my cousin Amy one night. I had several highballs and somehow, I ended up alone in a vacant room with one of the colored boys they'd hired to serve. Bless my soul, one thing led to another . . ." Miss Viola dipped her head and gave me a mysterious smile, like she was waiting for me to figure out where she was going. I figured out what she couldn't say in words. This prissy, respectable white woman had done the unthinkable: had sex with a colored man.

"Oh," was the most fitting thing I could think to say. But I wanted to scream and laugh at the same time.

"It was an experience I will never forget. My first time ever. Then there was another party and another boy. To make a long story short, I had relationships with four in all. Poor Garth. He was so naïve. He was a virgin when we got married. I claimed to be one, too, and he didn't know the difference." Miss Viola paused again, and a wistful look crossed her face. "Lord, how I miss being close to a man in the Biblical sense!"

"Oh," was all I could say again. I was not about to ask this white woman no questions about her sex life, and I sure wasn't going to discuss mine. I couldn't figure out what it was about me that made a woman like Miss Viola tell me things she should have kept to herself. No white person had ever discussed anything of a sexual nature with me before. What she'd just confessed took me aback so far, I suddenly "remembered" I had to get the clothes off the line. She never mentioned her sex life to me again after that day.

I often wondered if Reverend Spivey still had an interest in sex. One thing I knew was that old age didn't always mean the end of sex. Daddy proved that to me because there was several times when I overheard him and Miss Maddie going at it in his bedroom when they thought I was asleep. Both of them was in their late sixties at the time.

I scolded myself for letting my mind run wild. Sex was the last thing I needed to be thinking about.

I was glad Miss Viola decided to go visit one of her neighbors right after lunch. I liked being in the kitchen alone because it was so quiet. I could sit at the table and think. I was glad I had things other than Jacob and Homer to reflect on. One thing that left me reeling was the way some people shared "secrets" with me. Like the one about Annie Lou being colored. According to the law in the South, one drop of colored blood made a "white" person colored. What I couldn't understand was that if it was so important, why did Reverend Spivey risk Annie Lou being exposed by sharing it with me? Why did Annie Lou tell me she was colored? For all they knew, I could have blabbed that information to the world and caused them a major scandal. Now here I was saddled with the information that not only had Miss Viola deceived Reverend Spivey about being a virgin, but she had also confessed to me that she'd had sex with several colored men. I guess she never thought about the fact that if they fired me, I'd get back at them by letting that cat out of the bag.

When I got tired of running things through my mind, I started leafing through the Sears Roebuck catalogue. After that I stared out the window for several minutes. It reminded me of the times I used to go to the lake to fish so I could clear my mind. I was too spooked to go back there now because it was where I'd met Homer.

I wished Miss Viola had not brought up sex with me. I thought about what Ethel Mae had said on her last visit about me finding a boyfriend. I missed having sex, even with Jacob. It was hard to accept that my sex life was over at the age of thirty-six. I knew there was some good men out there, but searching for one would be like looking for a black cat in a dark room. I decided not to waste no more time today thinking about sex and men.

Just before noon, I started getting everything ready for lunch.

Reverend Spivey loved my crab cakes and hush puppies and smothered potatoes. I was standing over the sink peeling the potatoes when I heard somebody tap on the side window. I was horrified when I turned around and seen Homer peeping in!

I still had the knife in my hand when I ran outside to confront him. But he was gone by the time I got there. I told myself that the bus and the window-peeping incidents was all he was going to do. I didn't even believe that myself. Homer was going to do just what he said: make the rest of my life a living hell.

CHAPTER 36

FOR THE NEXT FEW DAYS, I KEPT MYSELF AS BUSY AS I COULD TO help keep my mind off Homer, not to mention my responsibility to Jacob. Homer could stop tormenting me when he got tired, but in Jacob's case, I'd been handed a life sentence in a prison I never imagined.

I did things for myself that used to make me feel good. The last Saturday morning in April, Lula came to sit with Jacob so I could do some shopping and go get my hair done. I went to the five-and-dime store and bought myself a few items I had run low on. When I got home, I rearranged everything in my kitchen cabinets and closets.

The following week I made new curtains for every window in my house. When I finished the last one, I turned on the radio to listen to a comedy show. On all the stations I could get, it was one report after another about trouble brewing in foreign countries that could lead to another world war. I knew that no matter where the mess started, somehow America would get involved in it. If and when that happened, a heap of families I knew had sons in the military who could end up maimed or dead.

I hadn't seen Homer since I'd caught him peeping in Reverend Spivey's kitchen window. The first week in May, I experienced something a lot more frightening. It had already been a bad night. Around midnight Jacob had puked so hard, it woke me up. It was hard to take off his clothes and scrub him off by myself. Then I had to pull him by his arms and legs around the bed so I could put on some clean kivver. Even though Lula had told me I could call her if I needed her any time of day or night, I wasn't about to disturb her in the middle of the night. When I got through, I was dead tired. To my surprise, I was a little hungry, so I went to the kitchen to fix myself a snack.

While I was spreading mayonnaise on a slice of bread, somebody tapped on the back kitchen window. I whirled around so fast I almost fell. I screamed bloody murder when I spotted Homer's face. I wasn't brave or stupid enough to go outside at night and confront a man who *had* to be crazy, so I lifted the window high enough to lean my head out. "Homer, you need to leave me alone and move on with your life!"

"What life? My life ain't worth a plugged nickel after what you done to me." He was speaking in such a calm tone, you would have thought we was still on good terms.

I didn't try to hide my anger. "Well, I can't do nothing about that now!" I hissed as I wagged my finger in his direction. "Why don't you leave here?"

Homer dropped his head and when he looked back up, I was shocked to see tears sliding down his face. What I couldn't understand was how he had got so wrapped up in me when a man like him could have had any other woman he wanted. There was so many younger and prettier women in Lexington looking for a man. Why didn't he go after one of them? Why couldn't he go on to Michigan and take advantage of all the opportunities he'd told me about? I couldn't get in his head, so I couldn't answer none of them questions. "Where do you expect me to go?" he boomed.

"To hell for all I care!"

Homer smiled and narrowed his eyes, which was still filled with tears. "When I do that, I'm taking you with me. And that ain't no threat, it's a promise."

Before I could say anything else, he spun around and casually walked away. I was shaking so hard, I could barely move my feet as I went back to the table. I didn't want nothing to eat now so I put the bread back on the counter and the baloney and mayonnaise back into the icebox.

I wasn't able to go back to sleep. I laid in bed and stared up at the ceiling until daybreak. When Lula got to the house a couple of hours later, she noticed the dark circles around my eyes. "You been crying," she accused.

"Um . . . yeah." I told her I had just heard on the radio about the *Hindenburg* blimp exploding in New Jersey yesterday. "You know how emotional I get when I hear about a big tragedy. Even if I don't know the people involved."

Lula let out a loud sigh. "I heard the news. That was sad about all them folks getting killed in New Jersey. At least it took your mind off Jacob. Bless your soul. Always concerned about other folks. I know some white folks can be downright stupid, but they didn't have no business getting on a damn blimp— whatever the hell a blimp is—in the first place. Here you are sitting way down here in Alabama boo-hooing for them." Lula blew out a loud breath and gazed at me with a shy smile on her face. "God's got His eye on you and He's taking notes. I wish I could be more like you."

I never expected to hear such a comment from a spitfire like Lula. I didn't bother to mention Jacob puking and the hard time I'd had cleaning him up and changing the bed kivver. And that had only been part of the reason I couldn't sleep. Since Homer was coming onto my property now, I had something new to fret about, so there'd be more nights that I wouldn't be able to sleep.

"I'm going to spend the next couple of nights with you so you can get some sleep," Lula said.

I held up my hand. "No! You ain't got to do that. You do enough for me already. I don't want Lewis to start thinking I'm taking up too much of your time."

"He can think whatever he wants. Do you think he's crazy enough to get in my business?"

Somehow, I managed to laugh. "I know he ain't. But you don't need to spend the night with me. I'll be fine."

Even if Lula had stayed a couple of nights with me, I still would have had trouble getting to sleep. Just the thought of Homer showing up again and her seeing him, sent shivers up my spine. I'd have to give her a explanation that made sense. But what could I tell her?

"All right, Naomi. But if you change your mind, just let me know."

As bad as I wanted to tell Lula and Reverend Spivey what was going on, I couldn't bring myself to do it. Lula would probably hunt Homer down and use her knife on him or bash his head in with a brick. That was the last thing I wanted to happen. She was a tough cookie, but I didn't know what Homer was capable of. He was a lot bigger and stronger than she was, so there was no telling what he might do to her if she confronted him. Anybody as mentally disturbed as he turned out to be probably had all kinds of tricks up his sleeve to use if he needed to defend hisself.

Letting Reverend Spivey know I'd cheated on my husband was definitely out of the question. If he had disowned his own daughter for being an adulteress, he'd fire me in a heartbeat. He was so kind to me, I never wanted to disappoint him.

Two days went by, and Homer hadn't come back around. Not seeing him was almost as bad as seeing him. I didn't know if he was holed up somewhere plotting his next move or if he'd left town. That kind of uncertainty was hellish.

CHAPTER 37

B Y JUNE I WASN'T AS TENSE AS I'D BEEN THE MONTH BEFORE. I predicted that before the end of the year, I'd have put Homer completely out of my mind. However, as hard as I tried, I couldn't wipe out all the times he'd made me happy. Them memories was hard to forget.

I still liked to listen to the news on the radio. Even though the reception in our area was always weak during the day, I could make out most of what was being reported. While I was dusting off things in the living room on a hot evening in June, the newsman announced that a twenty-three-year-old colored boxer named Joe Louis was the new world heavyweight champion of the world. I stopped dusting and turned the radio up louder. I didn't care one way or the other about no sports, but I got excited when I heard that the man Joe Louis had beat in a Chicago arena yesterday was white. I never thought I'd live long enough to see the day when a colored man could beat up a white man and not get lynched. A boxing match between a colored and a white man could never take place in the South. My heart felt like somebody was tugging it every time I thought about the life I might have had in Michigan without segregation.

The news about Joe Louis traveled fast. When I went out to walk to the market ten minutes after I turned off the radio, I bumped into several neighbors who had heard about the fight. "It's about time we started beating their behinds," the old man who lived next door growled. He was a used-to-be slave who had been treated real bad by the family who'd owned him. He had so much contempt for white folks, he got hopping mad every time he seen one in our neighborhood.

People had stopped talking about Joe Louis by the time the Fourth of July rolled around. They was busy getting ready to celebrate the holiday. I had bought two slabs of ribs and three pounds of chicken wings, but I was no longer in the mood to have a cookout. Jacob had puked up a storm again the night before. I'd had to clean him off as well as I could by myself, the bed, and this time the floor. He did it again a hour later. I had slept less than two hours the previous night so I was as tired as I could be.

I called up my out-of-town relatives and wished them a happy Fourth of July and to catch up on what was going on in their lives. As much as I loved conversating with my family on the telephone, sometimes they depressed me. All they talked about was their numerous health issues, who died, and their other random problems.

"You don't know how lucky you are, baby sister. Your life ain't as bad as you think it is," my brother Dobie told me. His wife had some kind of blood disorder and they had to cut off her leg last year. My brother Grady's son fell off a boat three months ago while he was fishing and drowned. Claudette had recovered from her heart attack, but now she had sugar diabetes. I couldn't keep up with what was wrong with who. I decided that compared to the rest of my family, I was lucky.

After I finished making telephone calls, I decided to stretch out on the couch and take a nap. Before I could get comfortable, Ethel Mae showed up out of the blue around 10 A.M. She had wrote and told me she was going to celebrate the holiday with some friends, so I was surprised to see her. This time she didn't bring no boyfriend. What she did bring was a huge appetite. She barbecued the ribs and chicken wings, and I threw together a few side dishes.

Before I could finish setting the table, Ethel Mae sat down

and started eating. When I sat down, she suddenly stopped gnawing long enough to give me a compliment. "Mama, you look so much better than you did the last time I was here."

"I am much better, baby. Thank God Lula is still able to help me out." I sniffed. "How come you didn't bring a boyfriend with you this time? You ain't seeing nobody?"

A mysterious smile crossed Ethel Mae's face. "I'm seeing somebody, but he wants to take things real slow." She paused and suddenly got real excited. It had been a while since I'd seen such a sparkle in her eyes. "Guess what? He only likes big-boned women like me, so I don't have to listen to him scold me when I eat too much."

I had to think hard to come up with a good response. "Well, some men like large women, some like small women. Some like them all. That way, there's somebody for everybody."

We was so different it was hard for me to find things to talk to her about. I had to be careful not to bring up a subject that would upset her, like her eating and dating habits. "How is your job?"

She groaned and rolled her eyes. "Don't ask. The woman I work for now is mean and stingy. She don't pay me when she's supposed to and sometimes she shortchanges me. I'm thinking about looking for something else."

"White folks are always looking for good help. One of the young girls at church just got hired to do laundry three days a week for a lawyer's wife. I'm sure you'll find a better job soon."

"I hope so. I'd rather shovel shit than keep working for the old peckerwood I'm with now."

"Stop cussing and calling white folks ugly names," I scolded. "You know I hate that."

"I'm sorry, Mama."

"But I'd probably feel the same way if I was in your shoes." We laughed.

I got sad when Ethel Mae left. She had come over on the bus, so she had to leave a few minutes later so she'd have enough time to catch the last one before they ended service for the day.

Lula came over about a hour later. "I'm glad I caught you before you went to bed," she told me. "Something's come up."

Them words made my chest tighten. I was so sick of hearing bad news, I didn't know what I'd do when I heard something good. "Sweet Jesus. What now?"

Lula held up her hand and chuckled. "It ain't nothing bad. See, I'm going to have to take a break from taking care of Jacob. It'll only be for a week or two."

I didn't like hearing that, but I was glad it wasn't something bad enough to push me over the edge. "You going out of town?"

"No, I'm going to have a out-of-town houseguest. Cousin Maisie wants to get away from her husband for a while. He's about to drive her crazy. She says she's going to divorce him."

"Oh. I'm sorry to hear that. Maisie is good people." Lula's cousin was a very scary woman (more about her later). She lived in Hartville with her one-eyed husband, Silas. Their four grown children were on their own. Maisie liked to kick up her heels, so I was going to ask Lula if I could go out with them a couple of times.

"Me and her plan to do a lot of running around, visiting folks and whatnot. She likes to drink as much as I do, so we'll be spending a lot of time visiting the moonshiners. I'll see if I can get one of the ladies I sew for to come stay with Jacob until Maisie leaves. But you'll have to pay them. I will offer them a big discount on the next thing they want me to sew, if they will agree not to charge you too much."

I was grateful for all the help I was already getting from Lula. But I was so disappointed because of what she'd just told me, a lump rose up in my throat. Even though I didn't mean to, I whined, "I'm having such a hard time paying bills now, I can only pay somebody for one or two days a week. On the other days, I'll have to load Jacob into the car and take him to work with me. He can stay in the car until I get off. I'll go out to feed him and make sure he's doing all right."

Lula's mouth dropped open so wide, it looked like a big dipper. "Good God! What's wrong with you, Naomi? It takes two of

us to lift him into that wheelbarrow and load him in and out of
the car. Even if you could do it by yourself, you can't leave Jacob
laying in the back seat of a car all day, even for one day! There
ain't no telling what Reverend Spivey or his neighbors would do
if they seen him, a disabled colored man, laying in the backseat
of a car. And that's another thing, your car."

"What about the car?"

"That's a nice car for colored folks to own. You know how
some white folks don't like to see us looking too prosperous. Remember when that white girl spit on that cute dress you wore
downtown one day?"

I gave Lula a thoughtful look as I recalled that incident. To
this day, it still turned my stomach. The thought of somebody
causing damage to the car Jacob had loved so much, turned my
stomach, too. "Well, I'd rather keep taking the bus to and from
work anyway."

"So, like I was saying, leaving Jacob in the car is a bad idea.
One of that preacher's neighbors would call the sheriff and
trust me, he'd find something to charge you with."

"You got a point there. I didn't think about all that," I admitted. Then I thought of what Ethel Mae had said about wanting
to quit her job. "I'm going to call up Ethel Mae and see if she
can come and stay here until you come back. She told me today
that she is going to look for another job."

"Well, that would be nice for you and Jacob. Maisie told me
she'd probably get here this weekend, so you need to get in
touch with Ethel Mae as soon as you can. If she can't come, I'll
help you find somebody else." We hugged and Lula left.

I waited another hour before I called up Ethel Mae. I was sure
she had made it home by now and got settled in. She answered
right away. "Mama, is something wrong with Daddy?"

"No, that ain't why I'm calling. Lula told me a little while ago
she needs to take some time off. Her cousin Maisie is coming for
a visit, and they got a lot of things planned." I couldn't stop my
voice from cracking as I went on. "I'll need to get somebody else
to look after Jacob until Lula comes back."

Ethel Mae took her time replying. "Oh. And you want me to do it?"

"I don't make enough to pay nobody to do it, and I can't take him to work with me. I ain't got no choice." I figured this was a good time to lay some guilt on Ethel Mae. "Besides, he is your daddy . . ."

"All right, then. Tomorrow I'm going to tell that old witch I work for I quit. How soon do you need for me to come?"

"Maisie is coming this weekend."

"Okay. I'll call you back to let you know when I'm coming. I done already paid my rent for this month, but I'll need a few dollars to pay my light bill."

"I got a little bit of money saved up so I can help you out. I can help cover your bills until you go back to your place."

"Okay, Mama. I'll try to get there in the next couple of days. What about food? You know I like to eat."

I sighed and rolled my eyes. "Tell me about it. I got a mess of beans in the pantry, chicken backs and necks I canned, and all kinds of jelly I made. Reverend Spivey buys so much food, he won't notice if I swipe a few items out of his pantry. Besides, he is always passing it out to folks that need it, anyway."

"All right, Mama. I ain't looking forward to wiping Daddy's behind and putting fresh underwear on him! You know I'm squeamish."

I held my breath to keep from losing my cool. I didn't want to make Ethel Mae mad so she wouldn't come at all. "I been wiping his butt and putting clean underwear on him and a lot more since he had his stroke," I reminded. "And . . . I'm . . . so tired." I had cried so much in the last few months, it was easy for me to choke up some fake sobs.

"Mama, stop crying. I'll come help take the load off you." I had never heard Ethel Mae sound so contrite in her life.

Chapter 38

Maisie slid into town three days later on Wednesday evening. She and Lula didn't waste no time going to Elmo's house that night. They both woke up with hangovers Thursday morning, but Maisie still accompanied Lula to my house. She wanted to keep her company while I was at work. Ethel Mae had promised she'd come by Friday evening.

When I got home from work on Thursday, Lula insisted on staying long enough to help feed Jacob and tuck him into bed for the night. In the meantime, me and her and Maisie sat at the kitchen table and listened to Maisie go over some of the same reasons we'd heard a dozen times already as to why she was going to divorce Silas. The only bad things she could say about him was that he was slow, dumb, and too generous to his trifling relatives. Lula kicked my foot under the table so many times, I was surprised she didn't rupture my corns.

Maisie had the same slanted black eyes Lula had, but her jowly face was not half as cute as it used to be before she gained a hundred pounds in the last two years. Silas made good money driving for a rich white doctor, so she didn't have to work. Maisie was spoiled and even snooty at times, but she was always nice and generous to me and Ethel Mae. One Christmas she gave me some of the most expensive smell-goods available, and Ethel Mae a basket filled with candy.

I offered Maisie some cider, she laughed and waved her thick arms and slapped the side of her thigh. "What's wrong with you, girl? You know I need something a lot stronger than cider to get me through the day. That one-eyed fool I'm married to got me so stressed out I can't even think straight."

Maisie's husband had lost his left eye two years ago when some white hoodlums attacked him on the street for smiling at a white woman. The same day he got home from the clinic wearing a black eye patch, Maisie blackened his other eye for the same "crime." She didn't carry a knife in her brassiere like Lula, but she was even more ferocious. Her huge hands and feet was the only weapons she needed. When her first husband cheated on her, she knocked out all of his front teeth and broke his arm in two places before she divorced him. Silas knew all that, but he married her anyway.

"I can't wait to get another divorce," Maisie snickered.

Me and Lula didn't think she was serious about a divorce, but we went along with it to humor her. "What all is Silas doing?" I asked. I liked Silas. He was a meek, squirrelly little man more than a hundred pounds lighter than Maisie and a head shorter. According to Lula, Maisie had that poor man wrapped around her finger so tight, he cashed his check every payday and gave every dime to her. She paid all the bills and gave him a allowance like he was a child. He had never cheated on her—as far as we knew. I would have traded places with Maisie in a heartbeat. Women like her had no idea what it was like to be married to a man like Jacob or knowing one like Homer.

"Well, he don't like to see me drinking, and he throws a fit when I don't give him enough money. He's better than a lot of other men, but I'm still going to divorce him. Colored men ain't the prizes they used to be." Maisie paused and gave me a pensive look. "By the way, how are you coping with Jacob?"

"As well as can be expected," I replied with my voice cracking.

"Lord Jesus. Girl, you got a major mess on your hands." Maisie drew in a sharp breath and shook her head. "Be glad you ain't got to worry about him beating on you or chasing women no more. That was bad, but what you got to deal with now is way worse. I wouldn't trade places with you for all the money in the world. You got every ounce of sympathy I can muster up." The

pitying look Maisie gave me was so profound it made me flinch.
I liked receiving sympathy, but I didn't like people feeling so
sorry for me that they "wouldn't trade places with me for all the
money in the world."

"Poor Jacob. He enjoyed life so much," Lula commented.

"He ain't dead, Lula," I said sharply. I didn't like what she said
because if Jacob hadn't "enjoyed life so much" I never would
have got involved with Homer.

"I'm sorry. I didn't mean that the way it sounded. I'm just trying to help you feel better," Lula said. "Now what's the deal with
Ethel Mae? Is she coming to help out?"

"She said she'd get here tomorrow evening," I said, forcing
myself to sound cheerful.

Lula suddenly snapped her fingers, and a grin crossed her
face. "Since Ethel Mae's going to be here for a while, we ought
to throw a little welcome-home party for her. You feel up to it,
Naomi? Me and Maisie can cook up some snacks and we can in-
vite a few friends and neighbors."

"I feel up to it. I don't know why I hadn't thought of it myself.
I'll go to the market on my way home tomorrow and pick up a
few things."

I was glad Lula and Maisie stayed until it was almost time for
me to turn in for the night. After they left, my house became so
quiet, and I felt so lonely. It felt like I was the last person left on
earth. I put on my nightgown and sat at the foot of the bed with
Catty curled up in my lap watching Jacob sleep. His breathing
was so shallow, his chest looked like it barely moved. When it
stopped, I panicked. But before I could check on him, he started
snoring again.

Since Jacob's stroke, Catty had not hid under the couch. It
was like she knew the coast was finally clear and she could strut
around in the house all the time and not have to worry about
Jacob abusing her. So now when I went to work, I let her stay inside. Lula let her out when she needed to find a spot to use as a
toilet, and she would stay out and wait for me to come home so
she could greet me.

When I got home from work on Friday and went to get in the

car to go to the market to pick up a few things for Ethel Mae's party, Catty followed me to the car and as soon as I opened the door, she leapt in. She was about to ride in the car Jacob had vowed "that critter" would never set her paws in. If my life wasn't so bleak, recalling his comment would have made me laugh. Catty sat in the passenger seat and stared out the window until I finished my shopping. I made sure my groceries included a huge mess of pig ears for her.

In addition to some healthy items like vegetables and fruit, I picked up some peanut brittle and Moon Pies for Ethel Mae. I didn't like helping her eat like a hog, but I knew by now that it didn't do no good to scold her when she did. I just wanted her to enjoy her visit with me.

I was glad to see Maisie and Lula had made some crab cakes and fried some frog legs when I got back home. Martha Lou had brought some fried chicken wings. We laid everything out on the kitchen table just in time, because the neighbors I invited had already started filing in.

Before everybody started eating, Lula had two of the men lay Jacob on the couch. She thought he would enjoy hisself as much as he could. Maisie was nice enough to feed him. I was so glad they was doing so much because I was so weary, I needed all the help I could get.

Everybody I had invited had already showed up so when I heard heavy footsteps on the front porch, I knew it was Ethel Mae. She opened the door and barged in like a gangbuster, and she wasn't alone. With a huge smile on her face, she led her companion through the door by his hand. They each set a big suitcase on the floor. I couldn't believe what happened next.

"Hi, y'all!" Ethel Mae hollered. I hadn't seen her look so excited since every Christmas morning when she was a little girl. "I want everybody to meet my fiancé!" She continued babbling, but I didn't hear nothing else she said. My eyes felt like somebody had stuck a hot fire poker in them, but I could still see that my future son-in-law was Homer Clark, my used-to-be lover/tormentor!

Chapter 39

I PRAYED FOR A LOT OF THINGS, BUT I NEVER THOUGHT I'D SEE THE day when I wished for my house to explode with me in it. I couldn't think of a better way for me to get out of the mess I was in. My body felt like it had turned to stone. You would have thought I was paralyzed too, because for a few moments, my eyes was the only things on my body I could move.

Martha Lou was standing next to me. She gasped when she seen Homer and turned her head so fast to look at me, I was surprised her neck didn't snap. "Don't say nothing. Me and you will talk later," I whispered.

"Ain't he cute?" Ethel Mae squealed. There wasn't too many frocks Ethel Mae could wear that didn't look like carnival tents. She had on a long blue skirt with white ruffles on the tail, and a white blouse with balloon-like sleeves. Her hair was pulled back into a bun, which, unfortunately, made her look ten years older. Homer had on a red plaid shirt that had lost the top button. I'd sewed it back on with a different color thread a week before we broke up. He had on the same black pants he wore the last time I was at his house.

"I call him Homie because Homer don't fit him. That's a ugly old geezer's name," Ethel Mae said as she gently pushed Homer toward me.

"I'm so happy to meet you, Naomi. Ethel Mae done told me so much about you, I feel like I already know you," he said as he wrapped his arms around my neck and squeezed. It couldn't have been worse if he had used a noose because that was what it felt like. In a way, he probably had, but I would die a lot slower. Then he whispered in my ear, "I'm going to make you sorry you was ever born."

I unwrapped his arms from around me, leaned my head back, and looked him straight in the eyes as bile rose in my throat. I had to cough and clear it before I could speak. "I'm glad to meet you, Homer."

Ethel Mae rushed over and gave me a hug. Then she showed me the engagement ring on her finger. "Mama, ain't it pretty? It's real gold but it looks white when the light hits it." It was the same engagement ring Homer had gave me! He wasn't pouring salt into my wounds; he was pouring acid.

There was at least two dozen folks in the room, not counting Jacob. They all crowded around Ethel Mae and oohed and aahed over her ring.

"I can't believe you found a ring like this in America. I ain't seen nothing this bodacious since I was in the Army stationed in Europe," one of the men hollered. "If this ain't a sign of true love, nothing is."

Ethel Mae guided Homer around the room and introduced him to everybody. When she got to Maisie, I noticed a look on her face I hadn't seen since her mama's funeral ten years ago.

While the guests was still crowded around Ethel Mae admiring her ring, Homer glanced at me and winked. I shuddered so hard, my stomach felt like it had turned upside down. All this was happening because I'd gone against my vows. Hell was the only punishment worse than what I was going through now.

"How long do y'all plan on staying, Ethel Mae?" another neighbor asked.

"I ain't sure yet. At least until Lula can come take care of Daddy again. But Homie wants us to stay long enough for him to get real acquainted with Mama," Ethel Mae replied. "My landlord said he'd hold my place so long as we send the rent every month. If Lula can continue looking after Daddy during the day, I'm going to get a job working them hours and Homie is going to find something to do at night. Like a night watchman or something. That way, Mama can find other things to do with her evenings and weekends. That was Homie's idea, too." Ethel Mae giggled and rubbed the side of Homer's arm. "Mama, I hope you got my room ready. Homie, wait until you see the curtains Mama made for me."

Catty suddenly padded into the room. She stopped in front of Ethel Mae's feet and started rubbing against her leg. "Homie, this is the stray cat I told you I dragged home one day. Mama treats her like she's her second child." She lifted Catty off the floor and held her up to Homer's face. I'd read in a magazine that animals had senses folks didn't have. They can sense all kinds of things, especially bad ones. As soon as Homer reached his arms out to hold Catty, she snarled, gnashed her teeth, and arched her back. The next thing I knew, she jumped to the floor and shot out of the room.

"My Lord. I wonder what spooked her." Ethel Mae gave me a stupefied look. Everybody else was stunned, too.

"She did the same thing to your Daddy when you brough her home, remember?" I reminded. Catty's reaction had to be a bad omen, as if Homer's presence wasn't enough of one. "Um . . . Ethel Mae, I put fresh linen on your bed a little while ago," I said in a raspy tone. "Why don't y'all take the suitcases to your room and come enjoy some of the good food we prepared."

Less than five seconds after Ethel Mae and Homer left the room with their suitcases, Lula rushed over to me with a frantic look on her face. Her lips was quivering when she spoke. "We got to leave right now. Maisie don't feel good."

I looked at her and blinked. "What's wrong with her?"

"I . . . I don't know. She said she can't tell me until we get to my house." I had never seen Lula look so frightened. I didn't want none of my other guests to get spooked, so I walked her and Maisie to the door real fast.

When I turned back around, Martha Lou beckoned me to join her in the kitchen. "What in the world is going on, Naomi?

That's the same Homer who used to live next door to my trick Vinnie and I—"

I held up my hand. "I know." I looked into her eyes and shook my head. "I didn't know about him and my daughter until now."

"Do you think he told her about you and him?"

I shook my head. "If she knew, she wouldn't be with him."

"Well, I advise you to tell her before he does. And you need to tell her *now*."

My jaw dropped. "You out of your mind? With all these folks in the house? I ain't going to say nothing until he tells me what he's up to."

Martha Lou wrung her hands and gave me a thoughtful look. "Maybe he didn't know she was your daughter."

"He knew. I told him about her the first day I met him," I said in a tired tone.

"Say what? You must have told him a heap of things about her if he found her."

I nodded. "I told him everything; even where she lived and worked. I needed somebody to talk to that day and he was such a good listener. Besides, he told me his life story."

"Knowing he's the kind of man who will mess around with a woman *and* her daughter, I don't want to know his life story. I declare, I can smell a disaster coming your way."

Martha Lou was right. I expected a disaster of Biblical proportions. I lifted my hands and waved them. "Let's drop this for now. I feel bad enough. Let's get back out there. But first"—I paused and shook my head—"um . . . you still ain't going to tell nobody about me and Homer?"

Before Martha Lou answered, she hugged me. "Naomi, I got too many secrets of my own. A lot of folks would be hurt if they knew them. I done told you, but I'll tell you again: I ain't never going to blow the whistle on you."

Fifteen minutes after me and Martha Lou got back to the living room, Ethel Mae and Homer strolled back in, holding hands and giggling. I was glad when the telephone rang so I could go back out of the room before I passed out. It was Lula calling. "Girl, you need to get to my house lickety-split. Maisie got something to tell you."

I couldn't imagine what Maisie had to tell me that was so important she needed to see me right away. "Can't it wait until tomorrow? I'm so tired." Seeing Homer with my daughter had shocked and drained me so bad, I knew I wouldn't get much sleep when I went to bed.

"Look-a-here, Naomi, *you need to come to my house as soon as you can.* Don't ask no more questions, just drag your tail over here."

"Okay," I mumbled. There ain't but four or five guest folks left, and Ethel Mae and Homer said they was so tired they can't wait to get to bed. I'll be there in the next ten or fifteen minutes. I need to put Jacob to bed first."

After Homer carried Jacob back to bed, I told him and Ethel Mae that Lula had forgot to take some of the leftover food, and I needed to take it to her. I threw a few chicken wings into a bowl and covered it with a towel before I rushed out the front door.

When I walked through Lula's living-room door, she was pacing back and forth with a frantic look on her face. Maisie was sprawled on the couch fanning her sweaty face with a rolled-up magazine.

"Maisie, you got something to say that concerns me?" I asked as I set the bowl on the coffee table.

"Uh-huh. But first you better sit down and brace yourself," Maisie replied. "It's about Homer. And it ain't good."

Chapter 40

As tight as Maisie's face looked and the way she was sweating, I could tell it wasn't easy for her to let everything out. She blew out several loud breaths before she started talking again. "Homer ain't from Toxey like he told everybody at the party. He grew up one house over from me in Hartville. His real name is Moses Finch."

When I seen Homer walk through my door with Ethel Mae, I didn't think there was nothing that could cause me more distress. I was wrong. Maisie went on to tell me that Homer/Moses had always been so violent, the relatives he had left in Hartville was so afraid of him they all kept shotguns close by in case he returned.

"H-how do you know for sure he's the same man?" I whimpered.

"Pffftt! I knew who he was the minute I seen him, and the scar on his face proved it. He got it when he was sixteen. He'd beat up his girlfriend and she gouged his face with a piece of glass. She got away and hid with some friends until her family was able to ship her to some relatives in Texas."

I kept my face straight, but there was such a grimace on Maisie's it seemed like she was in as much pain as I was.

"Homer found out where the girl was and went to visit her. Two days after he got to her, she disappeared and ain't been seen since. A year later, he 'accidentally' shot and killed his own mother with one of his deceased daddy's old hunting rifles." When Maisie paused again and stopped fanning her face, I thought she was finished.

"Thank you for telling me this," I mumbled. "Accidentally killing his mama must have devastated him."

"I ain't through yet. There's a heap more!" Maisie hollered.

I didn't think it was possible for my body to tense up more, but it did and even harder.

"Everybody knew Homer had made his girlfriend disappear, but nobody could prove nothing. I was the only one who didn't buy his story about him killing his mama by accident. I'd heard them arguing a hour before it happened. And I'd heard him threaten her a heap of times before that day."

I rubbed the side of my head and cleared my throat. "Did he get arrested?"

Lula and Maisie gave me disgusted looks. "Girl, please! Since when did them peckerwoods do much about colored folks killing colored folks in the South? When Homer killed his mama, the sheriff came and scribbled a few notes on a pad and that's where the investigation ended!" Maisie snarled.

"The worst is still to come," Lula tossed in. "Go on, Maisie."

Maisie snorted and continued. "After he killed his mama, his grandmama took him and his younger sister in. He joined the Army when he turned eighteen and was dishonorably discharged a few months later for threatening a officer. He moved back in with his grandmama. By now she had his number and told him he had a month to get a job and place of his own. They found her dead two days later."

I gasped. I didn't know if I could stand to hear anymore, but I knew it was important for me to know everything there was to know about the devil my daughter had brought into our family. "He killed his grandmama, too?"

"His story was that she went to feed the bull she kept in her backyard and the bull went berserk and stomped her to death. His sister was so scared of him, she left town and only told her close family members where she was going. Homer sold everything in his grandmama's house and married a girl he had met a month earlier." Maisie stopped talking for a moment to clear her throat, but she had a lot more to say. "After five years and one son, the wife was ready to leave Homer. The day after she told him she wanted a divorce, she died in a freak accident. According to him, she'd fell down their front porch steps and hit her head on a big rock. He dumped their three-year-old son off on his wife's mama. A week later he had a new girlfriend who had a four-year-old son. Homer moved in with her. She was new in town and didn't know nothing about him.

"Folks didn't waste no time putting a bug in her ear, and he showed his true colors within a month. The new woman had told me that if anything ever happened to her, Homer did it because he'd threatened to kill her, her son, and her mother if she ever left him." Maisie was getting so emotional, she had to pause again and fan her face. When she started talking again, the look of disgust on her face was so severe, it looked like she had put on a mask. "Less than a week later, that woman, her little boy, and her mama disappeared. Homer claimed they'd gone to live with some relatives in Florida. Nobody in the woman's family, in Florida or Alabama, could verify his story. This time everybody believed Homer was responsible. The police brushed it off, too. But the woman's younger brother vowed that he would make Homer pay. When one of Homer's few friends told him about the threat, he packed up and skipped town the same night.

"The next day, somebody burned his house to the ground. That was ten years ago and ain't nobody in Hartville seen him since. What you got to say about everything I just told you, Naomi?"

I was in such a state of disbelief and fear, a few seconds passed before I was able to answer. When I opened my mouth, it was so dry you would have thought my tongue had been sandpapered. "If you recognized him at the party, he probably recognized you. You could be in danger," I warned Maisie.

She shook her head. "Humph! I'm almost twice as big as I was ten years ago. The rouge, face powder, and other props I wear nowadays done changed my looks so much, some of my kinfolks didn't recognize me at our last family reunion." Maisie was right. Her appearance had changed so drastically, I wouldn't recognize her on the street if I didn't already know who she was.

"But your name didn't change," I pointed out.

"There was two other girls in our neighborhood besides me named Maisie."

"I . . . I can't believe the same monster is going to marry my only child. How is it that a man with the same name as Moses—one of the most frequently mentioned individuals in the Bible—could be so evil?"

"Naomi, since you know your Bible, you know that Satan was also one of the most frequently mentioned individuals in it," Maisie brought to my attention.

I wanted to stand up, but I couldn't feel my legs, so I just stayed on the couch. My stomach felt like somebody had tied everything in it into one big knot.

Lula stood up and started waving her arms. "That's a lot to swallow, but let's be fair and not jump to conclusions," she said. "All them things happened years and years ago."

Me and Maisie gasped at the same time. "So?" Maisie asked.

"Well, I know there is evil in the world. I know it's hard to believe, but some of the most despicable people I know have turned their lives around completely." Lula sat back down next to me. Her last statement puzzled me because I didn't know where she was going with it. "My oldest brother's best friend shot and wounded a man for cheating in a card game. He'd done a lot of other dirt before that. Anyway, he went to prison for twenty years. By the time he got out, he was a changed man. He'd found Jesus before it was too late and is now a deacon at the church some of my folks belong to. Ethel Mae said Homer joined the church she goes to in Branson. At least that's one good sign. Right?"

Maisie looked like she was deep in thought. "You got a point there, Cousin Lula. I know folks can change over the years. Maybe Homer—I got to remember not to call him Moses—did come to Jesus. As Christians, we need to look at everything from a Godly perspective. Maybe he is a changed man."

A changed man? I wanted to scream my head off and tell them that Homer was still a monster! But I couldn't let out everything without exposing myself. I just sat there like a bump on a log listening and burning up inside.

"Ethel Mae seems so happy. It took her a long time to find a man willing to marry her, so I don't think we should bust her bubble just yet," Lula added.

"Y'all don't think I should tell her about the real Homer?" I asked, looking from Lula to Maisie.

"Good God, not yet!" Maisie yelled. "If he's still crazy, it won't take long for him to show some signs. Keep both eyes on him, though. If he don't do or say nothing to cause you some concern in the next few weeks, give him a chance. But I advise you to *never* let your guard down. It could be the last thing you ever do."

Lula and Maisie surprised me by suggesting that Homer could be a changed man, especially because they distrusted most men. I couldn't tell them how wrong they was about Homer yet, though. I had a feeling it wouldn't be long before I would have no choice but to come clean.

CHAPTER 41

MY HOUSE WAS AS QUIET AS A TOMB WHEN I GOT BACK FROM MY visit to Lula's. I didn't go into my bedroom first to check on Jacob the way I usually did after I'd been out. Once I tucked him in for the night, he usually didn't wake up until morning.

My body was so stiff as I moved through my living room, you would have thought I was walking a tightrope. This was one of the few times I was sorry I didn't drink alcohol. I needed something to wet my dry mouth and give a jolt to my brain, and it had to be something potent like icy cold water or a bottle of pop. When I got to the kitchen, I was surprised and disgusted to see Homer standing in front of the ice box guzzling my last Dr Pepper. All he had on was a pair of the red and white striped undershorts I had bought him. He had really let hisself go since the last time I'd pampered him five months ago. He looked a mess. I used to clip his toenails and slather lotion over most of his body. Now his feet looked like bear claws and his skin was so ashy, I could have wrote my name with my finger on one of his legs. He had also put on about ten pounds. The hard, flat stomach I used to lay on top of looked like a mound of brown mush now.

Homer grinned when he spotted me. "Hello, Mother. I hope you don't mind if I start calling you that in advance. Me and Ethel Mae plan to get hitched maybe as soon as next month. That will give us enough time to find a dress big enough to fit her wide ass, and to work out the details with Reverend Sweeney."

I glanced around to make sure Ethel Mae wasn't close by. Then I got so close up in Homer's face, I could smell his foul breath. "I don't care what you call me, you funky black devil! I will never be a mother to you!" I was real offended that a man who was older than me would even hint at wanting to call me "Mother." I gulped in some air and continued. "And I don't appreciate you roaming around my house half naked."

Homer snickered and set the empty pop bottle on the counter. "I remember how much you used to love looking at my half-naked body at my house. If you worried you might get excited and want to give me some poontang for old times' sake, so be it." He lowered his voice and added, "I miss how you used to wrap your legs—"

I cut him off as fast as I could. "Hush up, you nasty buzzard you! I wouldn't let you mount me again if your pecker was a magic wand." I couldn't believe I'd let them words out of my mouth *again*. The last time Homer made love to me, I told him that's what his pecker was to me. Now I felt like biting off my tongue for saying such a thing.

He blew out a loud breath so hard, his lips quivered. Then he raised his hands high above his head, as if I'd pulled a gun on him. "Why, *Mother*! I'm scandalized! What would Ethel Mae think if she heard you talking to me in such a unkind way?"

"How did you find my daughter?" I was amazed at how gruff my normally soft voice sounded.

Homer sucked on his teeth and widened his eyes before he answered. "You told me exactly where to find her big sloppy ass, fool."

"Me?"

"Yes, you!" He went on to remind me that the first day we met at the lake last year, I told him so much about my daughter, a blind man could have found her. I had told him Ethel Mae's name and the location of the barbecue restaurant where she ate at almost every Friday evening. I had no idea why I also told him she lived across the street from the only colored funeral home in Branson in a little red shingled house with a glider on the front porch. I'd even told him how promiscuous she was and that all it took for a good-looking man to lure her to bed was some sweet words and something good to eat.

"I went to the rib joint one Friday night and the first thing I seen when I walked through the door was your daughter the sow, slopping up food like she was at a hog trough. You was right. All I had to do was say something sweet and offer to cook supper for Honey Hog. She practically dived into my bed. You know the rest. Any questions?"

"Why do you need to do anything else to me? Ain't you done enough?"

"You'll know when it's enough to satisfy me."

"Being in my house is bad enough. But *please* don't come back to Reverend Spivey's house. I'll forget about you peeping in his kitchen window. You know I need my job."

He laughed. "Humph. I could get you fired in a heartbeat if I really wanted to."

"If you go up to Reverend Spivey and tell him about us, I'll deny it! I'll tell him you ain't nothing but one of them deranged, love-struck men who used to be shut up in the asylum my church ministers to from time to time. Well . . ." I had to pause because I was making up stuff as I went along. "I was with my church members on one of their visits to the asylum. You took a shine to me right away. When they turned you loose, you seen me on the street one day and started following me around." The story I'd just spun sounded ridiculous, even to my own ears. But I couldn't come up with a better one at the time.

Homer laughed again. "Sister, when it comes to making up stories, you ain't no Charles Dickens. If that peckerwood preacher is stupid enough to buy a cock-and-bull story that flimsy, *he* needs to be in the asylum. I'll show him that birthday card you gave me with all of them mushy words and your name signed on it."

"Sweet Jesus!" Before I knew what was happening, tears was

rolling down my cheeks. "Don't show nobody that card," I pleaded.

"I will if I have to. Now I'm going back to bed and wake my fiancée up so I can make love to her." Homer started to walk away and then he stopped and turned back around. "By the way, you was much more fun in bed than she is. She got so much flesh and folds between her thighs—"

I couldn't stand to listen to him insult my child. "You stop that!" I hollered. I said it too loud because before I could say anything else, Ethel Mae came rushing into the kitchen with her floor-length white gown flapping like sails.

She looked from me to Homer and back. "What's going on out here, y'all? Mama, what do you want Homer to 'stop'?"

"Baby, I'm sorry we woke you up," Homer said real quick. He hurried up to her and put his arm around her shoulder. "I was just telling your mama about the carp I caught the last time I went fishing. When I told her how big it was, she thought I was fibbing and told me to 'stop that.' Ain't that right, Mother?" He looked at me and winked.

"Um . . . he's right, sugar." Somehow, I was able to make myself chuckle. "Every time men tell me about the big fish they caught, they stretch the truth. I was just teasing Homer."

"Aww. That's so sweet. I'm so glad to see you two are getting better acquainted so soon," Ethel Mae chirped.

"I better get to bed. I need to go back to the market in the morning to pick up a few things I forgot on my last trip, and I need to gas up the car," I mumbled.

The way Homer's face lit up turned my stomach. "If you don't mind, I'd like to go with you. I used to work in a grocery store so I can help you pick out a few things—and I can carry the bags."

"That would be nice." Them words felt like a knife pricking my tongue as I pushed them out. "Ethel Mae, you can come, too."

"Mama, somebody needs to stay here with Daddy since Lula won't be doing it again until Maisie goes back to Hartville. It'd be nice for you and Homie to spend some time alone without me breathing down your neck. Why don't y'all go over to Carson Lake tomorrow and fish for a little while? Mama, maybe you'll catch a big carp."

I couldn't respond fast enough. "I don't feel like fishing at that lake no more because it would bring back some sad memories."

Ethel Mae rubbed my shoulder. "I understand, Mama. Is it because you and Daddy had your first date there?"

"Uh-huh." With my face as hot as a burning bush, I added, "Just thinking about that place now makes me sick to my stomach."

There was a tight look on Homer's face. I knew he was recalling our first encounter at the lake, and the ones after that.

After Ethel Mae and Homer went back to bed, I went to my bedroom. I plopped down in the rickety metal chair we kept in front of the window. I cried until I couldn't cry no more.

CHAPTER 42

I WANTED TO SPEND AS LITTLE TIME AS POSSIBLE ALONE WITH HOMER. When I got up Saturday morning right after it got light, I eased out of bed, and grabbed the closest dress in sight. Before I could get out the front door, Ethel Mae popped up in the living-room doorway. "Mama, where you going this time of morning?"

"Um . . . oh, I thought I'd do my shopping early today."

"Ain't none of the stores opened yet."

"I know. But first I thought I'd drop in on the old blind lady in the red house down the street and see how she's doing. She might need something from the market."

"Oh. Get me a few Moon Pies and some more Dr Pepper. That's Homie's favorite pop." I wondered what else Homer had already told her that he'd also told me. I had to hold my breath to keep from screaming.

I got in the car and headed to Lula's house. When I parked, I dragged my feet up her porch steps like I was on my way to the electric chair. When I got to the front door, I let myself in. Lewis heard it open and shut and came rushing into the living room in his striped flannel pajamas. The love of Lula's life was one of the nicest men I knew. He was kind and generous to everybody. He had a fairly nice body for a man in his middle forties. But because of his square-shaped, coffee-colored face and large, round black eyes, he reminded me of a owl.

"Great balls of fire, Naomi! You scared the daylights out of me," he yelled. "What you doing here this early? Lula ain't even woke up yet."

"I'm sorry for showing up this time of morning. But I needed to go to the market, and I was short on cash. I wanted to see if I could borrow a dollar or two from Lula."

"Is that all? I ain't going to wake her up for that. I can lend you some money. Let me go get my wallet." He was already turning to go back to the bedroom.

"I would still like to talk to her about something . . ."

Lewis stopped in his tracks and turned back around with a puzzled expression on his face. Lula had trained him so good; he would never do nothing to upset her. "Can't it wait until she wakes up? She don't like to be woke up unless it's for something real important."

"It is real important," I insisted.

"All right, then. But if she bites my head off, I'm holding you responsible." I stood in front of the door, shifting my weight from one foot to the other, until Lula shuffled into the room wearing a fuzzy white bathrobe. Her long-toed bare feet looked like they belonged to a chicken.

"What's the matter?" she asked as she yawned and stretched her arms above her head.

I looked over her shoulder to make sure Lewis hadn't started back to the living room. "Remember what we talked about last night?" I whispered.

She gasped and widened her eyes. "Did he do something crazy?"

"Not yet. It's just, well . . . I . . . I'm having a hard time trying not to let him know that I know who he is and what he done to all them other folks."

Lula put her arm around my shoulder and guided me into her neat little kitchen, where a mess of chitlins was soaking in a pan on the counter. We plopped down at the table. She glanced toward the doorway before she started whispering. "I don't want Lewis to hear us talking. You listen to me, you can't let Homer know what you know if he ain't gave you no reason to expose him," she said in a firm tone.

"If I wait until then, it might be too late. I want him out of my house *now*." My head felt like it weighed more than everything else on my body put together. I didn't know how much longer I could keep the secret about my affair with him from Lula. But I didn't think now was the time to confess.

Lula looked at me with her mouth gaped open like a hole in the ground. "Girl, the man is engaged to your daughter. If you tell him to leave, what will you tell Ethel Mae?" She went on to remind me how fragile my daughter was and how important it was for me to let her live her life the way she wanted to. I knew everything she was saying to be true, but I reminded her about Homer's violent past. I felt better when she suggested that he might get tired of Ethel Mae and leave on his own. "In the meantime, I advise you to respect him, and to just be cautious."

"I read articles in some of my detective magazines about criminals like him. They can be real nice up front, and then something makes them snap and they'll commit even more crimes. What if something like that happens with Homer? You know how long it would take Sheriff Zachary to come, if he comes at all."

Lula stood up straight and narrowed her eyes. "Please stop working yourself up like this. Your imagination is working overtime."

"Answer my question!"

Lula sniffed and gave me a serious look, which I was glad to see. I hoped she was about to say something that would show she was on my side. And she did. "Well, if Homer was to hurt you or Ethel Mae, he'll have to deal with me. You won't need to call the sheriff; you'll need to call the undertaker."

Before I could respond to her grim words, Maisie waddled into the kitchen. She looked as big as a hot-air balloon in her yellow and white floor-length nightgown. "Who'll need the undertaker?" she asked.

"I was telling Naomi that if Homer hurt her or Ethel Mae, I'd put his lights out for good," Lula answered. She folded her arms and scrunched up her face so tight her nose looked like it was about to slide down and touch her lips. "This would be one time he won't commit a crime and get away with it."

Maisie looked from Lula to me and shook her head. "I thought we all agreed he might be a changed man." Despite what Maisie had just said, there was a skeptical look on her face.

"I know we did, but I still don't like having him in my house," I wailed.

"You ain't got no choice. If you ask him to leave, Ethel Mae will go with him," Lula insisted. I could tell that she was getting exasperated with me. "If she's alone with him someplace, there ain't no telling what he might do to her. So long as they're under your roof, you can keep a eye on things. When Maisie leaves, I'll start coming back to the house to look after Jacob and keep a eye on Homer."

It had been so long since I'd felt completely at ease, I had almost forgot what it felt like. Hearing Lula say that made me feel a little better. "I can't wait for you to come back."

Maisie cleared her throat. "Well, I think I'll cut my visit real short this time and leave next week."

I touched Maisie's hand. "I hope you ain't leaving on my account just so Lula can start taking care of Jacob again."

"No. I need to go home and do some housecleaning. Silas called me up last night and told me his sorry brother showed up yesterday with his equally sorry wife. He said they was planning to stay until I got back home. I'm going to give them fifteen minutes to pack up and get out of my house."

"Oh. I'm sure you won't have no trouble getting rid of them." I swallowed the huge lump that had suddenly blew up in my throat and said to Lula, "Ethel Mae told me they was both going out today to look for work. By the time you come back to look after Jacob, they might be working during the day. Then you won't have to worry about being around Homer much."

Lula looked like she wanted to laugh. "Aw shuck it! Honey, I ain't got to worry about him. Like I said, if he gets loose, y'all won't need to call the sheriff," she said with a firm nod.

The market wouldn't open for another hour, so I decided to stay with Lula and Maisie to kill time.

CHAPTER 43

I GOT BACK HOME A FEW MINUTES BEFORE 11:30 A.M. ETHEL MAE had bathed Jacob, changed his underwear, and cooked bacon, eggs, grits, and toast. She was sitting at the kitchen table with a huge plate in front of her. "Mama, Homie said he was sorry he didn't get up in time to go to the market with you," she told me with bits of egg on her bottom lip.

I set the bag of groceries on the counter and sat down across from her. "I don't like no man breathing down my neck when I go shopping. Tell him I said that." I pressed my lips together to keep some harsh words from slipping out of my mouth. Catty wandered in, leapt into my lap, and started rubbing her face on my hand. I flipped her onto her back and Ethel Mae started rubbing her belly. "This cat is starting to act more like a dog," I chuckled.

Ethel Mae blew out a huff and shook her head. "And that fleabag critter is another thing. Homie said it ain't fitting for folks to get too attached to pets."

I was sick of her referring to that beast as "Homie." I wanted so bad to tell her his *real* name was Moses. But if I did, she'd want to know how I knew, and it wouldn't stop with just his name. "Catty ain't never had fleas!" I snapped. I glared at Ethel Mae as she went on to tell me that Homer told her to prepare herself to console me because Catty was on her last legs. He also had the nerve to tell her, *"I'll console her, too. I will help you keep your Mama comfortable in her old age. She is such a lovely woman."*

I swallowed hard so I could stay as composed as possible. "What makes him think Catty is on her last legs?" I snapped. "We didn't know how old she was when you found her. She could have only been a year or two old." I had to stop to catch my breath before I could go on. "The next time he brings up this subject, tell him I said to mind his own business because Catty is part of our family and—"

Ethel Mae cut me off. "And he ain't?"

"I didn't say that."

"I had a feeling that was what you was going to say."

She was right. As far as I was concerned, Homer would never be as much a part of my family as Catty was. We didn't say nothing for a few moments and then Ethel Mae suddenly reared her head back and gasped. "Homie is going to be part of our family, too. Just like the children we plan to have." I was anxious to have grandchildren, but not if it meant they would come from demon seeds. I was praying Homer would get tired of playing his unholy games and leave before Ethel Mae got pregnant.

I decided to ask the question that had been burning a hole in my head since that snake slithered into my house. "How well do you know Homer?"

She wiped her greasy lips with the back of her hand and gave me a curious look. "I know him as well as I need to. Why?"

"Don't you wonder why he ain't told us nothing about none of his relatives?"

"Other than a cousin in Michigan, he ain't got none."

"So he claims. Everybody has folks in their background somewhere, and if they don't have a relationship with them, there is a good reason why. He could be as dangerous as a mad dog for all you know."

Ethel Mae guffawed like a hyena. When she stopped, she looked at me like I'd lost my mind. And she wasn't too far from the truth. "Homie could be *dangerous*? He's as harmless as a lamb! I declare, Mama. How could you even fix your lips to say such a thing?" She went on to blast me for judging Homer when I married her daddy, who had been "as dangerous as a mad dog" as far back as she could remember.

"You're right, sugar," I muttered with a heavy sigh. I knew when I was defeated so I steered the conversation in a different direction. Homer was still the subject. "Where is he now?"

"He went to look for a job. I'm going to do the same thing myself after I finish eating."

I didn't want them to find work now. If they didn't, then they could go on back to Branson when Lula was able to return to take care of Jacob. However, I knew Homer would find another reason for them to stay in Lexington. "Y'all should wait until Monday to go job hunting. I don't think many folks do much hiring on weekends."

Ethel Mae shook her head. "Uh-uh. We don't want you to spend no more money feeding us than you have to. I was going to take the bus over to Arch Street where most of the lazy white women live. The sooner we find work, the easier your life will be. By the way, I was going to feed and bathe Daddy while you was gone, but Homie insisted on doing it." Ethel Mae practically swooned. "Ain't you glad I found a man who is so considerate? And another thing, you got to give him credit for accepting a fat slob like me."

"First of all, you ain't a slob."

Ethel Mae lifted her thigh and slapped it. "But I'm fat!"

"There are men who love hefty women. You told me Homer said he did."

Ethel Mae dipped her head and gave me a woeful look. "But you act as if you don't like him. Is it because you think he's too old for me? He is old enough to be my daddy, but there are a heap of younger women in this very neighborhood married to men twice as old as them. Or is it that you think a handsome man like Homie is too good for me? And sex is all he wants from me?"

It saddened me to see such a hurt look on her face, so I had to backtrack. It wasn't easy, but I managed to crack a smile. "I don't think Homer is too old or too good for you, and I don't think he is only after sex."

"Most of them fools I messed around with before wouldn't

even be seen in public with me. You ought to see how proud Homie looks when we go out together."

I had to force myself not to grit my teeth or leap up and punch the wall. "All I care about is Homer being good to you. Now I don't want to talk about this no more today." Ethel Mae left the house a hour later to go visit one of her old friends from school. I was scared to death Homer would return before she did.

I managed to make it through the first two weeks without clashing with Homer again. I'd been in the same room alone with him several more times since our encounter in the kitchen the night he arrived. He'd been a perfect gentleman. By now, Ethel Mae had paraded him around town so much, almost everybody I knew had met him. Folks came up to me at the market and on the street and told me how blessed I was that I was going to have such a wonderful son-in-law.

The third week of my ongoing nightmare, Homer announced that he was going to go to church with us that Sunday. He acted so giddy, something told me he was going to use this opportunity to jab at me in some way.

He was so strong he carried Jacob to the car by hisself and into the church. He gently laid him in the back row pew and helped me prop him up with the pillows I always brought when Lula and Lewis helped get him to church. My whole body was saturated with shame and disgust when Homer winked at me. No matter how bad Jacob had treated me, he didn't deserve to be used to taunt me by the same man I'd cheated on him with.

When Reverend Sweeney finished his morning sermon, he did what he did every Sunday: asked if anybody had something good they wanted to share with the congregation. When Ethel Mae raised her hand, my heart almost stopped. I held my breath as she led Homer up to the pulpit and announced their engagement. They was both beaming like light bulbs and grinning like fools.

When Reverend Sweeney asked Homer if she was the "wonderful woman" he had told the church about last year, Homer looked nervous. Ethel Mae looked puzzled. Then he "admitted" that at the time, he had only seen Ethel Mae from afar while he was visiting somebody else in Branson. He went on to explain that he asked around about this "lovely, saintly woman." Homer had been told so many positive things about her, he assumed she was the one God had sent to him.

When they returned to their seats, tears was streaming down Ethel Mae's face. Homer pulled out a handkerchief and dabbed her eyes and nose. "See, Mama. Homie was finding out all he could about me before we even met. That was a omen that the Lord set us up."

Everybody must have fell for his lame story because they whooped and hollered and clapped. Them same two gossips who had made them comments the first time Homer went up to the pulpit, gave me puzzled looks. I avoided them until we left.

After Homer loaded Jacob back into the car, he offered to drive. As much misery as Jacob had caused me, I was not about to disrespect him even more by letting the man I'd cheated on him with drive his car. I would get rid of it or crash it before I ever let Homer drive it! "No, I'd rather do it myself. Jacob is real particular about who drives his car," I explained.

Ethel Mae looked at me with her face twisted up. "Mama, Daddy wouldn't know if this car was on fire. How would he know who was driving it?"

I turned around and glanced at Jacob. His eyes was wide-open and I knew he could hear everything. "Other than you and Lula, I ain't letting nobody else drive this car," I said in a firm tone.

Nobody said nothing else for the first couple of blocks. Homer broke the silence. "I really enjoyed church today. The spirit went all through me." He paused and grabbed Ethel Mae's hand and kissed it. "I am the happiest man alive. I love both of y'all with all my heart and I declare, I'm going to change y'all's lives in ways y'all never imagined."

I don't know how I was able to keep from screaming.

Chapter 44

B<small>Y THE END OF</small> J<small>ULY,</small> I <small>FELT A LITTLE MORE RELAXED BECAUSE A</small> couple of positive things had happened. Lula had started taking care of Jacob during the day again, and Ethel Mae and Homer found work. She would be doing laundry and housework every weekday for one of the ladies I used to work for. Elmo Petrie hired Homer to work nights at his place. With all the rowdy people who went to drink moonshine and dance at Elmo's house, he needed a husky man like Homer to help keep them in line when they got too rowdy. The man he had working for him now couldn't handle them drunks by hisself. I didn't think of it as a real job, but at least it would get that devil out of my sight every evening and he'd be bringing some money into the house.

On Homer's first night at his new "job," he tried to stop a drunk from hassling the women and the man socked him. He came home with a black eye, but it didn't bother him. Ethel Mae put some salve on his eye and told him she wanted him to find a safer job soon. He told her Elmo was paying him good money and he was having too much fun listening to the latest records and getting to know some of the local folks. That ended the argument. Three nights later, when he tried to break up a fight between two men, one pulled a knife on him and wouldn't leave until Elmo gave back all the money he'd spent.

For the next two weeks Ethel Mae told me about more violent incidents Homer encountered at work. In one week, there had been a ruckus three nights in a row. "Mama, he won't listen to me. I keep telling him that working for Elmo is too dangerous. His luck is going to run out eventually. Can you help me talk him into getting a job on a farm or at one of the mills? Better yet, ask Reverend Spivey if he's got something Homer can do. He'd make a good handyman or driver. Everybody knows how much your boss likes to help colored folks. Even his cousin Judge Smoot got a colored man driving him around."

My ears felt like they was on fire! The thought of me and Homer working at the same place was so upsetting, it almost brought me to my knees. I'd quit my job before I let that happen! "Um . . . I don't know if I should. If things didn't work out, Reverend Spivey might take it out on me. And you know I can't risk losing my job."

"Okay, Mama." Ethel Mae looked disappointed but that was nothing compared to how I felt. "Well, will you pray for Homie then?"

"Yes, baby. I'll do that every day and every night."

Some mornings I left for work before Homer got up so I wouldn't have to look at him. He had to go to Elmo's place right after supper, so I didn't have to see his face too much during the day.

I had some concerns about how his presence was going to affect Catty. Jacob was no longer a threat, so she didn't have to hide from him. But now she had to hide when Homer was around. When I was still involved with that maniac, I had told him more than once how important Catty was to me. I figured that was the reason he had tried to befriend her in front of me and the other folks at the party we'd had. But she had sensed right away that he was from hell.

One day last week when Homer picked Catty up, she clawed the back of his hand. "Mama, I don't like the way that cat behaves around Homie. She's going to have to go. The Bonner kids across the street told me they was looking for a new pet. Their dog died last week," Ethel Mae said while me and her was in the kitchen getting supper ready.

It was the last Thursday morning in August. I had planned to leave for work real early again, but Homer and Ethel Mae got up the same time I did. We had already ate breakfast and now he was outside washing the car. Not only did he do a lot of chores around the house, he helped bathe, feed, and put diapers on Jacob.

Ethel Mae continued. "I don't know what we'd do without Homie helping us. Besides, I love him to death. I ain't going to stand by and let a mangy old cat become a thorn in my fiancé's side. Shoot. One of my friend-girl's man broke up with her because her dog didn't respect him."

I was so horrified it took me a few moments to respond. "Hush your mouth! Catty's been a member of our family a lot longer than Homer! She ain't going nowhere! Don't you never ask me to get rid of my pet again!"

Ethel Mae replied in a voice so low, I could barely hear her. "I won't, Mama."

Homer insisted on cooking some of our meals and every time he mentioned preparing one of the dishes he used to cook for me at his house, he'd look at me and wink. Eating at the same table with him and Ethel Mae was straight-up torture. Friday morning when Ethel Mae left the breakfast table to go feed Jacob, Homer reached under the table and squeezed my knee. I jumped up and ran to the back porch and threw up. He was right behind me. Catty was stretched out on the ground at the bottom of the steps. When she seen Homer, she shot off like a bullet.

"I've been going easy on you so far, but don't ever think I ain't going to finish what I started," he said with his teeth clenched.

"You've already ruined my life. Ain't that enough?" I was still leaning over the porch banister. Homer was right beside me.

"No, it ain't." He slapped my butt and continued. "You and your baby hippo will celebrate your birthdays next month. Me and her will probably get married between them two days. So, we'll have three big events to celebrate in September."

I gave him the most menacing evil eye I could come up with.

"I ain't going to celebrate nothing with you!" I shot back. "The only thing I will celebrate that involves you, is you leaving my house!"

Homer folded his arms and snickered, "Why should I leave this lovely home? And wasn't the main reason me and Ethel Mae came to Lexington was to help you take care of that *thing* you married?"

I looked into Homer's eyes, hoping I'd see a trace of the compassion he used to have for me. All I seen was the black evil of the Devil. "I can't live like this too much longer," I said, choking on my words. "Can't you go back in your mind and remember the good times you had with me? I'm the same woman you fell in love with and treated you like Prince Charming because you'd had such a sad life. Don't I deserve something for that?"

Homer gave me a sympathetic look and for a moment, I seen the man I had fell in love with. I recalled all the passion we had enjoyed, the fun we'd had, and the fact that he had treated me so good the whole time before things blew up. But the *real* Homer came back a split second later. "And you getting just what you deserve," he growled.

After he went back inside, I threw up again.

Somehow, I managed to go to work and get through the day without falling apart. I was glad Reverend Spivey left right after lunch to go to Mobile and price some new pews for his church. Miss Viola had a beauty parlor appointment, and a tea party to attend at a neighbor's house. Annie Lou was in her room working on another puzzle. I had cooked a pork butt and all the fixings and left everything on the table so that when everybody got home, supper was ready to eat.

I was so exhausted, I went to sleep on the bus for the first time in my life. If the lady sitting next to me hadn't woke me up, I would have missed my stop.

I was surprised Catty didn't come to meet me when I got to my block. I assumed she was outside chasing smaller creatures or lounging on the ground by our back porch. Lula was gathering up her stuff and getting ready to leave when I walked through the front door. She told me Ethel Mae hadn't made it home from work yet and Homer had went to Elmo's house early to do a few chores around his house. "You seen Catty?" I asked as I glanced around the room.

She gave me a puzzled look. "Now that you mentioned her, I ain't seen her at all since this morning. Hmmm. She usually scratches at the door to be let in every time she sees Homer leave the house. She's probably out chasing squirrels again, or looking for a boyfriend . . . hint, hint," Lula joked.

I rolled my eyes and waved her out the door.

Before I looked in on Jacob, I went outside to look for Catty. I started in front of the house. I found her when I got to the back-yard.

She was laying on the ground at the bottom of the porch steps with her head twisted all the way around.

Chapter 45

*S*OME OF MY SIBLINGS HAD OWNED PETS WHEN WE WAS GROWING UP. My brothers had dogs, and one time Grady even had a pet coon. My sister Claudette brought home a baby frog one day. She kept it in a bucket but when it got big enough to leap out, it would hop all over the house. Daddy got mad and told her to take it back to the lake. Well, Claudette didn't, and that frog ended up in Daddy's frying pan. My sister cried like a baby and never had another pet.

Most of my brothers' dogs died of old age, one got stole, and another died when he got hit by a car. Each time a pet departed, it caused a lot of grief in our house. All that had stopped me from getting a pet of my own. But because I "inherited" Catty and we had hit it off from day one, I promised myself that she'd be happy as long as she stayed with me.

Now she was gone and in the worst possible way—murder.

I was crying so hard I couldn't see straight. Somehow, I managed to scoop up my beloved pet and carry her into the kitchen, hoping I could revive her. I knew nothing could still be alive with their head twisted around completely in the opposite direction, but I gently shook Catty and called her name anyway. She still didn't move or make a sound. The pain I experienced was so deep, it felt like my soul had left my body. But I was able to pull myself back together right away. I stumbled into my bedroom and got a pillowcase to use as a shroud for Catty. I wanted to bury her as soon as possible.

I dug a grave close to the back of the house. "I'm so sorry I couldn't protect you," I sobbed as I shoveled dirt on top of her. After I said a prayer, I scrambled up off the ground and sat on the porch steps until I had composed myself.

When I returned to the kitchen and sat down at the table, I stared off into space until the telephone rang. I wiped my eyes and nose with the tail of my dress and wobbled up out of my chair to answer it. It was Homer.

"Hello, Naomi." He sounded as cold as a block of ice.

"Ethel Mae ain't here!" I snapped. "I'll tell her you called!"

"I called to talk to you." My heart started racing. "I'm using Elmo's telephone so I can't talk long," he said in a low tone. And then he whispered, "Did you find Catty yet?"

I gasped so hard I seen double. Then I heard something pop inside my head. I thought I was having a stroke myself. Surprised that I was able to speak in such a strong tone. "You killed my cat?" We had a couple of unruly boys in our neighborhood who had chased and tortured a few dogs and cats. My mind was so mushy that before Homer called, I had convinced myself that one of them boys killed Catty. But in my heart, I knew that wasn't true—even before he called. He was the only person I knew who would do something so evil. I recalled the time I told him if something ever happened to Catty, I would never get over it. Homer had assured me that if anything happened to her, he'd find me another female cat and I could name her Catty. I thought it was one of the sweetest things a man could tell a woman.

"I didn't know it was so easy to break a neck," he taunted. "You keep that in mind." He snickered and added, "You got a mighty thin neck . . ."

He hung up before I could say anything else. After I rubbed my neck, I read a few pages in my Bible. That didn't make me feel no better or safer. I called up Lula, but she didn't answer. I couldn't sit or stand still so I paced the living-room floor for the next ten minutes. When I got tired of pacing, I sat down at the kitchen table.

For some reason, I looked at the window by the side of the

stove. This time I seen something even worse than Homer's face peeping at me. Smack dab in the middle of the window was a bullet hole.

"Oh, my Lord!" I hollered. I looked at the wall behind me and seen where the bullet had lodged. I got a knife and dug it out. I couldn't throw it into the trash can fast enough. I took the calendar off the wall next to one of the cabinets and tacked it over the bullet hole.

Before I could do anything else, Lula called. The first thing she said was, "Did you find Catty yet?"

"She's dead," I blurted out. "I found her in the backyard right after you left this evening."

"No, no, no! How did she die?"

"Um . . . old age, I guess. You know we never knew how old she really was."

"Hmmm. She didn't seem that old. I seen her chasing a squirrel two days ago. She was so sharp and active, I would have guessed she was only seven or eight."

I was praying that Lula wouldn't talk too long. My head was throbbing like somebody had clobbered me with a blunt object. "Well, that's old for a cat. She walked into the wall and the couch leg yesterday. I think she was going blind."

"Being blind ain't that bad. When my brother's dog lost his sight, he still lived for two more years. Maybe Catty got bit by a snake."

"Yeah! That's probably what happened. I been seeing a heap of snakes in our backyard lately." There was no way I was going to tell Lula that Catty had been murdered. That would have opened up a humongous can of worms. Knowing her, she probably would have accosted every single one of the unruly kids in our neighborhood. I realized Lula wasn't going to end this call anytime soon. "Can I call you back later? I don't feel like talking right now."

"I understand. I'll pray for Catty. If God allows animals in heaven, she's up there. The cat that belongs to the Baker kids next door gave birth to six kittens day before yesterday. You want me to get dibs on one for you?"

"No, I don't think so. I got enough on my hands taking care of Jacob right now."

"All right, then. Call me when you feel better."

Less than a minute after I hung up the telephone, it rung again. It was Homer. "You check that window by the stove yet?" he asked, talking so casual, you would have thought he was asking about the weather.

"You shot into my house," I accused.

"Yup. The next bullet I shoot got your name on it," he said with a snort.

I hung up as fast as I could because I heard Ethel Mae come through the front door. She started talking before she got into the kitchen. "Sorry I'm late. I missed my bus. I—Mama, you look upset."

"Catty died."

She gave me a blank look at first. "That's a shame. Well, I ain't surprised. I hope you don't grieve too much. Shoot. Catty was just a cat." Her callous words felt like bricks going upside my head. I kept my cool because I didn't want to say nothing that would make her say something even worse. She laid her purse on the table and exhaled. "I'm so hungry I could bite a fish-hook! You want me to cook dinner?"

"Yeah, if you don't mind," I muttered.

She looked around the room. "Is Homie here?"

"Um, he left to go to work already." I started walking toward my room. "I'm going to check on Jacob." I glanced at Jacob, but the next thing I did was grab my Bible and pray. "Lord, please stop Homer from torturing me."

God must have thought I'd suffered enough for a while because Homer didn't bother me for a whole month. But I knew my ordeal wasn't over yet.

CHAPTER 46

I MISSED POOR CATTY SO MUCH I COULD BARELY STAND TO LOOK AT none of the other cats roaming around our neighborhood without getting tears in my eyes. Every time I went out the back door and seen her grave, I cried. It felt like I had lost a member of my family, and as far as I was concerned, I had.

I hated Homer so much now, just the sight of him made my blood boil. Either he was going to get out of my house, or I was. That's what it had come down to.

There hadn't been no brawls at Elmo's place this week until last night. Homer had come home early because his bottom lip got split open during another ruckus. Ethel Mae made a fuss over him and put some salve on his lip. She made a big fuss about it, but he didn't. "That sucker had more than a busted lip by the time I got his tail out the door," Homer bragged.

As much as I despised him, I did want him to find a safer job for Ethel Mae's sake. I wasn't going to say nothing to Homer about it because I didn't want to be no more involved with him than I already was.

Sunday evening after church, while I was in the kitchen washing the greens I was going to cook for supper, Homer crept up behind me and whispered, "Boo!"

I whirled around so fast, I was surprised my neck didn't snap.

"You scared me!" I scolded. "What's the matter with you? I almost had a heart attack."

He reared back on his legs and folded his arms. "Ethel Mae told me you said you'd pray for me."

"I will pray for you." I paused and looked him straight in the eyes. "But I'm praying that you will pack up and buy yourself a one-way ticket to *anywhere*."

"Well, your prayer ain't going to be answered because I ain't going no place. And if you run away, I will hunt you down like a bloodhound."

Before I could respond, Ethel Mae came gliding into the kitchen like she had wheels for feet. "Mama, Daddy smiled just now," she announced. Then she went up to Homer and wrapped her arms around his waist. "Baby, I'm so happy we are helping lighten up Mama's load. Taking care of Daddy ain't as much trouble as I thought it would be. Maybe we should plan on staying in Lexington permanently." She sniffed and looked at me. "Mama, would you like that?"

"Yes . . . I would," I said in a meek tone. I turned back around and started washing the greens again. Ethel Mae and Homer went into the living room and turned on the radio. Some swing music was blasting. When I heard them giggling, I went to the doorway to see what they was up to. They was dancing and twirling around like they didn't have a care in the world. Homer looked over Ethel Mae's shoulder and winked at me.

My birthday was coming up next week; this time I didn't want to make a fuss like I usually did, but Lula thought differently. "Maisie is coming back. We want to take you out to a nice restaurant for your birthday. After that, we'll go to Elmo's and dance up a storm."

I would never go back to Elmo's place as long as Homer was working for him. We was sitting on my couch that Thursday evening. Ethel Mae was visiting one of her old friend-girls and Homer was at Elmo's house. Lula exhaled and went on. "I went to Elmo's last night. Homer had to rough up one of them hot-headed Mitchell boys for trying to sneak a free drink."

"So, what else is new?" I muttered. When I was fooling around with Homer, he would get so sad when we discussed stories we'd read in the newspaper or heard on the radio about violent incidents. One time he had the nerve to tell me he would walk away from a fight before he put his hands on another human being.

I was so deep in thought, I didn't realize Lula had said something else until she waved her hand in front of my face. "I asked what you was going to wear for your birthday celebration?"

I jumped back to attention. "Oh! I'm sorry. My mind wanders off like a loose wheel sometime." I faked a laugh.

"Especially lately," Lula said in a sarcastic tone.

"Um . . . I don't want to go out. Let's celebrate at your house."

Lula looked disappointed. "If that's all you want to do, that's fine with me." She squeezed my hand and gazed upside my head. "Naomi, I know you and I know something is bothering you. You still concerned about Homer getting loose?"

"Well, I'm concerned about that and everything else I'm going through right now."

She squeezed my hand even harder and gave me a pitying look. "You poor thing you. It breaks my heart to know you're hurting so much. What else can I do to help more?"

"Nothing. You do enough already." I stood up and smiled at Lula. "Thank you for being such a good friend. Now I think I'll go take me a bath and splash on one of my smell-goods."

"If Homer gets out of line, just let me know." Lula stood up and shook her head. "You poor little thing. Too bad you ain't got nothing to really take your mind off Homer, like a good hump. Since Jacob is out of commission, you should get a friend."

"I don't need no man," I insisted.

"Dagnabbit! The hell you don't! I'm talking about a *maintenance* man to keep your body tuned up. And he could take you out once in a while. I don't think nobody would hold that against you."

"With my job and taking care of Jacob I wouldn't have time for that."

"You ain't got to see nobody on a regular basis. Before me and

Lewis got together, I had a friend I seen only when we both got the urge to go at it." Lula chuckled. "I didn't tell you about him because he was just a temporary *feel-good* substitute to me until I found another full-time sweetie. Besides, he was a happily married man and wasn't about to risk losing his wife, so we never went out in public."

I reared my head back and gave Lula one of my sternest looks. "Lula, I'm scandalized! I didn't know you fooled around with married men!"

"See there. I knew you'd judge me. That's why I never told you or nobody else."

"I ain't judging you. But I ain't interested in no boyfriend, so don't bring it up no more."

I woke up in the middle of the night and seen what I thought at first was a ghost standing at the foot of my bed. It was Homer, buck naked! Before I could say anything, he left.

I was so spooked I got up ten minutes later and went to get a glass of water. Before I could fill my glass, Homer came into the kitchen in his long-john underwear. I covered my mouth to stifle a yelp as he grabbed the butcher knife off the counter and pressed it against my neck.

"If I decide to slit your throat, I'll do it with a dull knife so it will take longer and be more painful," he whispered. He suddenly put the knife down and wrapped his arms around me so tight I could barely breathe. He kissed me long and hard.

I leaned my face away from his as fast as I could. "Why don't you just hurry up and kill me and put me out of my misery. I done gave up," I whimpered.

"Nope. I ain't letting you off that easy. I want to see you suffer some more before I kill you dead." He kissed me again. His arms was still around me. I didn't know what I would say to Ethel Mae if she walked in and seen him kissing me. My mind was so scrambled, I couldn't do nothing but stand stock-still and listen. "And another thing, you ain't the only one going to pay for ruining my life."

My whole body felt like it had frozen up. Homer's breath was so hot and foul, I winced. "W-what do you mean?" I stammered.

"Jacob will be going to hell with you. If it wasn't for him, me and you would be living like kings in Michigan by now! If I take him and you out, I can't leave Ethel Mae behind to grieve herself to death. I'll put her out of her misery, too. I'll make it quick for Jacob. A pillow over his face would be the most humane punishment, I guess. I ain't sure how I'm going to do away with Ethel Mae. But it won't be quick or pretty, and she'll get it before you because I want you to watch her die."

"The white folks won't even bother to take you to trial. They'll strap you in the electric chair as soon as the sheriff brings you in."

Homer glared at me and snickered. "You think I ain't thought about that? My record is as clean as God's hands. *Would you like to hear how many times I done got away with murder?*"

Him confirming what Maisie had told me and Lula was like a bomb exploding inside my head. I unwrapped his arms from around me and ran to my bedroom.

I locked the door for the first time since me and Jacob got married.

CHAPTER 47

I DIDN'T SLEEP MUCH FRIDAY NIGHT. AS TIRED AS I FELT, ALL I COULD do was lie next to Jacob and think about everything Homer had said to me so far. When I got up Saturday morning and seen him at the kitchen table, my chest tightened and my stomach turned. I could hear Ethel Mae outside yip-yapping with our next-door neighbor.

Homer nodded at the chair facing him. "Have a seat, Mother. I done the cooking this morning. I made some of that gravy for the grits you always liked." He leaned toward me and added in a whisper, "Remember how I used to cook for you at my house?"

Every time he made a reference to anything me and him used to do, I shuddered. "I ain't hungry," I said in a raspy tone. The last threats he'd made was ringing in my ears like jingle bells.

He looked toward the door before he stood up and got close to my face. "Good news. I decided to let you and your family enjoy one more Thanksgiving and Christmas together. You still got about three and a half months to live, so I advise you to make every single day count."

I gave him the evilest eye I could muster, but he didn't even flinch. "I hate your guts!" I blasted.

While Homer was laughing, I skittered back to my bedroom. When Jacob seen me, tears pooled in his eyes. It dawned on me that he had heard everything me and Homer said in the kitchen. There was no telling what Homer might have said to Jacob when he was in the bedroom alone with him. "Jacob, I'm sorry I brought the Devil into our lives. I thought you was the only devil I'd have to deal with." I let out a strange cackle and he did, too.

I dabbed his tears with one of the napkins I kept on the nightstand. About two minutes later, while I was staring out the window, I heard gurgling noises behind me. I turned around as fast as I could. I had a hard time believing my eyes: Jacob's lips was quivering, and it looked like he was trying to speak. I sprinted across the floor and sat down on the bed and held his hand. "Jacob, can you hear me?" He blinked three times. "Can you say something?"

Instead of blinking, he licked his lips and blew out a few breaths first. And then he said in a very raspy tone, "Na . . . Naomi, I . . . I'm sorry for the way I messed up your . . . life."

"You didn't. You gave me a wonderful home, a beautiful daughter, and we did have a few good times together."

"Not . . . enough . . . good times." He sounded stronger now, but when he laughed it was weak and low. "And you ain't . . . fat. I said you was . . . because I wanted to needle you. It . . . it made me feel better . . . about my own lard ass."

I laughed and squeezed his hand. "I didn't pay you no mind so don't even worry about that."

"My . . . mama always told me that God don't like ugly. Now I know she was right. I . . . I was as ugly as a hog's butt to you and this is my payback."

"Don't put the blame on God. If we only did things He wanted us to do, He wouldn't have gave us the ability to make choices."

Jacob struggled to nod, but he did, and at the same time, he smiled. "For . . . give me . . . so . . . I . . . can die a happy man." His voice was getting weaker, and I didn't want to encourage him to talk no more for now.

"I forgave you a long time ago and you ain't going to die anytime soon. Now you get some rest."

He cleared his throat and tried to talk some more, but all he could do now was gurgle. It pleased me to know that Jacob was remorseful. I kissed his forehead before I left the room. I couldn't wait to tell Ethel Mae and Lula and the people who cared about him that he'd spoke. But I didn't want to tell nobody in front of Homer because he didn't deserve to share that milestone with us.

When I got back to the kitchen, Ethel Mae was sitting across from Homer. There was a mighty big plate of food in front of her. "Mother, ain't you going to eat? I'd hate to think you don't like my cooking," Homer said with a smirk.

"It ain't that. I woke up with heartburn. If I eat, it'll get worse," I explained, as I wrung my hands. "Uh . . . Maisie was supposed to get back last night. I'm going to Lula's house to see if she made it," I said as I moved toward the front door. "Poor Maisie. Her husband's getting on her nerves and she's threatening to divorce him."

Ethel Mae rolled her eyes and snickered. "Again? I declare, she's been threatening to divorce Mr. Silas for years. Don't worry about Daddy. Me and Homie will tend to him until you get back."

"Mother, Ethel Mae promised that lady next door she'd come braid her hair in a little while. Can you skip going to Lula's house and go fishing at Carson Lake with me for a couple of hours? You remind me so much of my mama, I'd like to spend more time with just me and you. We been bonding real good." I couldn't believe Homer could let them words out of that hole in his face!

"Awww, that's so sweet," Ethel Mae said, swooning like she was in the presence of the Lord.

"Not today. I promised Lula I'd come this morning and I'm going to be there for a spell," I replied.

I ran all the way to Lula's house. Halfway there, I tripped over a lizard and came out of my shoes. Lula and Maisie was sitting at the kitchen table drinking coffee when I barged in holding my shoes and huffing and puffing like a overworked bull.

"What's wrong with you?" Maisie asked me. "You look like you seen the Devil hisself."

I forgot all about telling them that Jacob had spoken. "I did. *I seen the Devil hisself in the flesh.*"

Lula and Maisie looked at each other and hunched their shoulders. Lula was the first one to say something. "Naomi, I don't know nobody saner than you. What the hell are you talking about?"

"It's a long ugly story and I can't keep it in no longer," I answered.

Lula glanced at the big round clock on the wall above her stove and gently said, "We got time."

I put my shoes back on and composed myself as much as I could. My lips was moving but nothing was coming out. The next thing I knew, I crumbled like a stale tea cake. I hit the floor babbling and flailing my arms. Lula and Maisie yelped at the same time. Lula dashed across the floor and pulled me up. She wiped snot and tears off my face with a napkin. "Girl, we can't help if you don't tell us what's the matter!" she hollered.

Lula held onto my arm as I staggered to the table and plonked down in a chair. She sat down next to me. "All right, then." I sniffled. I took a very deep breath and told them everything from my first "date" with Homer to us planning to run away together. They yelped again when I told them he had killed Catty. When I told them how he had went after Ethel Mae to get back into my life so he could kill me, her, and Jacob, Lula screamed bloody murder. Maisie called Homer some vile names and slammed her huge fist down on the table so hard, the window rattled. When I stopped talking, their faces looked like they had turned to stone.

Lula scooted her chair closer to me and put her arm around my shoulder. "Girl, when I think of a wolf in sheep's clothing, I picture the wolf in plain ordinary clothes. In your case, the wolf is wearing a *tuxedo!*"

"Amen," Maisie agreed. "And handmade, Eye-talian shoes!"

Lula sniffed and continued. "Shame, shame, shame on you, Naomi! I can't believe you been carrying such a heavy load all this time by yourself! How come you didn't tell me? How come you ain't told Ethel Mae?"

"I was too scared to tell anybody, especially Ethel Mae. What if I tell her and she don't believe me? She'd never forgive me. She already thinks I'm trying to sabotage her love life."

"If you don't tell her and Homer hurts or kills her, how will you feel knowing you could have stopped him?" Lula asked.

It felt like a thousand-pound rock had been lifted off my chest. I scolded myself for not confessing before now. I was surprised Maisie had got so quiet. But the muscles under her eyes was twitching up a storm. I had no idea what she was thinking now.

"I don't know what to do," I said in a small, defeated voice.

"Whatever you do, you better do it *quick*. I don't care if he did say he was going to let y'all live through Thanksgiving and Christmas. Maniacs can say one thing and do another. If you want to borrow my knife, you're welcome to it."

I sucked in so much air, I felt like somebody had blew me up like a balloon. My jaw dropped and I stared at Lula like she'd pulled her knife on me. "You want me to kill him? What's the matter with you, Lula? I'm scandalized!" I had to stop talking and catch my breath. "If I killed Homer, I'd go to prison and what would happen to Jacob? What would become of Ethel Mae if I killed her fiancé?"

Lula sighed and said in a gentle tone, "She wouldn't have to know you done it. We'll bury him behind my chicken coop. I'll write a note saying he went to California and address it to Ethel Mae from him. I guarantee you, ain't nobody going to look for him."

Maisie cleared her throat and finally spoke again. "I hate to interrupt y'all, but I just thought of something. I know I just got here, but I need to find somebody to drive me back to Hartville."

Me and Lula looked at her at the same time. "How come you leaving already?" Lula asked.

"Um . . . I can't remember if I hid the money I borrowed from my brother to pay for my divorce. In case I didn't, I better drag my tail back home lickety-split before Silas finds it. I'll come back in time for your birthday celebration, Naomi. And I'm glad you told us about Homer . . ." Maisie abruptly got up, grabbed her purse off the coffee table, and waddled toward the front door.

Lula stared at the door and then at me. "What do you think about that?"

I was just as baffled as she was. "There ain't no way in the world Maisie left no money laying around where Silas could spot it," I said.

"Maybe my cousin is getting senile, bless her heart." Lula shook her head. "Why don't you spend the rest of the day with me? And the night. We'll figure out what to do about that devil! After what you told me he said to you today, I'm worried about what he might do to you if you go home."

I shook my head. "Staying away from my house won't help. It's my home and I ain't going to let Homer run me away from it. Besides, I need to be there in case he tries to do something to my daughter or my husband." I bit my bottom lip and added, "If he hurts them . . . I will kill him."

CHAPTER 48

M E KILL HOMER? THAT WAS AS FAR-FETCHED AS ME KILLING PRESident Roosevelt. There was no way I could kill another human being, so I didn't understand how I was able to say such a thing to Lula.

I stayed at Lula's house so long, Ethel Mae called to see when I was coming home. "Mama, you been over there for hours. Is Lula sick, or is she on one of her marathon gossip binges?"

"She's fine, baby. She's just feeling lonely since Maisie left to go back home this morning."

"Huh? Didn't Maisie just get back here?"

"Um . . . she forgot to do something before she left her house and she had to go back and take care of it. She said she'd be back soon."

"All right, Mama. You ain't got to worry about Daddy. Homie fed him before he went to Elmo's house. You can spend the night over there if you want to."

"I don't think so. I'm only going to stay a little longer."

"Okay. Mama"—Ethel Mae paused—"I just want to let you know how pleased I am you are showing Homie more love. He thinks the world of you. I know I'll be very happy being married to him. And guess what? He wants us to give you and Daddy a grandchild as soon as possible."

As bad as I wanted to be a grandmama, I prayed Ethel Mae wouldn't get pregnant. I also prayed that if Homer got out of the picture, she'd meet a nice man and have as many children as she could. "That's nice, baby," I mumbled. "Lula needs to use the phone, so I have to hang up now."

Two hours later, Maisie strolled back through Lula's front door. Me and Lula was sitting on the couch. "What the heck—I didn't expect you back so soon. I hope you hid your money where Silas can't find it," Lula said.

"Everything is fine now." Maisie looked at me and gave me a mysterious smile. "Naomi, you seem a little more relaxed than you was before I left. How are you feeling?"

I dropped my head. "No better, no worse."

Lula poured great big glasses of moonshine for herself and Maisie. She gave me a bottle of Dr Pepper. I immediately took a long pull. "I know y'all ain't going to tell nobody what I said about me and Homer. I had to let somebody know that if something happens to my family, Homer done it." I let out a long, loud sigh. "I guess I should go on back home. The longer I stay away, the harder it'll be to go back."

Lula and Maisie tried to talk me into staying, but I reluctantly got up and left. When I got home, Ethel Mae and Homer was sitting on the couch listening to the radio. His arm was around her shoulder. She looked like she was deep in the heart of Heaven. Homer glanced at me and winked as I walked by.

He didn't say or do nothing to irritate me in the next few days. But he had the nerve to come up to me and give me a hug for my birthday the third Saturday in September. "I wish I could have bought you a nice gift, but you know me and Ethel Mae need every penny we make so we can help you pay the bills. I think that by the end of the year, I'll be able to spare enough to get you a new washboard or a mop."

"Hush up, Homie. You need to learn more about women," Ethel Mae scolded as she wagged her finger in his face. "Mama bought a new washboard last year and there ain't nothing wrong with the mop she got." Then she turned to me with a sympathetic expression on her face. "Mama, I know how much you love to hear Bessie Smith sing. We are going to chip in and buy you one of them wind-up Victrola phonographs and a copy of her record 'Gimme a Pigfoot and a Bottle of Beer.' That's more like it!" Ethel Mae exclaimed as she pinched Homer's hand. "Groom, I got a lot to teach you about how to make a woman feel special."

It was irritating enough to hear her call him "Homie" but to hear her call him "groom" was even worse. It was obvious to me that she was getting even more anxious to marry this monster.

"Elmo got a old phonograph sitting in his closet collecting dust. I'm sure he'll let me have it real cheap. There ain't nothing I'd rather do than make you feel special, Mother," Homer said with a wink. One of the first things he'd promised to buy for our home when we got to Michigan was a phonograph player and some Bessie Smith records, all because he wanted to make me feel special.

"Y'all don't have to buy me nothing for my birthday. Just having y'all here with me is enough of a gift." I couldn't believe I'd let them words leave my mouth.

It had been a week since I'd told Lula and Maisie about me and Homer. They hadn't brought it up since then and I hadn't, but I knew it would come up this evening during the so-called birthday supper they was fixing for me.

I didn't put on no special outfit to celebrate my birthday, the way I usually did every year. I wore the same striped blouse and black skirt I'd had on all day. I didn't know when I'd be in a party mood again. But I would at least go through the motions.

I decided to go to Lula's at 6 P.M. Ethel Mae had just fed Jacob and was going to tend to him until I got back. Her monthly had started. She had cramps and didn't feel well enough to go with me. "Have fun, Mama. Stay as long as you want. Homie said he'd try to come home early tonight so he can help me turn Daddy over and change his underwear."

Lula had cooked a chocolate cake and fried some chicken wings. The food had been set on the kitchen table right next to a huge jar of moonshine. Maisie filled glasses to the brim for herself and Lula. I had a glass of cider. I knew they was itching to discuss my dilemma with Homer, and I was, too. Before we could, Lewis rushed through the door with his arms flailing like a bat flying in from hell. There was a frantic look on his face.

"Cock your pistols because y'all ain't going to believe what done happened!" Before either one of us could say a word, he blurted out, "Homer done got shot to death!"

Me and Lula yelped and stood up at the same time. Maisie didn't make a sound and didn't budge. She had the same stone-faced look she had when I told her about me and Homer. My legs felt like they was going to buckle so I sat back down. "What happened?" I hollered.

"Who shot him? Why did they shoot him?" Lula yelled.

Lewis grabbed Lula's glass of moonshine and took a long pull. After he let out a mighty belch and wiped his wet lips with his sleeve, he answered. "Y'all know all kinds of hoodlums hang out at them moonshiners' houses. Some are strangers just passing through. Well, one started a kerfuffle with one of Elmo's regulars tonight. When Homer tried to break them up, the stranger pulled out a gun and started shooting. He missed his target and hit poor Homer! Oh Lord. This is going to kill Ethel Mae."

I was so stunned, a gnat could have knocked me down. "How do you know he's dead?" I asked with my voice trembling. "You could be wrong. Maybe he just got wounded."

Lewis dismissed my words with a wave of his hand. "Woman, don't dispute me. I fought in the big war we had with them Germans way back when. I seen more death than an undertaker so I know 'dead' when I see it. *Homer is dead!*" Lewis drunk some more moonshine. "I stayed there until the Fuller Brothers showed up with their hearse. Naomi, I'm glad you was here so I wouldn't have to come to your house to break the news. I'm going to go back over there and wait until Sheriff Zachary comes."

Lula went up to Lewis and grabbed his hand. "Baby, maybe you should wait until things get settled before you go back over there. The man who done the shooting might come back and shoot some more. If he hears how close you and Homer was, he might aim at you just to be mean."

"Humph! If you had seen the way that man was running, you would know he ain't *never* coming back this way." Lewis finished what was left in the jar and rushed back out the door.

"Homer . . . is . . . dead." It took a few seconds for me to realize I was talking. I looked from Lula to Maisie. They had blank expressions on their faces. "Um . . . I guess I better get home to Ethel Mae. She's going to need me more than ever now."

Maisie stared at me with a tight smile on her face before she said, "Happy birthday, Naomi." And then she winked.

CHAPTER 49

ETHEL MAE WAS SOUND ASLEEP ON THE COUCH WHEN I GOT home from Lula's house. My baby looked so peaceful laying there, I didn't have the heart to wake her up and tell her Homer was dead. She had been predicting something bad was going to happen to him ever since he started working for Elmo. Even after all them times he had came home with black eyes and other injuries, I didn't think she ever thought somebody would *kill* him.

Now she would never have to know about me and Homer. I scolded myself for having such a thought. My daughter's feelings was a lot more important than mine now. I was going to do all I could to help ease her grief. I didn't know what was going to happen next. One thing I did know was that Homer wasn't going to hurt or kill me, Ethel Mae, and Jacob now, and I didn't scold myself for rejoicing over that.

I wanted to get all the facts about what happened first, so I tiptoed into the kitchen and called Elmo's house. The man who answered had to go find Elmo. While I was waiting, my heart was racing, and I was sweating bullets because I was worried Ethel Mae might wake up before I could talk to Elmo.

Several minutes later, I finally heard Elmo's voice. He was surprised to hear mine because I had only called his house once to get information about a church program I was helping his wife put together. "Naomi, I can't tell you how sorry I am about what happened to Homer. He was a good egg." Elmo had to pause and clear his throat because he was choking on his words. "Excuse me, sugar. I'm so distressed I don't know what to do." After he composed hisself he went on, talking slower this time. "A ruckus like the one we had tonight is bad for my business. It is the *third* murder in my house this year!"

"Lewis said a stranger killed Homer by mistake," I said.

"Yup. That's what happened. He tried to break up a fight and got shot for his trouble. Bless his soul. The man who shot him had come by hisself, so we don't know where he came from. He had to be from out of town because I know almost every spook in Lexington and I ain't never seen him before. Anyway, that sucker bolted out the door right after the shooting. It was dark and by the time we all made it outside, he wasn't nowhere in sight. I declare, it was like he was a ghost because he disappeared into thin air!"

"Do you think they'll find him?"

"Humph. I wouldn't count on it. You know the only way them crackers will spend money or time looking for a colored man on the run is if he killed somebody white or raped one of their women. But if me or some of my friends run into that sucker again, we will put a hurting on him! I called up the sheriff and reported the shooting, and I told him point blank there was over two dozen witnesses, but nobody knew the shooter. Sheriff Zachary said if we couldn't give him enough information for him to get started on, there ain't nothing he can do. He claims he'll come to my house tomorrow when he comes from fishing and make out a report, though."

"Thank you, Elmo. I'm sorry this happened in your house."

"I am, too. I'm tired of sopping up blood off my floors! How did Ethel Mae take it?"

"Um . . . I ain't told her yet. I'm fixing to."

"Naomi—oh shit! Another fight is fixing to break loose. I have to hang up now before these drunks tear my house down to the ground! Let me know when you're going to have Homer's funeral. Bye, Naomi." Elmo hung up before I could say anything else.

I went back into the living room and shook Ethel Mae until she woke up. She sat up, rubbing her eyes and looking around. "What time is it? I didn't mean to go to sleep." She yawned. "I hope you enjoyed celebrating your birthday with just Lula and Maisie. Next year we'll do something big on the same day for both our birthdays." Ethel Mae sniffed and looked around some more. "Did Homie make it back yet?"

I looked at my poor lovestruck child and wondered if she would ever find true love and happiness. I prayed that she (and me) would eventually find it someday. I knew she had thought Homer was the right one. Now that he was gone, I didn't see no reason to bust her bubble and try to convince her that he wasn't. I had already tried to tell her that, and all it had done was make her mad at me.

I sat on the edge of the couch and exhaled before I started breaking the news to her. "Baby, something real bad happened at Elmo's house tonight."

Ethel Mae waved her hands in the air and yelped. She was wide-awake now. "Here we go again! Did Homie get another black eye or did one of them roughnecks break one of his limbs?"

I shook my head.

Ethel Mae blinked. "Was it something worse?"

I nodded.

"Talk to me, Mama! What could be worse than some of the stuff he done already been through?" Ethel Mae's eyes got big, and she covered her mouth for a few seconds. "He got fired, didn't he?" She let out a sigh of relief. "Well, now he ain't got no choice but to look for more honorable work. Now you'll ask Reverend Spivey to give him a job, right?"

My legs felt like jelly when I stood up and started wringing my hands. "Baby, Homer ain't never coming back home." I had to take a mess of deep breaths before I could tell Ethel Mae all I knew. By the time I finished, she was a mess. She wobbled up off the couch and started pacing back and forth with a wild-eyed look on her face.

"What am I going to do now? Homie was the best thing that ever happened to me." Within seconds, tears was gushing from her eyes and she started howling like a sick baby. "Aaarrrgghh! Aaarrrgghh! My man is dead! Why *me*?" I got up and wrapped my arms around her. She howled even louder and by now her bosom was heaving so hard, it felt like somebody was pumping it from the inside.

"Be strong, baby," I said in the gentlest tone I could as I rubbed her back. "We'll get through this. What we need to do now is get in touch with the undertaker."

When I got the last word out, Ethel Mae pulled away from me and started pacing the floor again and howling even louder. I eventually managed to calm her down enough to get her to lay down on her bed. Even though I had closed the door to her bedroom behind me, I could still hear her screaming bloody murder.

Ethel Mae was so distraught, me and Lula had to make all the arrangements for Homer's funeral. Other than the cousin in Michigan he had told me about, I didn't know of any other kin-folk I could contact. Maisie said he had a bunch in Hartville, but they had disowned him years ago. When somebody mentioned his name to them, they got cussed out. Despite the monster he had become, it saddened me to know that his own blood relatives hated him so much, they didn't care if he was dead or alive.

To add insult to injury, I had to use part of the money I had saved up to run away with that devil to help pay for his funeral. Ethel Mae, Lula, and Lewis chipped in as much as they could and so did Elmo. He felt some responsibility because Homer had been killed while working for him.

CHAPTER 50

W E HAD HOMER'S FUNERAL THREE DAYS AFTER HE GOT KILLED. It was the most pathetic homegoing I ever attended. Most of the same folks who attended every funeral, whether they knew the deceased or not, showed up. Lula and Lewis shared the front pew with me and Ethel Mae.

Reverend Sweeney didn't know enough about Homer to go on and on about what a "good person" he was, the way he did with people he had known for a long time. When he had to preach the funeral for a despicable, Godless person, he made up stuff about how we was all God's children and He loved us unconditionally. In Homer's case, he added a few words about how unfortunate it was he wouldn't get to marry him and Ethel Mae.

After Reverend Sweeney finished preaching, he asked if anybody wanted to say a few words about Homer. Everybody started whispering and looking around. The only person who responded was Ethel Mae. One of the ushers took her hand and escorted her up to the podium. I braced myself. The same way I had the day Homer went up there. When Lula poked my side with her elbow, I just looked at her and hunched my shoulders.

Ethel Mae sniffled and dabbed tears from her eyes before she started talking. "God sent me the most amazing man he could find. I had only a few short months with him, but they was the most wonderful months I ever spent with a man. Homie was such a good man, I know he's with God now, so I don't feel as bad as I did when I heard what had happened to him. Thank all of y'all for coming." She blew her nose, managed to give a weak smile, and returned to her seat.

After the choir sung four more long, sad songs in a row, Reverend Sweeney made a few closing remarks. Right after he finished, some of the mourners stampeded into the dining area to eat, which was the reason some of them came in the first place. This was the first funeral I ever attended that I didn't bring no home-cooked dishes to.

Lewis, Maisie, and her husband, Silas, came. Maisie was still sobbing when she came up to hug me and Ethel Mae. I had seen Lewis crying earlier, but his eyes was dry now. Silas wore a black patch over the spot where his missing eye used to be. His one good eye was red and dry, but he kept dabbing it with a white handkerchief. They all had to leave right after the service because they had to go to Clarksdale, Mississippi, to attend Lula and Maisie's family reunion.

Ethel Mae insisted on going to the burial. She looked so pitiful I couldn't let her go by herself, so I went with her. I was glad a few of the usual stragglers also went. One was a skinny, pointy-nose woman who'd been at church the day Homer went up to the podium and made his announcement about how God had sent him the perfect woman. The woman's name was Libby Dawson, but folks called her "Lippy" behind her back because she gossiped so much.

"Naomi, I'm so sorry for your loss. I never would have thought your baby girl was the woman Homer was talking about that day he went up to the podium." Lippy adjusted the flat-topped, wide-brimmed hat on her head and gave me a side-eye look. "I almost ran myself ragged roaming all over town asking folks about him. Nobody could tell me nothing. He sure was a mysterious man."

"He was real private, so he didn't tell folks too much of his business." I wasn't defending Homer. I was trying to cut the conversation short.

"Hmmm." Libby scratched the side of her neck. "I even went up to Elmo one night and asked him if he knew Homer's background and he didn't. He did tell me that Homer used to live on Franklin Street next door to my stepbrother, Vinnie."

"Um . . . I think Homer did mention that."

"You know me, I went up to Vinnie and asked him about Homer. Vinnie said he used to hear him and a woman going at it in bed two or three times a week—especially on Sundays—but he never seen who the woman was. So, Homer couldn't have been that private if he had another woman before he met Ethel Mae. I wonder who she was. I'll keep asking around about him. If I find out anything you and Ethel Mae need to know, I'll—"

I cut Libby off. "That's all right. The man is dead now so there ain't no reason for us to find out nothing else about his background. Don't say nothing to Ethel Mae about Homer and that woman Vinnie used to hear him pestering in bed."

"All right, then. I'm sorry I didn't get to know Homer. I will say this much, though: for him to move in with you to help take care of Jacob, he had to be a righteous, God-loving, do-right man. Your daughter was so blessed. You was, too!"

"Thank you, Lip—*Libby*." I had almost slipped and called her Lippy. I didn't wait for her to say nothing else.

I wanted to get Ethel Mae home as soon as I could, so I hurried up to her, wrapped my arm around her shoulder, and guided her to the car. We was almost home before she said anything. "Mama, I'm glad everything is over with so I can get on with my life. But I am going to miss Homie so much!"

I patted her shoulder. "I am, too."

Ethel Mae busted out crying and so did I. We cried almost all the way home. When we got inside, she went to her room and cried some more. I was through crying.

Several hours later, Lula strolled into my living room and sat down on the couch. I was sitting in the chair across from her. "How was your family reunion?" I asked.

She rolled her eyes, clapped her hands, and guffawed. "Well, my crazy uncle Melvin got drunk and fell on top of the barbecue grill. It took my cousins a while to clean him off and dress his burns. Then it started raining cats and dogs so mud puddles was everywhere. Drunk, crippled old folks was slipping and sliding all over the place. Oh! It was such a fiasco; I don't even want to discuss it. Talk about anything else."

I didn't give much thought to what I said next. "I'm glad you're here." I cleared my throat before I went on. Then the words shot out of my mouth like I didn't have no control over them. "I need to ask you something I been holding off on. There's no need to answer if you don't want to. If you do, I want you to be honest."

Lula folded her arms and looked at me from the corner of her eye. "What is it?"

I stood up. "Can we go out on the porch? I don't want to take a chance on Ethel Mae hearing what I'm going to say."

We shuffled out my front door and stopped at the foot of the porch steps. I put my hands on my hips and stared at Lula. "Did you and Maisie have anything to do with Homer's killing?"

She did a double take and gazed at me with a tight expression on her face. "Wh-what's wrong with you, girl?"

I didn't like her gruff tone, but if somebody had asked me the same question, I would have reacted the same way. I touched her shoulder. "Because it happened so soon after I told y'all about my affair with him, and how he had started tormenting me."

"You heard what happened. Homer got shot trying to break up a fight."

I sighed and stared at Lula. "If y'all are behind it, I don't care. I just want to know so I can have some peace of mind."

Lula pressed her lips together and gave me a thoughtful look before she started talking again. "All right, then." Before she went on, she took a real deep breath. "Remember Homer's used-to-be girlfriend Maisie told us about who disappeared with her little boy and her mama?"

"I remember. Her brother believed Homer had something to do with them disappearing."

"Well, that woman's brother said he'd get revenge if he ever seen Homer again. When Maisie abruptly left right after you told us what Homer was doing to you, she went to find that woman's brother. He still lived in the same neighborhood, so he was easy to locate. Maisie told the brother where Homer was. That man got so anxious, he didn't waste no time. He got in his car and headed to Lexington. He parked a mile down the road from Elmo's house so nobody at the house would see what kind of car he was driving. When he got to Elmo's house, he picked a fight with another man and when Homer stepped in, well, you know the rest." Lula stopped talking and stared at me with her eyes narrowed. "I advise you not to never tell nobody what I just told you. That man already told Maisie that if she blabbed on him, she was next. And, if he couldn't find her, her kids and grandkids wouldn't be hard to find."

I was glad Lula had come clean because I never would have guessed what really happened. I was stunned and didn't know what to say. I was also glad Homer was out of my life—and Ethel Mae's—for good, but I was sorry he'd been killed. He died not knowing he'd been set up. I almost wished he had pushed me to kill him, so he'd know I got the last word. But he wasn't worth me spending the rest of my life in prison for. I couldn't never live with myself if I killed somebody, even Homer.

"I'll never tell nobody. You know you can trust me." I paused and blinked at Lula. "I'm sorry it had to end this way."

"What other way could it have ended? It was either him, or you and your family." Lula held her hand up to my face and her tone suddenly got real soft. "I don't want to conversate about this no more. You never know who might be lurking close enough to hear something. Let's forget about this murder."

I looked at the ground for a few moments before I said with a straight face, "What murder?"

CHAPTER 51

THE DAY AFTER HOMER'S FUNERAL, REVEREND SPIVEY TOLD ME TO take the rest of the week off and the first couple of days of next week if I wanted to. His wife and Annie Lou was going to ride the train to Montgomery to spend a week with Miss Viola's sister. While they was gone, he planned to eat his meals at some of his favorite restaurants, and with members of his congregation.

I spent Thursday doing laundry and a few other chores around the house. The worst chore I ever had was getting rid of Homer's things. Ethel Mae was too distressed to do it, so Lula helped me. We put everything in a pile in my backyard and burned it.

Ethel Mae was still grieving but she went back to work two days after Homer's funeral to keep from moping around the house like she'd been doing since his death.

I got antsy and decided not to wait until next week to go back to work like Reverend Spivey had suggested. I got up Friday morning and put on my work uniform. I had tried to reach him by telephone Thursday evening and again on Friday morning to let him know I would be coming back sooner than he thought, but he didn't answer his phone.

When I got to Reverend Spivey's house at my usual time, I let myself in the back door like I always did. His car was in the driveway, so I knew he was at home. Right after I got into the kitchen and shut the door, I heard a woman laugh real loud in the living room. She sounded like one of them vulgar women who hung out at Elmo's house. I assumed Reverend Spivey was giving somebody some spiritual guidance. But when he did that, he almost always went to the person's house. I got nosy and tiptoed to the doorway so I could hear better. "My dear, if you ever stop meeting up with me, I couldn't go on." That line really got my attention. I couldn't count the number of times Homer had said something like that to me.

I was so confused and curious I had to massage my temples and shake my head to clear it. Who could Reverend Spivey be talking to? I wondered. The first thing I thought was that Miss Viola had come back home earlier than she was supposed to. But what I'd just heard didn't sound like something a man would say to his wife. Besides that, Miss Viola was too ladylike and dainty to let out a guffaw like the one I'd just heard.

What I heard next made my heart jump so hard, I thought I was having a heart attack. "Don't worry, sugar. So long as you keep treating me good, I'll keep seeing you." Good God! It was *Martha Lou's* voice!

"Well, we've been doing business for nigh on to fifteen years, I see no reason to stop. I'm so glad you didn't mind coming over so early in the morning. This way, we can have several hours together before I meet with my deacons this evening to begin preparing this coming Sunday's program." Reverend Spivey chuckled. "Nothing puts me in a spiritual mood like a good romp with you. Give me some sugar!" I stumbled when I heard kissing noises and moans coming from the living room. "Boy, you sure got my blood flowing," Reverend Spivey panted. "By the way, you can start looking for the new car you've been pining for. You deserve it. I'm concerned about the one you have now after you told me about the problem with the brakes last week. I wish you had told me before today."

"I tried to get in touch with you before our scheduled date. Every time I called your house, either your wife or Annie Lou answered the telephone, so I just hung up."

"You did the right thing. Nobody can ever know about us. I'd be shunned and run out of town on a rail, and there is no telling what would become of you. I have some very active members of the Ku Klux Klan in my congregation."

I couldn't believe my ears! It was hard to believe Reverend Spivey was the same pious man who had disowned his own daughter for not living up to the high Christian standards he claimed to live by.

I knew that if he caught me eavesdropping my goose would be cooked. Just as I was about to ease back out the door and go home, I heard him say, "Well, now! I think it's time for us to take a stroll to the bedroom!"

"Whatever you say," Martha Lou giggled.

"By the way, I'll have the whole house to myself for another four or five days. Can you come back tomorrow and spend the night? I declare, you got me hotter than a smoking gun. Heh, heh, heh."

"That depends . . ."

"I know, I know. I'll have to pay extra for an all-night episode. Well, that ain't never been a problem before, *Buttercup*. Giddy-up!"

The next thing I heard was bare skin being slapped and a yelp. "Ow! I done told you to stop spanking me!" Martha Lou hollered before she laughed again. "I'll pay you back when you get out of the rest of them clothes and into bed."

I didn't want to hear nothing else. I slipped out the door and crept back down the street to the bus stop. I couldn't stop thinking about what I had stumbled upon. For some strange reason, I felt relieved now. I'd been scolding myself for my un-Christian behavior. If a preacher could backslide as far as Reverend Spivey had, a regular woman like me didn't need to feel so bad. I knew now that *nobody* was what they appeared to be. Who would have thought that a devout, well-respected preacher like Reverend Spivey was having sex outside of his marriage with a *colored* woman? And that Miss Viola used to be a hoochie coochie woman who had fooled around with colored men? As far as I was concerned, their behavior was just as blasphemous as mine. I was in good company, but that didn't make me feel no better about my behavior. I didn't even want to think about some of the secrets other folks was hiding! Reverend Spivey and Martha Lou was on my mind the rest of the weekend.

When I got home from church on Sunday, I put some flowers on Catty's grave. My grief wasn't so bad now, but I still missed her so much, I hadn't been able to cook no pig ears since she was murdered.

I had a hard time looking Reverend Spivey in the face when he came into the kitchen to eat breakfast Monday morning. I already had everything on the table. "I'm so pleased you're back, Naomi. You looked well rested. The time off I gave you benefited you tremendously, eh?"

"Yes, sir. I feel so much better now."

Reverend Spivey sat down in the chair at the head of the table. I filled his coffee cup, and he spurted in some milk. He took a huge gulp before he started talking again. "Mrs. Spivey and Annie Lou will be back home tomorrow. I can't wait to see them."

"I bet you got mighty lonesome in this big house by yourself . . ."

Reverend Spivey drunk some more coffee. "Not inordinately, praise the Lord. I kept myself busy. I found a heap of things to do." He burped and wiped his lips with the back of his hand.

I cringed when I pictured his wrinkled, age-spotted, naked body flopping around in bed with a buxom, much younger woman like Martha Lou. In a strange way, I liked knowing he still got some physical pleasure since Miss Viola couldn't give him none no more. I wondered if he'd ever fooled around with other women besides Martha Lou.

I wasn't going to let what I'd found out about my boss change the way I felt about him, or how I acted around him. Now that I knew he'd been "doing business" with Martha Lou for fifteen years, I wondered how come he'd never tried to make a move on me. I was just as attractive as she was. Then it dawned on me that maybe he liked my cooking so much, he didn't get no ideas about me because he didn't want to scare me off. I knew a lot of colored women who'd been approached by men in the families they worked for. Several of my previous male employers had tried to lure me into bed. I turned them all down and each one suddenly found a reason to fire me.

I suffered another tragedy two weeks after Homer's funeral. I got up to bathe and feed Jacob that Sunday morning to get him ready for church and he was as cold as ice. I screamed and Ethel Mae came running into the room. She took one look at Jacob and then she screamed.

We had Jacob's funeral three days later. Nary one of them heifers he used to fool around with showed up, but a lot of other folks did. Even Reverend Spivey, Miss Viola, and Annie Lou. "I want you to take off the next week," Reverend Spivey told me as he hugged my neck before the service started. Over his shoulder I seen Martha Lou looking in my direction with a blank expression on her face. She was the next person to come up and give me a hug.

"I'm so sorry Jacob had to suffer so much before the Lord took him. If you need me for anything, just let me know," she sobbed.

I noticed how Martha Lou never got too close to Reverend Spivey. But I seen them smiling at each other from across the room a heap of times.

I was glad Jacob had died of natural causes. For some strange reason, with Homer and Jacob gone, I felt like I had been let out of prison and in a way I had. I didn't feel the least bit guilty about the way I felt. I had really meant it when I told Jacob I forgave him for treating me so bad. I didn't know if I would ever be able to forgive Homer, though. And I didn't feel guilty about that, neither.

I loved my house and didn't want to move, even though Lula told me I should. I did get rid of the bed me and Jacob had shared, though. Some men from church hauled it to a dump site. I bought a new one the same day.

"You don't seem nervous or sad no more. And you seem at peace," Lula told me, a week after Jacob's funeral.

"I am." I made sure I looked fine on the outside, but inside I was still in pain. Some nights I had nightmares about Jacob; other nights it was Homer. When they haunted me together in the same dream, I woke up screaming.

I thought about getting some spiritual guidance from Reverend Sweeny and Reverend Spivey. But I couldn't tell them what was burning me up inside without telling them everything. Besides, I believed I would heal myself as time went on.

I was still surprised that things had moved so fast once I told Lula and Maisie how Homer had been torturing and threatening me. There was no doubt in my mind that if I hadn't told them in time, he would have carried out his final threat. And, he would have got away with murder again.

EPILOGUE

September 26, 1938

BESSIE SMITH DIED A YEAR AGO TODAY. SHE WAS ONE OF MY FA-vorite singers and one of the greatest blues singers of all time, in my opinion. She died in a bad car accident near Clarksdale, Mississippi, the same town where Lula's family had their family reunion last year.

Bessie's death had saddened all of my friends. Some was mad because they heard that the hospital near the accident had refused to admit her because she was colored. We all believed that if they had treated her, she wouldn't have died. Now people was saying that story wasn't true. But no matter what was true and what wasn't, a woman I had admired was dead. I used the rest of the money I had saved up to run off with Homer to buy myself a Victrola phonograph and as many of her records as I could find.

So much was happening, I didn't have time to dwell on the past that much.

Lula and Lewis got married in September in her house two weeks after my thirty-eighth birthday. It was a wedding I would never forget. It seemed more like a circus. When Reverend Sweeney got to the "Do you take this woman?" part, he had to pause because one of Lula's cats dragged a dead mouse across the floor in front of his feet. Everybody in the room roared with laughter until Maisie chased the cat out of the house. A minute after the ceremony continued, somebody dropped some glasses on the kitchen floor. The noise was so loud, Reverend Sweeney had to pause again. Right after he pronounced Lula and Lewis man and wife, she threatened to de-ball Lewis if he ever cheated on her or disrespected her—and she said it right in front of Reverend Sweeney! Lewis laughed along with everybody else, but I knew he knew Lula meant what she said. I didn't believe she would cut his balls off, but she'd probably put something on Lewis a doctor couldn't take off.

Maisie stopped threatening to divorce Silas and realized what a good man she had because the week after Lula's wedding, Maisie and Silas renewed their vows. I was so happy for them I hosted their wedding reception at my house. I was in the kitchen making more lemonade when Martha Lou popped in to get another dish. "I declare, Naomi, you been in a real chipper mood lately. Just being around you, uplifts me," she told me. The next thing I knew she hugged my neck. And then a wistful look crossed her face. "Guess what? I ain't told nobody else yet, but one of my generous white men friends hired a detective to track down my children. It took him several months, but he found them."

"Oh, my God!" I hollered as I patted Martha Lou's back. "Where did he find them at?"

"They live in Chicago and got families of their own. So, I'm a grandmama! I talked to both girls three times this week. They can't wait to see me again. Their low-down, funky black dog of a daddy died two years ago. He had told them when they was real little that I was dead! They grieved for years and my youngest took it so hard, she had to take nervous pills. Can you believe somebody would do that to their own kids?"

I shook my head. "That's a devil for you."

Martha Lou swallowed hard and gave me a pensive look. "As soon as I can pack up my house, I'm hopping on a train to Chicago."

"Will you tell your kids what you been doing all these years? Um . . . for a living, I mean."

A sad look crossed Martha Lou's face and she shrugged. "I

don't plan on coming back this way, but my kids might. One of these big mouths will let the cat out of the bag. So, I'm going to tell them first. We both know how much damage secrets can cause."

I sighed. "Tell me about it. I wish you all the luck in the world. I want to throw a going-away party for you so please give me enough time to put one together. After you get settled in Chicago, write, and call me as often as you can."

"I will. Naomi, you are the closest thing I ever had to a best friend. I'm glad for that."

I sniffed and looked into Martha Lou's eyes. "I'm glad for that too, *Buttercup.*"

She gasped and stumbled a step back. "W-who . . . how . . . *you know about me and Reverend Spivey?* He gave me that nickname and is the only one who calls me by it."

I looked toward the doorway before I whispered. "I know about y'all. When his wife and sister went out of town last year, he told me to take some time off after Homer's funeral. He didn't tell me when to come back, but I decided to go sooner than he thought I would. You and him was in the living room, I was in the kitchen . . ."

"Aw shuck it!" Martha Lou laughed. "Oh, well. I guess it ain't a secret no more. What all did you hear?"

I patted her shoulder. "It don't matter. Y'all been doing business for fifteen years and nobody knew. I found out by mistake. You know I won't tell nobody. Besides, you kept my secret about me and Homer."

"Anybody else know about you and Homer?"

"Well, I eventually told Lula and Maisie. But they promised they wouldn't blab." I didn't see no reason to tell Martha Lou the whole story, especially the part about Homer tormenting me and his killing being set up by Maisie.

"I owe you. Let's go fishing next Saturday. I went last weekend, and the blue gills was biting."

I hadn't been back to Carson Lake since my episode with Homer and I missed going there. I felt comfortable enough now to return. "You got a date."

"We can ride in my brand-new Lincoln. Um . . . *he* bought it for me."

"I know. I heard him tell you he would. He always does what he says he's going to do."

The look on Martha Lou's face got real smug. "And I'm going to milk that cow while the milking is good. When I get to Chicago, I'm going to need serious money to get me a nice house . . ."

The reception went on for another hour. I couldn't remember the last time I seen Lula, Maisie, and Martha Lou so happy. I was happy, too. And not just fairly, I was *real* happy. But I hope there was more to come for me . . .

Annie Lou passed away the day before Halloween. Reverend Spivey had her buried in the same plot with the rest of his family, just like he promised their daddy he would.

Two of the nicer ladies I used to work for called me up out of the blue and told me that if I ever wanted to work for them again, they'd be glad to have me back. They promised to pay me more and give me some benefits. I was glad to know that, so that when Reverend Spivey and Miss Viola passed, I'd have another job to fall back on.

Reverend Sweeney hosted a Thanksgiving celebration at our church. The dining room table had so much food on it, I got dizzy looking at it. I had contributed a turkey and several side dishes.

Everybody had a good time, especially Ethel Mae. That girl was eating like she was at the Last Supper. She finally put her fork down when a tall, dark, handsome young man in an Army uniform went up to her and started talking. Bobby Joe Stargen had grown up in our neighborhood and had just been honorably discharged from the military. I used to pay him a nickel two or three times a week to go to the market for me, but him and Ethel Mae had never been close friends. Ethel Mae used to say he was too lame for her because he never showed her enough attention the way the other boys did. Because she was older and wiser (I hoped) now, she realized he wasn't as lame as she thought. She went to the movies with him the following evening. The next thing I knew, they was courting up a storm.

Bobby Joe was kindhearted, respectful, and he treated Ethel Mae like a queen. He introduced her to his family and didn't pressure her to hop into bed with him. Only a few of the men she had fooled around with took her out in public and introduced her to their relatives. Even with all the good qualities Bobby Joe had, I was still a little wary of him because Homer's "good qualities" was what had lured me into his trap. I decided not to compare other men to that devil because I knew some of them really was the "Prince Charming" they appeared to be.

I encouraged Ethel Mae to get to know everything there was to know about Bobby Joe and his family, and I even did some snooping around myself. He had a few relatives who was a little on the rough side, but I wasn't going to hold that against him. Bobby Joe was a good man, and I knew he'd make my daughter a good husband. To my surprise and relief, Ethel Mae was even happier with him than she'd been with Homer.

As far as my love life went, I wasn't in no hurry to get seriously involved with nobody anytime soon. I did date, though. But I was so aloof with the last two men I went out with, they never asked me out again. When I drove past Homer's old house or seen a man who looked even a little bit like him, I shuddered.

I promised myself that the next time I met a man I liked, I would take my time to get to know *everything* about him and his family. But I believed that if there was a *real* Prince Charming for me, I'd find him.

I finally figured out that the dread I'd felt the day I got involved with Jacob, and a repeat of it the day I met Homer, was something trying to warn me about them two devils. I promised myself and God that if I ever felt that dread again about a man, I was going to run like hell.

DISCUSSION QUESTIONS

1. Naomi married Jacob to please her father. When she realized she'd made a mistake, should she have ended the marriage?

2. Do you think Jacob repeatedly cheated on Naomi because he no longer found her attractive or because she let him get away with it?

3. Ethel Mae caused Naomi almost as much grief as Jacob. Naomi disciplined her and tried to talk some sense into her but it didn't do any good. What would you do with an unruly child?

4. Ethel Mae was so out of control; Naomi was glad when she finished high school and moved to another town. Do you think Ethel Mae's low self-esteem was the reason she let men take advantage of her?

5. Naomi began her affair with Homer only a few days after she met him. Were you surprised she no longer cared about being a "virtuous" woman after being one for over twenty years?

6. Do you think Naomi would have been unfaithful if Jacob hadn't cheated on her? Was Homer so charming and handsome she would have cheated with him anyway?

7. Naomi met Homer in October and by November he was madly in love with her. He was so jealous he didn't even want her to have sex with her own husband. Should Naomi have realized then that he was unhinged?

8. Do you think Naomi would have agreed to run away with Homer if she hadn't caught Jacob in their bed with another woman?

9. When Jacob had a stroke, Naomi felt obligated to take care of him and cancel her plans to run away with Homer. Did you expect Homer to react the way he did when she told him?

10. Did you think Homer's threat to make the rest of Naomi's life "a living hell" was only a threat, or did you think he was serious?

11. Homer stalked Naomi for a few weeks and then abruptly stopped. She believed it was over, but did you?

12. How surprised were you when Ethel Mae moved back home to help take care of Jacob and brought along her fiancé, who turned out to be Homer?

13. When Lula and Maisie tell Naomi about Homer's murderous past, Naomi tells them everything about her relationship with him. Should Naomi have told Ethel Mae he was a monster then?

14. Did you suspect Homer's murder was set up by Maisie before Lula revealed the details to Naomi?